The Unveiling of

by Edmund Ca

CONTENTS

CHAPTER I

THE CAUSES OF THE EXPEDITION

PAGES

A retrospect--Early visitors to Lhasa--The Jesuits--The Capuchins--Van der Putte--Thomas Manning--The Lazarist fathers--Policy of exclusion due to Chinese influence--The Nepalese invasion--Bogle and Turner--The Macaulay Mission--Tibetans invade Indian territory--The expedition of 1888--The convention with China--British blundering--Our treatment of the Shata Shap?-The Yatung trade mart--Tibetans repudiate the convention--Fiction of the Chinese suzerainty--A policy of drift--Tibetan Mission to the Czar--Dorjieff and his intrigues--The Dalai Lama and Russian designs--Our great countermove--Boycotted at Khamba Jong--The advance sanctioned--Winter quarters at Tuna 1-21

CHAPTER II

OVER THE FRONTIER

From the base to Gnatong--A race to Chumbi--A perilous night ride--Forest scenery--Gnatong three years ago and now--Gnatong in action--A mountain lake--The Jelap la and beyond--Undefended barriers--Yatung and its Customs House--Chumbi--The first Press message from Tibet--Arctic clothing--Scenes in camp--A very uncomfortable 'picnic' 22-34

CHAPTER III

THE CHUMBI VALLEY

The Tomos--A hardy race--Their habits and diversions--Chinamen in exile--A prosperous valley--But a cheerless clime--Kasi and his statistics--Trade figures--Tibetan cruelties--Kasi as general provider--Mountain scenery--The spirit of the Himalayas--A glorious flora--The Himalayas and the Alps--The wall of Gob-sorg--Chinamen and Tomos--A future hill-station--Lingmathang--A cosy cave--The Mounted Infantry Corps--Two famous regiments--Sport at Lingmathang--The Sikkim stag--Gamebirds and wildfowl--Gautsa camp 35-61

CHAPTER IV

PHARI JONG

Gautsa to Phari Jong--A wonderful old fortress--Tibetan dirt--A medical armoury--The Lamas' library--Roadmaking and sport--The Tibetan gazelle and other animals--Evening diversions--Cold, grime, and misery--Manning's journal--Bogle's account of Phari--History of the fortress--The town and its occupants--The mystery of Tibet--The significance of the frescoes--Departure from Phari--The monastery of the Red Lamas--Chumulari--The Tibetan New Year--Bogle's narrative--The Tang la and the road to Lhasa 62-82

CHAPTER V

THE ROAD AND TRANSPORT

A transport 'show'--Difficulties of the way--Vicissitudes of climate--Frozen heights and sweltering valleys--Disease amongst transport animals--A tale of disaster--The stricken Yak Corps--Troubles of the transport officer--Mules to the rescue--The coolie transport corps--Carrying power of the transport items--The problem and its solution--The ekka and the yak--A providentially ascetic beast--Splendid work of the transport service--Courage and endurance of officers and men--The 12th Mule Corps benighted in a blizzard--Rifle-bolts and Maxims frost-jammed--Difficulties of a Russian advance on Lhasa--The new Ammo Chu cart-road 83-98

CHAPTER VI

THE ACTION AT THE HOT SPRINGS

The deadlock at Tuna--Discomforts of the garrison--The Lamas' curse--The attitude of Bhutan--A diplomatic triumph--Tedious delays--A welcome move forward--The Tibetan camp at Hot Springs--The Lhasa Depon meets Colonel Younghusband--Futile conferences--The Tibetan position surrounded--Coolness of the Sikhs and Gurkhas--The disarming--A sudden outbreak--A desperate struggle--The action of the Lhasa General--The rabble disillusioned in their gods--A beaten and bewildered enemy--Reflections after the event--Tibetans in hospital--Three months afterwards 99-114

CHAPTER VII

A HUMAN MISCELLANY

In a doolie to the base--Tibetan bearers--A retrospect--A reverie and a reminiscence--Snow-bound at Phari--The Bhutia as bearer--The Lepchas and their humours--Mongolian odours--The road at last--Platitudes in epigram--Lucknow doolie-wallahs--Their hymn of the obvious--Meetings on the road--A motley of races--Through a tropical forest--The Tista and civilization 115-126

CHAPTER VIII

THE ADVANCE OF THE MISSION OPPOSED

The Tibetans responsible for hostilities--Their version of the Hot Springs affair--Treacherous attack at Samando--Wall-building--The Red Idol Gorge action--A stiff climb--The enemy outflanked--Impressed peasants--First phase of the opposition--Bad generalship--Lack of enterprise--Erratic shooting--All quiet at Gyantse--Enemy occupy Karo la--A booby trap--Colonel Brander's sortie--Frontal attack repulsed--Captain Bethune killed--Failure of flanking movement--A critical moment--Sikhs turn the position--Flight and pursuit--Second phase of the opposition--Advanced tactics--Danger of being cut off--The attack on Kangma--Desperate gallantry of the enemy--Patriots or fanatics? 127-151

CHAPTER IX

GYANTSE (BY HENRY NEWMAN)

A happy valley--Devastated by war--Why the Jong was evacuated--The lull before the storm--Tibetans massing--The attack on the mission--A hot ten minutes--Pyjamaed warriors--Wounded to the rescue--The Gurkhas' rally--The camp bombarded--The labour of defence work--Hadow's Maxim--Life during the siege--Tibetans reinforced--They enfilade our position--The taking of the 'Gurkha Post'--Terrible carnage 152-169

CHAPTER X

GYANTSE--continued

Attack on the postal riders--Brilliant exploit of the Mounted Infantry--Communications threatened--Clearing the villages--A narrow shave--Arrival of reinforcements--The storming of Palla--House-fighting--Capture of the post--A fantastic display--Night attacks--Seven miles of front--Advance of the relief column--The Tibetans cornered--Naini monastery taken--Capture of Tsaden--Our losses--The armistice--Tibetans refuse to surrender the Jong--A bristling fortress--The attack at dawn--The breach--Gallantry of Lieutenant Grant and his Gurkhas--Capture of the Jong 170-194

CHAPTER XI

GOSSIP ON THE ROAD TO THE FRONT

A garden in the forest--A jeremiad on transport--The servant question--Jung Bir--British Bhutan--Kalimpong--'The Bhutia tat'--Father Desgodins--An adventurous career--A lost opportunity--Chinese duplicity--Phuntshog--New arms and new friends for Tibet--A mysterious Lama--Dorjieff again--The inscrutable Tibetan 195-206

CHAPTER XII

TO THE GREAT RIVER

Failure of peace negociations--Opposition expected--Details of force--March to the Karo la--Villages deserted--The second Karo la action--The Gurkhas' climb--The Tibetan rout--The Kham prisoners--Hopelessness of the Tibetans' struggle--Their troops disheartened--Arrival at Nagartse--Tedious delegates--The victory of a personality--Brush with Tibetan cavalry--The last shot--The Shap 閣 despoiled--Modern rifles--Exaggerated reports of Russian assistance--The Yamdok Tso--Dorje Phagmo--Legends of the lake--The incubus of an army--Why men travel--Wildfowl--Pehte--View from the Khamba Pass--From the desert to Arcadia--The Tibetan of the tablelands--The

Tuna plateau--Homely scenes--A mood of indolence--The course of the Tsangpo--The Brahmaputra Irawaddy controversy--The projected Tsangpo trip--Legendary geography--Lost opportunities 207-238

CHAPTER XIII

LHASA AND ITS VANISHED DEITY

The passage of the river--Major Bretherton drowned--The Kyi Chu valley--Tropical heat--Atisa's tomb--Foraging in holy places--First sight of the Potala--Hidden Lhasa--Symbols of remonstrance--Prophecies of invasion--And decay of Buddhism--Medieval Tibet--Spiritual terrorism--Lamas' fears of enlightenment--The last mystery unveiled--Arrival at Lhasa--View from the Chagpo Ri--Entry into the city--Apathy of the people--The Potala--Magnificence and squalor--The secret of romance--A vanished deity--'Thou shalt not kill'--Secret assassinations--A marvellous disappearance--The Dalai Lama joins Dorjieff--His personality and character--The verdict of the Nepalese Resident--The voice without a soul--The wisdom of his flight--A romantic picture--The place of the dead 239-264

CHAPTER XIV

THE CITY AND ITS TEMPLES

Sullen monks--A Lama runs amok--The environs of Lhasa--The Lingkhor--The Ragyabas--The cathedral--Service before the Great Buddhas--The Lamas' chant--Vessels of gold--'Hell'--White mice--The many-handed Buddha--Silence and abstraction--The bazaar--Hats--The Mongolians--Curio-hunting--The Ramo-ch?-Sorcery--The adventures of a soul--Lamaism and Roman Catholicism--The decay of Buddhism--The three great monasteries--Their political influence--Depung--An ecclesiastical University--The 'impossible' Tibetan--An ultimatum--Consternation at Depung--Temporizing and evasion--An ugly mob--A political deadlock 265-285

CHAPTER XV

THE SETTLEMENT

An irresponsible administration--An insolent reply--Tibetan haggling--Release of the Lachung men--Social relations with the Tibetans--A guarded ultimatum--A diplomatic triumph--The signing of the treaty--Colonel Younghusband's speech--The terms--Political prisoners liberated--Deposition of the Dalai Lama--The Tashe Lama--Prospect of an Anglophile Pope--The practical results of the expedition--Russia discredited--Why a Resident should be left at Lhasa--China hesitates to sign the Treaty--The 'vicious circle' again--Her acquiescence not of vital importance--The attitude of Tibet to Great Britain--Fear and respect the only guarantee of future good conduct 286-304

THE UNVEILING OF LHASA

CHAPTER I

THE CAUSES OF THE EXPEDITION

The conduct of Great Britain in her relations with Tibet puts me in mind of the dilemma of a big boy at school who submits to the attacks of a precocious youngster rather than incur the imputation of 'bully.' At last the situation becomes intolerable, and the big boy, bully if you will, turns on the youth and administers the deserved thrashing. There is naturally a good deal of remonstrance from spectators who have not observed the byplay which led to the encounter. But sympathy must be sacrificed to the restitution of fitting and respectful relations.

The aim of this record of an individual's impressions of the recent Tibetan expedition is to convey some idea of the life we led in Tibet, the scenes through which we passed, and the strange people we fought and conquered. We killed several thousand of these brave, ill-armed men; and as the story of the fighting is not always pleasant reading, I think it right before describing the punitive side of the expedition to make it quite clear that military operations were unavoidable--that we were drawn into the vortex of war against our will by the folly and obstinacy of the Tibetans.

The briefest review of the rebuffs Great Britain has submitted to during the last twenty years will suffice to show that, so far from being to blame in adopting punitive measures, she is open to the charge of unpardonable weakness in allowing affairs to reach the crisis which made such punishment necessary.

It must be remembered that Tibet has not always been closed to strangers. The history of European travellers in Lhasa forms a literature to itself. Until the end of the eighteenth century only physical obstacles stood in the way of an entry to the capital. Jesuits and Capuchins reached Lhasa, made long stays there, and were even encouraged by the Tibetan Government. The first[1] Europeans to visit the city and leave an authentic record of their journey were the Fathers Grueber and d'Orville, who penetrated Tibet from China in 1661 by the Sining route, and stayed in Lhasa two months. In 1715 the Jesuits

Desideri and Freyre reached Lhasa; Desideri stayed there thirteen years. In 1719 arrived Horace de la Penna and the Capuchin Mission, who built a chapel and a hospice, made several converts, and were not finally expelled till 1740.[2] The Dutchman Van der Putte, first layman to penetrate to the capital, arrived in 1720, and stayed there some years. After this we have no record of a European reaching Lhasa until the adventurous journey in 1811 of Thomas Manning, the first and only Englishman to reach the city before this year. Manning arrived in the retinue of a Chinese General whom he had met at Phari Jong, and whose gratitude he had won for medical services. He remained in the capital four months, and during his stay he made the acquaintance of several Chinese and Tibetan officials, and was even presented to the Dalai Lama himself. The influence of his patron, however, was not strong enough to insure his safety in the city. He was warned that his life was endangered, and returned to India by the same way he came. In 1846 the Lazarist missionaries Huc and Gabet reached Lhasa in the disguise of Lamas after eighteen months' wanderings through China and Mongolia, during which they must have suffered as much from privations and hardships as any travellers who have survived to tell the tale. They were received kindly by the Amban and Regent, but permission to stay was firmly refused them on the grounds that they were there to subvert the religion of the State. Despite the attempts of several determined travellers, none of whom got within a hundred miles of Lhasa, the Lazarist fathers were the last Europeans to set foot in the city until Colonel Younghusband rode through the Pargo Kaling gate on August 4, 1904.

[1] Friar Oderic of Portenone is supposed to have visited Lhasa in 1325, but the authenticity of this record is open to doubt.

[2] When in Lhasa I sought in vain for any trace of these buildings. The most enlightened Tibetans are ignorant, or pretend to be so, that Christian missionaries have resided in the city. In the cathedral, however, we found a bell with the inscription, 'TE DEUM LAUDAMUS,' which is probably a relic of the Capuchins.

The records of these travellers to Lhasa, and of others who visited different parts of Tibet before the end of the eighteenth century, do not point to any serious political obstacles to the admission of strangers. Two centuries ago, Europeans might travel in remote parts of Asia with greater safety than is possible to-day. Suspicions have naturally increased with our encroachments, and the white man now inspires fear where he used only to awake interest.[3]

   [3] Suspicion and jealousy of foreigners seems to have been the guiding principle both of Tibetans and Chinese even in the earlier history of the country. The attitude is well illustrated by a letter written in 1774 by the Regent at Lhasa to the Teshu Lama with reference to Bogle's mission: 'He had heard of two Fringies being arrived in the Deb Raja's dominions, with a great retinue of servants; that the Fringies were fond of war, and after insinuating themselves into a country raised disturbances and made themselves masters of it; that as no Fringies had ever been admitted into Tibet, he advised the Lama to find some method of sending them back, either on account of the violence of the small-pox or on any other pretence.'

   The policy of strict exclusion in Tibet seems to have been synchronous with Chinese ascendancy. At the end of the eighteenth century the Nepalese invaded and overran the country. The Lamas turned to China for help, and a force of 70,000 men was sent to their assistance. The Chinese drove the Gurkhas over their frontier, and practically annihilated their army within a day's march of Khatmandu. From this date China has virtually or nominally ruled in Lhasa, and an important result of her intervention has been to sow distrust of the British. She represented that we had instigated the Nepalese invasion, and warned the Lamas that the only way to obviate our designs on Tibet was to avoid all communication with India, and keep the passes strictly closed to foreigners.

   Shortly before the Nepalese War, Warren Hastings had sent the two missions of Bogle and Turner to Shigatze. Bogle was cordially received by the Grand Teshu Lama, and an intimate friendship was established between the two men. On his return to India he reported that the only bar to a complete understanding with Tibet was the obstinacy of the Regent and the Chinese agents at Lhasa, who were inspired by Peking. An attempt was arranged to influence the Chinese Government in the matter, but both Bogle and the Teshu Lama died before it could be carried out. Ten years later Turner was despatched to Tibet, and received the same welcome as his predecessor. Everything pointed to the continuance of a steady and consistent policy by which the barrier of obstruction might have been broken down. But Warren Hastings was recalled in 1785, and Lord Cornwallis, the next Governor-

General, took no steps to approach and conciliate the Tibetans. It was in 1792 that the Tibetan-Nepalese War broke out, which, owing to the misrepresentations of China, precluded any possibility of an understanding between India and Tibet. Such was the uncompromising spirit of the Lamas that, until Lord Dufferin sanctioned the commercial mission of Mr. Colman Macaulay in 1886, no succeeding Viceroy after Warren Hastings thought it worth while to renew the attempt to enter into friendly relations with the country.

The Macaulay Mission incident was the beginning of that weak and abortive policy which lost us the respect of the Tibetans, and led to the succession of affronts and indignities which made the recent expedition to Lhasa inevitable. The escort had already advanced into Sikkim, and Mr. Macaulay was about to join it, when orders were received from Government for its return. The withdrawal was a concession to the Chinese, with whom we were then engaged in the delimitation of the Burmese frontier. This display of weakness incited the Tibetans to such a pitch of vanity and insolence that they invaded our territory and established a military post at Lingtu, only seventy miles from Darjeeling.

We allowed the invaders to remain in the protected State of Sikkim two years before we made any reprisal. In 1888, after several vain appeals to China to use her influence to withdraw the Tibetan troops, we reluctantly decided on a military expedition. The Tibetans were driven from their position, defeated in three separate engagements, and pursued over the frontier as far as Chumbi. We ought to have concluded a treaty with them on the spot, when we were in a position to enforce it, but we were afraid of offending the susceptibilities of China, whose suzerainty over Tibet we still recognised, though she had acknowledged her inability to restrain the Tibetans from invading our territory. At the conclusion of the campaign, in which the Tibetans showed no military instincts whatever, we returned to our post at Gnatong, on the Sikkim frontier.

After two years of fruitless discussion, a convention was drawn up between Great Britain and China, by which Great Britain's exclusive control over the internal administration and foreign relations of Sikkim was recognised, the Sikkim-Tibet boundary was defined, and both Powers undertook to prevent acts of aggression from their respective sides of the frontier. The questions of pasturage, trade facilities, and the method in which official communications should be conducted between the Government of India and the authorities at Lhasa were deferred for future discussion. Nearly three more years passed before the trade regulations were drawn up in Darjeeling--in December, 1903. The negotiations were characterized by the same shuffling and equivocation on the part of the Chinese, and the same weak-kneed policy of forbearance and conciliation on the part of the British. Treaty and regulations were alike impotent, and our concessions went so far that we exacted nothing as the fruit of our victory over the Tibetans--not even a fraction of the cost of the campaign.

Our ignorance of the Tibetans, their Government, and their relations with China was at this time so profound that we took our cue from the Chinese, who always referred to the Lhasa authorities as 'the barbarians.' The Shata Shap? the most influential of the four members of Council, attended the negotiations on behalf of the Tibetans. He was officially ignored, and no one thought of asking him to attach his signature to the treaty. The omission was a blunder of far-reaching consequences. Had we realized that Chinese authority was practically non-existent in Lhasa, and that the temporal affairs of Tibet were mainly directed by the four Shap and the Tsong-du (the very existence of which, by the way, was unknown to us), we might have secured a diplomatic agent in the Shata Shap?who would have proved invaluable to us in our future relations with the country. Unfortunately, during his stay in Darjeeling the Shap?s feelings were lacerated by ill-treatment as well as neglect. In an unfortunate encounter with British youth, which was said to have arisen from his jostling an English lady off the path, he was taken by the scruff of the neck and ducked in the public fountain. So he returned to Tibet with no love for the English, and after certain courteous overtures from the agents of 'another Power,' became a confirmed, though more or less accidental, Russophile. Though deposed,[4] he has at the present moment a large following among the monks of the Gaden monastery.

[4] The Shata Shap?and his three colleagues were deposed by the Dalai Lama in October, 1903.

In the regulations of 1893 it was stipulated that a trade mart should be established at Yatung, a small hamlet six miles beyond our frontier. The place is obviously unsuitable, situated as it is in a narrow pine-clad ravine, where one can throw a stone from cliff to cliff across the valley. No traders have ever resorted there, and the Tibetans have studiously boycotted the place. To show their contempt for the treaty, and their determination to ignore it, they built a wall a quarter of a mile beyond the Customs House, through which no Tibetan or British subject was allowed to pass, and, to nullify the object of the mart, a tax of 10 per cent. on Indian goods was levied at Phari. Every attempt was made by Sheng Tai, the late Amban, to induce the Tibetans to substitute Phari for Yatung as a trade mart. But, as an official report admits, 'it was found impossible to overcome their reluctance. Yatung was eventually accepted both by the Chinese and British Governments as the only alternative to breaking off the negociations altogether.' This confession of weakness appears to me abject enough to quote as typical of our attitude throughout. In deference to Tibetan wishes, we allowed nearly every clause of the treaty to be separately stultified.

The Tibetans, as might be expected, met our forbearance by further rebuffs. Not content with evading their treaty obligations in respect to trade, they proceeded to overthrow our boundary pillars, violate grazing rights, and erect guard-houses at Giagong, in Sikkim territory. When called to question they repudiated the treaty, and said that it had never been shown them by the Amban. It had not been sealed or confirmed by any Tibetan representative, and they had no intention of observing it.

Once more the 'solemn farce' was enacted of an appeal to China to use her influence with the Lhasa authorities. And it was only after repeated representations had been made by the Indian Government to the Secretary of State that the Home Government realized the seriousness of the situation, and the hopelessness of making any progress through the agency of China. 'We seem,' said Lord Curzon, 'in respect to our policy in Tibet, to be moving in a vicious circle. If we apply to Tibet we either receive no reply or are referred to the Chinese Resident; if we apply to the latter, he excuses his failure by his inability to put any pressure upon Tibet.' In the famous despatch of January 8, 1903, the Viceroy described the Chinese suzerainty as 'a political fiction,' only maintained because of its convenience to both parties. China no doubt is capable of sending sufficient troops to Lhasa to coerce the Tibetans. But it has suited her book to maintain the present elusive and anomalous relations with Tibet, which are a securer buttress to her western dependencies against encroachment than the strongest army corps. For many years we have been the butt of the Tibetans, and China their stalking-horse.

The Tibetan attitude was clearly expressed by the Shigatze officials at Khamba Jong in September last year, when they openly boasted that 'where Chinese policy was in accordance with their own views they were ready enough to accept the Amban's advice; but if this advice ran counter in any respect to their national prejudices, the Chinese Emperor himself would be powerless to influence them.' China has on several occasions confessed her inability to coerce the Tibetans. She has proved herself unable to enforce the observance of treaties or even to restrain her subjects from invading our territory, and during the recent attempts at negociations she had to admit that her representative in Lhasa was officially ignored, and not even allowed transport to travel in the country. In the face of these facts her exceedingly shadowy suzerainty may be said to have entirely evaporated, and it is unreasonable to expect us to continue our relations with Tibet through the medium of Peking.

It was not until nine years after the signing of the convention that we made any attempt to open direct communications with the Tibetans themselves. It is astonishing that we allowed ourselves to be hoodwinked so long. But this policy of drift and waiting is characteristic of our foreign relations all over the world. British Cabinets seem to believe that cure is better than prevention, and when faced by a dilemma have seldom been known to act on the initiative, or take any decided course until the very existence of their dependency is imperilled.

In 1901 Lord Curzon was permitted to send a despatch to the Dalai Lama in which it was pointed out that his Government had consistently defied and ignored treaty rights; and in view of the continued occupation of British territory, the destruction of frontier pillars, and the restrictions imposed on Indian trade, we should be compelled to resort to more practical measures to enforce the observance of the treaty, should he remain obstinate in his refusal to enter into friendly relations. The letter was returned unopened, with the verbal excuse that the Chinese did not permit him to receive communications from any foreign Power. Yet so great was our reluctance to resort to military coercion that we might even at this point have let things drift, and submitted to the rebuffs of these impossible Tibetans, had not the Dalai Lama chosen this moment for publicly flaunting his relations with Russia.

The second[5] Tibetan Mission reached St. Petersburg in June, 1901, carrying autograph letters and presents to the Czar from the Dalai Lama. Count Lamsdorff declared that the mission had no political significance whatever. We were asked to believe that these Lamas travelled many thousand miles to convey a letter that expressed the hope that the Russian Foreign Minister was in good health and prosperous, and informed him that the Dalai Lama was happy to be able to say that he himself enjoyed excellent health.

[5] A previous mission had been received by the Czar at Livadia in October, 1900.

It is possible that the mission to St. Petersburg was of a purely religious character, and that there was no secret understanding at the time between the Lhasa authorities and Russia. Yet the fact that the mission was despatched in direct contradiction to the national policy of isolation that had been respected for over a century, and at a time when the Tibetans were aware of impending British activity to exact fulfilment of the treaty obligations so long ignored by them, points to some secret influence working in Lhasa in favour of Russia, and opposed to British interests. The process of Russification that has been carried on with such marked success in Persia and Turkestan, Merv and Bokhara, was being applied in Tibet. It has long been known to our Intelligence Department that certain Buriat Lamas, subjects of the Czar, and educated in Russia, have been acting as intermediaries between Lhasa and St. Petersburg. The chief of these, one Dorjieff, headed the so-called religious mission of 1901, and has been employed more than once as the Dalai Lama's ambassador to St. Petersburg. Dorjieff is a man of fifty-eight, who has spent some twenty years of his life in Lhasa, and is known to be the right-hand adviser of the Dalai Lama. No doubt Dorjieff played on the fears of the Buddhist Pope until he really believed that Tibet was in danger of an invasion from India, in which eventuality the Czar, the great Pan-Buddhist Protector, would descend on the British and drive them back over the frontier. The Lamas of Tibet imagine that Russia is a Buddhist country, and this belief has been fostered by adventurers like Dorjieff, Tsibikoff, and others, who have inspired dreams of a consolidated Buddhist church under the spiritual control of the Dalai Lama and the military is of the Czar of All the Russias.

These dreams, full of political menace to ourselves, have, I think, been dispelled by Lord Curzon's timely expedition to Lhasa. The presence of the British in the capital and the helplessness of Russia to lend any aid in such a crisis are facts convincing enough to stultify the effects of Russian intrigue in Buddhist Central Asia during the last half-century.

The fact that the first Dalai Lama who has been allowed to reach maturity has plunged his country into war by intrigue with a foreign Power proves the astuteness of the cold-blooded policy of removing the infant Pope, and the investiture of power in the hands of a Regent inspired by Peking. It is believed that the present Dalai Lama was permitted to come of age in order to throw off the Chinese yoke. This aim has been secured, but it has involved other issues that the Lamas could not foresee.

And here it must be observed that the Dalai Lama's inclination towards Russia does not represent any considerable national movement. The desire for a rapprochement was largely a matter of personal ambition inspired by that arch-intriguer Dorjieff, whose ascendancy over the Dalai Lama was proved beyond a doubt when the latter joined him in his flight to Mongolia on hearing the news of the British advance on Lhasa. Dorjieff had a certain amount of popularity with the priest population of the capital, and the monks of the three great monasteries, amongst whom he is known to have distributed largess royally. But the traditional policy of isolation is so inveterately ingrained in the Tibetan character that it is doubtful if he could have organized a popular party of any strength.

It may be asked, then, What is, or was, the nature of the Russian menace in Tibet? It is true that a Russian invasion on the North-East frontier is out of the question. For to reach the Indian passes the Russians would have to traverse nearly 1,500 miles of almost uninhabited country, presenting difficulties as great as any we had to contend with during the recent campaign. But the establishment of Russian influence in Lhasa might mean military danger of another kind. It would be easy for her to stir up the Tibetans, spread disaffection among the Bhutanese, send secret agents into Nepal, and generally undermine our prestige. Her aim would be to create a diversion on the Tibet frontier at any time she might have designs on the North-West. The pioneers of the movement had begun their work. They were men of the usual type--astute, insidious, to be disavowed in case of premature discovery, or publicly flaunted when they had prepared any ground on which to stand.

Our countermove--the Tibet Expedition--must have been a crushing and unexpected blow to Russia. For the first time in modern history Great Britain had taken a decisive, almost high-handed, step to obviate a danger that was far from imminent. We had all the best cards in our hands. Russia's designs in Lhasa became obvious at a time when we could point to open defiance on the part of the Tibetans, and provocation such as would have goaded any other European nation to a punitive expedition years before. We could go to Lhasa, apparently without a thought of Russia, and yet undo all the effects of her scheming there, and deal her prestige a blow that would be felt throughout the whole of Central Asia. Such was Lord Curzon's policy. It was adopted in a half-hearted way by the Home Government, and eventually forced on them by the conduct of the Tibetans themselves. Needless to say, the discovery of Russian designs was the real and prime cause of the despatch of the mission, while Tibet's violation of treaty rights and refusal to enter into any relations with us were convenient as ostensible motives. It cannot be denied that these grievances were valid enough to justify the strongest measures.

In June, 1903, came the announcement of Colonel Younghusband's mission to Khamba Jong. I do not think that the Indian Government ever expected that the Tibetans would come to any agreement with us at Khamba Jong. It is to their credit that they waited patiently several months in order to give them every chance of settling things amicably. However, as might have been expected, the Commission was boycotted. Irresponsible delegates of inferior rank were sent by the Tibetans and Chinese, and the Lhasa delegates, after some fruitless parleyings, shut themselves up in the fort, and declined all intercourse, official or social, with the Commissioners.[6]

[6] Their attitude was thus summed up by Captain O'Connor, secretary to the mission: 'We cannot accept letters; we cannot write letters; we cannot let you into our zone; we cannot let you travel; we cannot discuss matters, because this is not the proper place; go back to Giogong and send away all your soldiers, and we will come to an agreement' (Tibetan Blue-Book).

At the end of August news came that the Tibetans were arming. Colonel Younghusband learnt that they had made up their minds to have no negociations with us inside Tibet. They had decided to leave us alone at Khamba Jong, and to oppose us by force if we attempted to advance further. They believed themselves fully equal to the English, and far from our getting anything out of them, they thought that they would be able to force something out of us. This is not surprising when we consider the spirit of concession in which we had met them on previous occasions.

At Khamba Jong the Commissioners were informed by Colonel Chao, the Chinese delegate, that the Tibetans were relying on Russian assistance. This was confirmed later at Guru by the Tibetan officials, who boasted that if they were defeated they would fall back on another Power.

In September the Tibetans aggravated the situation by seizing and beating at Shigatze two British subjects of the Lachung Valley in Sikkim. These men were not restored to liberty until we had forced our way to Lhasa and demanded their liberation, twelve months afterwards.

The mission remained in its ignominious position at Khamba Jong until its recall in November. Almost at the same time the expedition to Gyantse was announced.[7]

[7] The situation was thus eloquently summarized by the Government of India in a despatch to Mr. Brodrick, November 5, 1903: 'It is not possible that the Tibet Government should be allowed to ignore its treaty obligations, thwart trade, encroach upon our territory, destroy our boundary pillars, and refuse even to receive our communications. Still less do we think that when an amicable conference has been arranged for the settlement of these difficulties we should acquiesce in our mission being boycotted by the very persons who have been deputed to meet it, our officers insulted, our subjects arrested and ill-used, and our authority despised by a petty Power which only mistakes our forbearance for weakness, and which thinks that by an attitude of obstinate inertia it can once again compel us, as it has done in the past, to desist from our intentions.'

In the face of the gross and deliberate affront to which we had been subjected at Khamba Jong it was now, of course, impossible to withdraw from Tibetan territory until we had impressed on the Lamas the necessity of meeting us in a reasonable spirit. It was clear that the Tibetans meant fighting, and the escort had to be increased to 2,500 men. The patience of Government was at last exhausted, and it was decided that the mission was to proceed into Tibet, dictate terms to the Lamas, and, if necessary, enforce compliance. The advance to Gyantse was sanctioned in the first place. But it was quite expected that the obstinacy of the Tibetans would make it necessary to push on to Lhasa.

Colonel Younghusband crossed the Jelap la into Tibet on December 13, meeting with no opposition. Phari Jong was reached on the 20th, and the fort surrendered without a shot being fired. Thence the mission proceeded on January 7 across the Tang Pass, and took up its quarters on the cold, wind-swept plateau of Tuna, at an elevation of 15,300 feet. Here it remained for three months, while preparations were being made for an advance in the spring. Four companies of the 23rd Pioneers, a machine-gun section of the Norfolk Regiment, and twenty Madras sappers, were left to garrison the place, and General Macdonald, with the remainder of the force, returned to Chumbi for winter quarters. Chumbi (10,060 feet) is well within the wood belt, but even here the thermometer falls to 15?below zero.

A more miserable place to winter in than Tuna cannot be imagined. But for political reasons, it was inadvisable that the mission should spend the winter in the Chumbi Valley, which is not geographically a part of Tibet proper. A retrograde movement from Khamba Jong to Chumbi would be interpreted by the Tibetans as a sign of yielding, and strengthen them in their opinion that we had no serious intention of penetrating to Gyantse.

With this brief account of the facts that led to the expedition I abandon politics for the present, and in the succeeding chapters will attempt to give a description of the Chumbi Valley, which, I believe, was untrodden by any European before Colonel Younghusband's arrival in December, 1903.

I was in India when I received permission to join the force. I took the train to Darjeeling without losing a day, and rode into Chumbi in less than forty-eight hours, reaching the British camp on January 10.

CHAPTER II

OVER THE FRONTIER

CHUMBI, January 13.

From Darjeeling to Lhasa is 380 miles. These, as in the dominions of Namgay Doola's Raja, are mostly on end. The road crosses the Tibetan frontier at the Jelap la (14,350 feet) eighty miles to the north-east. From Observatory Hill in Darjeeling one looks over the bleak hog-backed ranges of Sikkim to the snows. To the north and north-west lie Kinchenjunga and the tremendous chain of mountains that embraces Everest. To the north-east stretches a lower line of dazzling rifts and spires, in which one can see a thin gray wedge, like a slice in a Christmas cake. That is the Jelap. Beyond it lies Tibet.

There is a good military road from Siliguri, the base station in the plains to Rungpo, forty-eight miles along the Teesta Valley. By following the river-bed it avoids the two steep ascents to Kalimpong and Ari. The new route saves at least a day, and conveys one to Rungli, nearly seventy miles from the base, without compassing a single tedious incline. It has also the advantage of being practicable for bullock-carts and ekkas as far as Rungpo. After that the path is a 6-foot mule-track, at its best a rough, dusty incline, at its worst a succession of broken rocks and frozen puddles, which give no foothold to transport animals. From Rungpo the road skirts the stream for sixteen miles to Rungli, along a fertile valley of some 2,000 feet, through rice-fields and orange-groves and peaceful villages, now the scene of military bustle and preparation. From Rungli it follows a winding mountain torrent, whose banks are sometimes sheer precipitous crags. Then it strikes up the mountain side, and becomes a ladder of stone steps over which no animal in the world can make more than a mile and a half an hour. From the valley to Gnatong is a climb of some 10,000 feet without a break. The scenery is most magnificent, and I doubt if it is possible to find anywhere in the same compass the characteristics of the different zones of vegetation--from tropical to temperate, from temperate to alpine--so beautifully exhibited.

At ordinary seasons transport is easy, and one can take the road in comfort; but now every mule and pony in Sikkim and the Terai is employed on the lines of communication, and one has to pay 300 rupees for an animal of the most modest pretensions. It is reckoned eight days from Darjeeling to Chumbi, but, riding all day and most of the night, I completed the journey in two. Newspaper correspondents are proverbially in a hurry. To send the first wire from Chumbi I had to leave my kit behind, and ride with poshteen[8] and sleeping-bag tied to my saddle. I was racing another correspondent. At Rungpo I found that he was five hours ahead of me, but he rested on the road, and I had gained three hours on him before he left the next stage at Rora Thang. Here I learnt that he intended to camp at Lingtam, twelve miles further on, in a tent lent him by a transport officer. I made up my mind to wait outside Lingtam until it was dark, and then to steal a march on him unobserved. But I believed no one. Wayside reports were probably intended to deceive me, and no doubt my informant was his unconscious confederate.

[8] Sheepskin.

Outside Rungli, six miles further on, I stopped at a little Bhutia's hut, where he had been resting. They told me he had gone on only half an hour before me. I loitered on the road, and passed Lingtam in the dark. The moon did not rise till three, and riding in the dark was exciting. At first the white dusty road showed clearly enough a few yards ahead, but after passing Lingtam it became a narrow path cut out of a thickly-wooded cliff above a torrent, a wall of rock on one side, a precipice on the other. Here the darkness was intense. A white stone a few yards ahead looked like the branch of a tree overhead. A dim shapeless object to the left might be a house, a rock, a bear--anything. Uphill and downhill could only be distinguished by the angle of the saddle. Every now and then a firefly lit up the white precipice an arm's-length to the right. Once when my pony stopped panting with exhaustion I struck a match and found that we had come to a sharp zigzag. Part of the revetment had fallen; there was a yard of broken path covered with fern and bracken, then a drop of some hundred feet to the torrent below. After that I led my beast for a mile until we came to a charcoal-burner's hut. Two or three Bhutias were sitting round a log fire, and I persuaded one to go in front of me with a lighted brand. So we came to Sedongchen, where I left my beast dead beat, rested a few hours, bought a good mule, and pressed on in the early morning by moonlight. The road to Gnatong lies through a magnificent forest of oak and chestnut. For five miles it is nothing but the ascent of stone steps I have described. Then the rhododendron zone is reached, and one passes through a forest of gnarled and twisted trunks, writhing and contorted as if they had been thrust there for some penance. The place suggested a scene from Dante's 'Inferno.' As I reached the saddle of Lingtu the moon was paling, and the eastern sky-line became a faint violet screen. In a few minutes

Kinchenjunga and Kabru on the north-west caught the first rays of the sun, and were suffused with the delicate rosy glow of dawn.

I reached Gnatong in time to breakfast with the 8th Gurkhas. The camp lies in a little cleft in the hills at an elevation of 12,200 feet. When I last visited the place I thought it one of the most desolate spots I had seen. My first impressions were a wilderness of gray stones and gray, uninhabited houses, felled tree-trunks denuded of bark, white and spectral on the hillside. There was no life, no children's voices or chattering women, no bazaar apparently, no dogs barking, not even a pariah to greet you. If there was a sound of life it was the bray of some discontented mule searching for stray blades of grass among the stones. There were some fifty houses nearly all smokeless and vacant. Some had been barracks at the time of the last Sikkim War, and of the soldiers who inhabited them fifteen still lay in Gnatong in a little gray cemetery, which was the first indication of the nearness of human life. The inscriptions over the graves were all dated 1888, 1889, or 1890, and though but fourteen years had passed, many of them were barely decipherable. The houses were scattered about promiscuously, with no thought of neighbourliness or convenience, as though the people were living there under protest, which was very probably the case. But the place had its picturesque feature. You might mistake some of the houses for tumbledown Swiss ch 鈒 ets of the poorer sort were it not for the miniature fir-trees planted on the roofs, with their burdens of prayers hanging from the branches like parcels on a Christmas-tree.

These were my impressions a year or two ago, but now Gnatong is all life and bustle. In the bazaar a convoy of 300 mules was being loaded. The place was crowded with Nepalese coolies and Tibetan drivers, picturesque in their woollen knee-boots of red and green patterns, with a white star at the foot, long russet cloaks bound tightly at the waist and bulging out with cooking-utensils and changes of dress, embroidered caps of every variety and description, as often as not tied to the head by a wisp of hair. In Rotten Row-- the inscription of 1889 still remains--I met a subaltern with a pair of skates. He showed me to the mess-room, where I enjoyed a warm breakfast and a good deal of chaff about correspondents who 'were in such a devil of a hurry to get to a God-forsaken hole where there wasn't going to be the ghost of a show.'

I left Gnatong early on a borrowed pony. A mile and a half from the camp the road crosses the Tuko Pass, and one descends again for another two miles to Kapup, a temporary transport stage. The path lies to the west of the Bidang Tso, a beautiful lake with a moraine at the north-west side. The mountains were strangely silent, and the only sound of wild life was the whistling of the red-billed choughs, the commonest of the Corvid?at these heights. They were flying round and round the lake in an unsettled manner, whistling querulously, as though in complaint at the intrusion of their solitude.

I reached the Jelap soon after noon. No snow had fallen. The approach was over broken rock and shale. At the summit was a row of cairns, from which fluttered praying-flags and tattered bits of votive raiment. Behind us and on both sides was a thin mist, but in front my eyes explored a deep narrow valley bathed in sunshine. Here, then, was Tibet, the forbidden, the mysterious. In the distance all the land was that yellow and brick-dust colour I had often seen in pictures and thought exaggerated and unreal. Far to the north-east Chumulari (23,930 feet), with its magnificent white spire rising from the roof-like mass behind, looked like an immense cathedral of snow. Far below on a yellow hillside hung the Kanjut Lamasery above Rinchengong. In the valley beneath lay Chumbi and the road to Lhasa.

There is a descent of over 4,000 feet in six miles from the summit of the Jelap. The valley is perfectly straight, without a bend, so that one can look down from the pass upon the Kanjut monastery on the hillside immediately above Yatung. The pass would afford an impregnable military position to a people with the rudiments of science and martial spirit. A few riflemen on the cliffs that command it might annihilate a column with perfect safety, and escape into Bhutan before any flanking movement could be made. Yet miles of straggling convoy are allowed to pass daily with the supplies that are necessary for the existence of the force ahead. The road to Phari Jong passes through two military walls. The first at Yatung, six miles below the pass, is a senseless obstruction, and any able-bodied Tommy with hobnailed boots might very easily kick it down. It has no block-houses, and would be useless against a flank attack. Before our advance to Chumbi the wall was inhabited by three Chinese officials, a dingpon, or Tibetan sergeant, and twenty Tibetan soldiers. It served as a barrier beyond which no British subject was allowed to pass. The second wall lies across the valley at Gob-sorg, four miles beyond our camp at Chumbi. It is roofed and loop-holed like the Yatung barrier, and is defended by block-houses. This fortification and every mile of valley between the Jelap and Gautsa might be held by a single company against an invading force. Yet there are not half a dozen Chinese or Tibetan soldiers in the valley. No opposition is expected this side of the Tang la, but nondescript troops armed with matchlocks and bows hover round the mission on the open plateau beyond. Our evacuation of Khamba Jong and occupation of Chumbi were so rapid and unexpected that it is thought the Tibetans had no time to bring troops into the valley; but to anyone who knows their strategical incompetence, no explanation is necessary.

Yatung is reached by one of the worst sections of road on the march; one comes across a dead transport mule at almost every zigzag of the descent. For ten years the village has enjoyed the distinction of being the only place in Southern Tibet accessible to Europeans. Not that many Europeans avail themselves of its accessibility, for it is a dreary enough place to live in, shrouded as it is in cloud more than half the year round, and embedded in a valley so deep and narrow that in winter-time the sun has hardly risen above one cliff when it sinks behind another. The privilege of access to Yatung was the result of the agreement between Great Britain and China with regard to trade communications between India and Tibet drawn up in Darjeeling in 1893, subsequently to the Sikkim Convention. It was then stipulated that there should be a trade mart at Yatung to which British subjects should have free access, and that there should be special trade facilities between Sikkim and Tibet. It is reported that the Chinese Amban took good care that Great Britain should not benefit by these new regulations, for after signing the agreement which was to give the Indian tea-merchants a market in Tibet, he introduced new regulations the other side of the frontier, which prohibited the purchase of Indian tea. Whether the story is true or not, it is certainly characteristic of the evasion and duplicity which have brought about the present armed mission into Tibet.

To-day, as one rides through the cobbled street of Yatung, the only visible effects of the Convention are the Chinese Customs House with its single European officer, and the residence of a lady missionary, or trader, as the exigencies of international diplomacy oblige her to term herself. The Customs House, which was opened on May 1, 1894, was first established with the object of estimating the trade between India and Tibet--traffic is not permitted by any other route than the Jelap--and with a view to taxation when the trade should make it worth while. It was stipulated that no duties should be levied for the period of five years. Up to the present no tariff has been imposed, and the only apparent use the Customs House serves is to collect statistics, and perhaps to remind Tibet of the shadowy suzerainty of China. The natives have boycotted the place, and refuse to trade there, and no European or native of India has thought it worth while to open a market. Phari is the real trade mart on the frontier, and Kalimpong, in British Bhutan, is the foreign trade mart. But the whole trade between India and Tibet is on such a small scale that it might be in the hands of a single merchant.

The Customs House, the missionary house, and the houses of the clerks and servants of the Customs and of the headman, form a little block. Beyond it there is a quarter of a mile of barren stony ground, and then the wall with military pretensions. I rode through the gate unchallenged.

At Rinchengong, a mile beyond the barrier, the Yatung stream flows into the Ammo Chu. The road follows the eastern bank of the river, passing through Cheuma and Old Chumbi, where it crosses the stream. After crossing the bridge, a mile of almost level ground takes one into Chumbi camp. I reached Chumbi on the evening of January 12, and was able to send the Daily Mail the first cable from Tibet, having completed the journey from Darjeeling in two days' hard riding.

The camp lies in a shallow basin in the hills, and is flanked by brown fir-clad hills which rise some 1,500 feet above the river-bed, and preclude a view of the mountains on all sides. The situation is by no means the best from the view of comfort, but strategic reasons make it necessary, for if the camp were pitched half a mile further up the valley, the gorge of the stream which debouches into the Ammo River to the north of Chumbi would give the Tibetans an opportunity of attacking us in the rear. Despite the protection of almost Arctic clothing, one shivers until the sun rises over the eastern hill at ten o'clock, and shivers again when it sinks behind the opposite one at three. Icy winds sweep the valley, and hurricanes of dust invade one's tent. Against this cold one clothes one's self in flannel vest and shirt, sweater, flannel-lined coat, poshteen or Cashmere sheepskin, wool-lined Gilgit boots, and fur or woollen cap with flaps meeting under the chin. The general effect is barbaric and picturesque. In after-days the trimness of a military club may recall the scene--officers clad in gold-embroidered poshteen, yellow boots, and fur caps, bearded like wild Kerghizes, and huddling round the camp fire in this black cauldron-like valley under the stars.

Officers are settling down in Chumbi as comfortably as possible for winter quarters. Primitive dens have been dug out of the ground, walled up with boulders, and roofed in with green fir-branches. In some cases a natural rock affords a whole wall. The den where I am now writing is warmed by a cheerful pinewood blaze, a luxury after the angeiti in one's tent. I write at an operating-table after a dinner of minal (pheasant) and yak's heart. A gramophone is dinning in my ears. It is destined, I hope, to resound in the palace of Potala, where the Dalai Lama and his suite may wonder what heathen ritual is accompanied by 'A jovial monk am I,' and 'Her golden hair was hanging down her back.'

Both at home and in India one hears the Tibet Mission spoken of enviously as a picnic. There is an idea of an encampment in a smiling valley, and easy marches towards the mysterious city. In reality, there is plenty of hard and uninteresting work. The expedition is attended with all the discomforts of a campaign, and very little of the excitement. Colonel Younghusband is now at Tuna, a desolate hamlet on the Tibetan plateau, exposed to the coldest winds of Asia, where the thermometer falls to 25?below zero. Detachments of the escort are scattered along the line of communications in places of varying cold and discomfort, where they must wait until the necessary supplies have been carried through to Phari. It is not likely that Colonel Younghusband will be able to proceed to Gyantse before March. In the meanwhile, imagine the Pioneers and Gurkhas, too cold to wash or shave, shivering in a dirty Tibetan fort, half suffocated with smoke from a yak-dung fire. Then there is the transport officer shut up in some narrow valley of Sikkim, trying to make half a dozen out of three with his camp of sick beasts and sheaf of urgent telegrams calling for supplies. He hopes there will be 'a show,' and that he may be in it. Certainly if anyone deserves to go to Lhasa and get a medal for it, it is the supply and transport man. But he will be left behind.

CHAPTER III

THE CHUMBI VALLEY

CHUMBI, February, 1904.

The Chumbi Valley is inhabited by the Tomos, who are said to be descendants of ancient cross-marriages between the Bhutanese and Lepchas. They only intermarry among themselves, and speak a language which would not be understood in other parts of Tibet. As no Tibetan proper is allowed to pass the Yatung barrier, the Tomos have the monopoly of the carrying trade between Phari and Kalimpong. They are voluntarily under the protection of the Tibetans, who treat them liberally, as the Lamas realize the danger of their geographical position as a buffer state, and are shrewd enough to recognise that any ill treatment or oppression would drive them to seek protection from the Bhutanese or British.

The Tomos are merry people, hearty, and good-natured. They are wonderfully hardy and enduring. In the coldest winter months, when the thermometer is 20?below zero, they will camp out at night in the snow, forming a circle of their loads, and sleep contentedly inside with no tent or roofing. The women would be comely if it were not for the cutch that they smear over their faces. The practice is common to the Tibetans and Bhutanese, but no satisfactory reason has been found for it. The Jesuit Father, Johann Grueber, who visited Tibet in 1661, attributed the custom to a religious whim:--'The women, out of a religious whim, never wash, but daub themselves with a nasty kind of oil, which not only causes them to stink intolerably, but renders them extremely ugly and deformed.' A hundred and eighty years afterwards Huc noticed the same habit, and attributed it to an edict issued by the Dalai Lama early in the seventeenth century. 'The women of Tibet in those days were much given to dress, and libertinage, and corrupted the Lamas to a degree to bring their holy order into a bad repute.' The then Nome Khan (deputy of the Dalai Lama), accordingly issued an order that the women should never appear in public without smearing their faces with a black disfiguring paste. Huc recorded that though the order was still obeyed, the practice was observed without much benefit to morals. If you ask a Tomo or Tibetan to-day why their women smear and daub themselves in this unbecoming manner, they invariably reply, like the Mussulman or Hindu, that it is custom. Mongolians do not bother themselves about causes.

The Tomo women wear a flat green distinctive cap, with a red badge in the front, which harmonizes with their complexion--a coarse, brick red, of which the primal ingredients are dirt and cutch, erroneously called pig's blood, and the natural ruddiness of a healthy outdoor life in a cold climate. A procession of these sirens is comely and picturesque--at a hundred yards. They wrap themselves round and round with a thick woollen blanket of pleasing colour and pattern, and wear on their feet high woollen boots with leather or rope soles. If it was not for their disfiguring toilet many of them would be handsome. The children are generally pretty, and I have seen one or two that were really beautiful. When we left a camp the villagers would generally get wind of it, and come down for loot. Old newspapers, tins, bottles, string, and cardboard boxes were treasured prizes. We threw these out of our cave, and the children scrambled for them, and even the women made dives at anything particularly tempting. My last impression of Lingmathang was a group of women giggling and gesticulating over the fashion plates and advertisements in a number of the Lady, which somebody's memsahib had used for the packing of a ham.

The Tomos, though not naturally given to cleanliness, realize the hygienic value of their hot springs. There are resorts in the neighbourhood of Chumbi as fashionable as Homburg or Salsomaggiore; mixed bathing is the rule, without costumes. These healthy folk are not morbidly conscious of sex. The springs contain sulphur and iron, and are undoubtedly efficacious. Where they are not hot enough, the Tomos bake large boulders in the ashes of a log fire, and roll them into the water to increase the temperature.

Tomos and Tibetans are fond of smoking. They dry the leaves of the wild rhubarb, and mix them with tobacco leaves. The mixture is called dopta, and was the favourite blend of the country. Now hundreds of thousands of cheap American cigarettes are being introduced, and a lucrative tobacco-trade has sprung up. Boxes of ten, which are sold at a pice in Darjeeling, fetch an anna at Chumbi, and two annas at Phari. Sahibs smoke them, sepoys smoke them, drivers and followers smoke them, and the Tomo coolies smoke nothing else. Tibetan children of three appreciate them hugely, and the road from Phari to Rungpo is literally strewn with the empty boxes.

There is a considerable Chinese element in the Chumbi Valley--a frontier officer, with the local rank of the Fourth Button, a colonel, clerks of the Customs House, and troops numbering from one to two hundred. These, of course, were not in evidence when we occupied the valley in December. The Chinese are not accompanied by their wives, but take to themselves women of the country, whose offspring people the so-called Chinese villages. The pure Chinaman does not remain in the country after his term of office. Life at Chumbi is the most tedious exile to him, and he looks down on the Tomos as barbarous savages. He is as unhappy as a Frenchman in Tonquin, cut off from all the diversions of social and intellectual life. The frontier officer at Bibi-thang told me that he had brought his wife with him, and the poor lady had never left the house, but cried incessantly for China and civilization. Yet to the uninitiated the Chinese villages of Gob-sorg and Bibi-thang might have been taken from the far East and plumped down on the Indian frontier. There is the same far-Eastern smell, the same doss-house, the same hanging lamps, the same red lucky paper over the lintels of the doors, and the same red and green abortions on the walls.

Much has been written and duly contradicted about the fertility of the Chumbi Valley. If one does not expect orange-groves and rice-fields at 12,000 feet, it must be admitted that the valley is, relatively speaking, fertile--that is to say, its produce is sufficient to support its three or four thousand inhabitants.

The lower valley produces buckwheat, turnips, potatoes, radishes, and barley. The latter, the staple food of the Tibetans, has, when ground, an appetizing smell very like oatmeal. The upper valley is quite sterile, and produces nothing but barley, which does not ripen; it is gathered for fodder when green, and the straw is sold at high prices to the merchants who visit Phari from Tibet and Bhutan. This year the Tibetan merchants are afraid to come, and the commissariat benefits by a very large supply of fodder which ought to see them through the summer.

The idea that the valley is unusually fertile probably arose from the well-to-do appearance of the natives of Rinchengong and Chumbi, and their almost palatial houses, which give evidence of a prosperity due to trade rather than agriculture.

The hillsides around Chumbi produce wild strawberries, raspberries, currants, and cherries; but these are quite insipid in this sunless climate.

The Chinese Custom's officer at Yatung tells me that the summer months, though not hot, are relaxing and enervating. The thermometer never rises above 70? The rainfall does not average quite 50 inches; but almost daily at noon a mist creeps up from Bhutan, and a constant drizzle falls. In June, July, and August, 1901, there were only three days without rain.

At Phari I met a venerable old gentleman who gave me some statistics. The old man, Katsak Kasi by name, was a Tibetan from the Kham province, acting at Phari as trade agent for the Bhutanese Government. His face was seared and parchment-like from long exposure to cold winds and rough weather. His features were comparatively aquiline--that is to say, they did not look as if they had been flattened out in youth. He wore a very large pair of green spectacles, with a gold bulb at each end and a red tassel in the middle, which gave him an air of wisdom and distinction. He answered my rather inquisitive questions with courtesy and decision, and yet with such a serious care for details that I felt quite sure his figures must be accurate.

If statistics were any gauge of the benefits Indian trade would derive from an open market with Tibet, the present mission, as far as commercial interests are concerned, would be wasted. According to Kasi's statistics, the cost of two dozen or thirty mules would balance the whole of the annual revenue on Indian imports into the country. The idea that duties are levied at the Yatung and Gob-sorg barriers is a mistake. The only Customs House is at Phari, where the Indian and Bhutanese trade-routes meet. The Customs are under the supervision of the two jongpens, who send the revenue to Lhasa twice a year.

The annual income on imports from India, Kasi assured me, is only 6,000 rupees, whereas the income on exports amounts to 20,000. Tibetan trade with India consists almost entirely of wool, yaks'-tails, and ponies. There is a tax of 2 rupees 8 annas on ponies, 1 rupee a maund on wool, and 1 rupee 8 annas a maund on yaks'-tails. Our imports into Tibet, according to Kasi's statistics, are practically nil. Some piece goods, iron vessels, and tobacco leaves find their way over the Jelap, but it is a common sight to see mules returning into Tibet with nothing but their drivers' cooking utensils and warm clothing.[9]

[9] The only articles imported to the value of ?,000 are cotton goods, woollen cloths, metals, chinaware, coral, indigo, maize, silk, fur, and tobacco.

The only exports to the value of ?,000 are musk, ponies, skins, wool, and yaks'-tails.

Appended are the returns for the years 1895-1902:

Year. Value of Articles Value of Articles Total Value of Imported into Exported from Imports and Tibet. Tibet. Exports. Rs. Rs. Rs. 1895 416,218 634,086 1,050,304 1896 561,395 781,269 1,342,664 1897 674,139 820,300 1,494,436 1898 718,475 817,851 1,536,326 1899 962,637 822,760 1,785,397 1900 730,502 710,012 1,440,514 1901 734,075 783,480 1,517,555 1902 761,837 805,338 1,567,075

Customs House Returns, Yatung.

At present no Indian tea passes Yatung. That none is sold at Phari confirms the rumour I mentioned that the Chinese Amban, after signing the trade regulations between India and Tibet in Darjeeling, 1893, crossed the frontier to introduce new laws, virtually annulling the regulations. Indian tea might be carried into Tibet, but not sold there. Tibet has consistently broken all her promises and treaty obligations. She has placed every obstacle in the way of Indian trade, and insulted our Commissioners; yet the despatch of the present mission with its armed escort has been called an act of aggression.

When I asked Kasi if the Tibetans would be angry with him for helping us, he said they would certainly cut off his head if he remained in the fort after we had left. There is some foundation in travellers' stories about the punishment inflicted on the guards of the passes and other officials who fail to prevent Europeans entering Tibet or pushing on towards Lhasa.

Some Chumbi traders who were in Lhasa when we entered the valley are still detained there, as far as I can gather, as hostages for the good behaviour of their neighbours. In Tibet the punishment does not fit the crime. The guards of a pass are punished for letting white men through, quite irrespective of the opposing odds.

The commonest punishment in Tibet is flogging, but the ordeal is so severe that it often proves fatal. I asked Kasi some questions about the magisterial powers of the two jongpens, or district officers, who remained in the fort some days after we occupied it. He told me that they could not pass capital sentence, but they might flog the prisoners, and if they died, nothing was said. Several victims have died of flogging at Phari.

The natives in Darjeeling have a story of Tibetan methods, which have always seemed to me the refinement of cruelty. At Gyantse, they say, the criminal is flung into a dark pit, where he cannot tell whether it is night or day. Cobras and scorpions and reptiles of various degrees of venom are his companions; these he may hear in the darkness, for it is still enough, and seek or avoid as he has courage. Food is sometimes thrown in to tempt any faint-hearted wretch to prolong his agony. I asked Kasi if there were any truth in the tale. He told me that there were no venomous snakes in Tibet, but he had heard that there was a dark prison in Gyantse, where criminals sometimes died of scorpion bites; he added that only the worst offenders were punished in this way. The modified version of the story is gruesome enough.

It is usual for Tibetan and Bhutanese officials to receive their pay in grain, it being understood that their position puts them in the way of obtaining the other necessaries of life, and perhaps a few of its luxuries. Kasi, being an important official, receives from the Bhutan Government forty maunds of barley and forty maunds of rice annually. He receives, in addition, a commission on the trade disputes that he decides in proportion to their importance. He is now an invaluable servant of the British Government. At his nod the barren solitudes round Phari are wakening into life. From the fort bastions one sees sometimes on the hills opposite an indistinct black line, like a caterpillar gradually assuming shape. They are Kasi's yaks coming from some blind valley which no one but a hunter or mountaineer would have imagined to exist. Ponies, grain, and fodder are also imported from Bhutan and sold to the mutual gratification of the Bhutanese and ourselves. The yaks are hired and employed on the line of communications.

It is to be hoped that the Bhutanese, when they hear of our good prices, will send supplies over the frontier to hasten our advance. But we must take care than no harm befalls Kasi for his good services. When I asked him how he stood with the Tibetan Government, he laid his hand in a significant manner across his throat.

LINGMATHANG, February.

Before entering the bare, unsheltered plateau of Tibet, the road to Lhasa winds through seven miles of pine forest, which recalls some of the most beautiful valleys of Switzerland.

The wood-line ends abruptly. After that there is nothing but barrenness and desolation. The country round Chumbi is not very thickly forested. There are long strips of arable land on each side of the road, and villages every two or three miles. The fields are terraced and enclosed within stone walls. Scattered on the hillside are stone-built houses, with low, over-hanging eaves, and long wooden tiles, each weighed down with a gray boulder. One might imagine one's self in Kandersteg or Lauterbrunnen; only lofty praying flags and mani-walls brightly painted with Buddhistic pictures and inscriptions dispel the illusion.

There is no lack of colour. In the winter months a brier with large red berries and a low, foxy-brown thornbush, like a young osier in March, lend a russet hue to the landscape. Higher on the hills the withered grass is yellow, and the blending of these quiet tints, russet, brown, and yellow, gives the valley a restful beauty; but in cloud it is sombre enough.

Three years ago I visited Yatung in May. In springtime there is a profusion of colour. The valley is beautiful, beyond the beauty of the grandest Alpine scenery, carpeted underfoot with spring flowers, and ablaze overhead with flowering rhododendrons. To try to describe mountains and forests is a most unprofitable task; all the adjectives of scenic description are exhausted; the coinage has been too long debased. For my own part, it has been almost a pain to visit the most beautiful parts of the earth and to know that one's sensations are incommunicable, that it is impossible to make people believe and understand. To those who have not seen, scenery is either good, bad, or indifferent; there are no degrees. Ruskin, the greatest master of description, is most entertaining when he is telling us about the domestic circle at Herne Hill. But mountain scenery is of all the most difficult to describe. The sense of the Himalayas is intangible. There are elusive lights and shades, and sounds and whispers, and unfamiliar scents, and a thousand fleeting manifestations of the genius of the place that are impossible to arrest. Magnificent, majestic, splendid, are weak, colourless words that depict nothing. It is the poets who have described what they have not seen who have been most successful. Milton's hell is as real as any landscape of Byron's, and the country through which Childe Roland rode to the Dark Tower is more vivid and present to us than any of Wordsworth's Westmoreland tarns and valleys. So it is a poem of the imagination--'Kubla Khan'--that seems to me to breathe something of the spirit of the Yatung and Chumbi Valleys, only there is a little less of mystery and gloom here, and a little more of sunshine and brightness than in the dream poem. Instead of attempting to describe the valley--Paradise would be easier to describe--I will try to explain as logically as possible why it fascinated me more than any scenery I have seen.

I had often wondered if there were any place in the East where flowers grow in the same profusion as in Europe--in England, or in Switzerland. The nearest approach I had seen was in the plateau of the Southern Shan States, at about 4,000 feet, where the flora is very homelike. But the ground is not carpeted; one could tread without crushing a blossom. Flowers are plentiful, too, on the southern slopes of the Himalayas, and on the hills on the Siamese side of the Tennasserim frontier, but I had seen nothing like a field of marsh-marigolds and cuckoo-flowers in May, or a meadow of buttercups and daisies, or a bank of primroses, or a wood carpeted with bluebells, or a hillside with heather, or an Alpine slope with gentians and ranunculus. I had been told that in Persia in springtime the valleys of the Shapur River and the Karun are covered profusely with lilies, also the forests of Manchuria in the neighbourhood of the Great White Mountain; but until I crossed the Jelapla and struck down the valley to Yatung I thought I would have to go West to see such things again. Never was such profusion. Besides the primulas[10]--I counted eight different kinds of them--and gentians and anemones and celandines and wood sorrel and wild strawberries and irises, there were the rhododendrons glowing like coals through the pine forest. As one descended the scenery became more fascinating; the valley narrowed, and the stream was more boisterous. Often the cliffs hung sheer over the water's edge; the rocks were coated with green and yellow moss, which formed a bed for the dwarf rhododendron bushes, now in full flower, white and crimson and cream, and every hue between a dark reddish brown and a light sulphury yellow--not here and there, but everywhere, jostling one another for nooks and crannies in the rock.[11]

[10] Between Gnatong and Gautsa, thirteen different species of primulas are

found. They are: Primula Petiolaris, P. glabra, P. Sapphirina, P. pusilia, P. Kingii, P. Elwesiana, P. Capitata, P. Sikkimensis, P. Involucra, P. Denticulata, P. Stuartii, P. Soldanelloides, P. Stirtonia.

[11] The species are: Rhododendron campanulatum, purple flowers; R. Fulgens, scarlet; R. Hodgsonii, rose-coloured; R. Anthopogon, white; R. Virgatum, purple; R. Nivale, rose-red; R. Wightii, yellow; R. Falconeri, cream-coloured; R. cinndbarinum, brick-red ('The Gates of Tibet,' Appendix I., J. A. H. Louis).

These delicate flowers are very different from their dowdy cousin, the coarse red rhododendron of the English shrubbery. At a little distance they resemble more hothouse azaleas, and equal them in wealth of blossom.

The great moss-grown rocks in the bed of the stream were covered with equal profusion. Looking behind, the snows crowned the pine-trees, and over them rested the blue sky. And here is the second reason--as I am determined to be logical in my preference--why I found the valley so fascinating. In contrasting the Himalayas with the Alps, there is always something that the former is without. Never the snows, and the water, and the greenery at the same time; if the greenery is at your feet, the snows are far distant; where the Himalayas gain in grandeur they lose in beauty. So I thought the wild valley of Lauterbrunnen, lying at the foot of the Jungfrau, the perfection of Alpine scenery until I saw the valley of Yatung, a pine-clad mountain glen, green as a hawthorn hedge in May, as brilliantly variegated as a beechwood copse in autumn, and culminating in the snowy peak that overhangs the Jelapla. The valley has besides an intangible fascination, indescribable because it is illogical. Certainly the light that played upon all these colours seemed to me softer than everyday sunshine; and the opening spring foliage of larch and birch and mountain ash seemed more delicate and varied than on common ground. Perhaps it was that I was approaching the forbidden land. But what irony, that this seductive valley should be the approach to the most bare and unsheltered country in Asia!

Even now, in February, I can detect a few salmon-coloured leaf-buds, which remind me that the month of May will be a revelation to the mission force, when their veins are quickened by the unfamiliar warmth, and their eyes dazzled by this unexpected treasure which is now germinating in the brown earth.

Four miles beyond Chumbi the road passes through the second military wall at the Chinese village of Gob-sorg. Riding through the quiet gateway beneath the grim, hideous figure of the goddess Dolma carved on the rock above, one feels a silent menace. One is part of more than a material invasion; one has passed the gate that has been closed against the profane for centuries; one has committed an irretrievable step. Goddess and barrier are symbols of Tibet's spiritual and material agencies of opposition. We have challenged and defied both. We have entered the arena now, and are to be drawn into the vortex of all that is most sacred and hidden, to struggle there with an implacable foe, who is protected by the elemental forces of nature.

Inside the wall, above the road, stands the Chinese village of Gob-sorg. The Chinamen come out of their houses and stand on the revetment to watch us pass. They are as quiet and ugly as their gods. They gaze down on our convoys and modern contrivances with a silent contempt that implies a consciousness of immemorial superiority. Who can tell what they think or what they wish, these undivinable creatures? They love money, we know, and they love something else that we cannot know. It is not country, or race, or religion, but an inscrutable something that may be allied to these things, that induces a mental obstinacy, an unfathomable reserve which may conceal a wisdom beyond our philosophy or mere callousness and indifference. The thing is there, though it has no European name or definition. It has caused many curious and unexplained outbreaks in different parts of the world, and it is no doubt symbolized in their inexpressibly hideous flag. The element is non-conductive, and receives no current from progress, and it is therefore incommunicable to us who are wrapped in the pride of evolution. The question here and elsewhere is whether the Chinese love money more or this inscrutable dragon element. If it is money, their masks must have concealed a satisfaction at the prospect of the increased trade that follows our flag; if the dragon element, a grim hope that we might be cut off in the wilderness and annihilated by Asiatic hordes.

Unlike the Chinese, the Tomos are unaffectedly glad to see us in the valley. The humblest peasant is the richer by our presence, and the landowners and traders are more prosperous than they have been for many years. Their uncompromising reception of us makes a withdrawal from the Chumbi Valley impossible, for the Tibetans would punish them relentlessly for the assistance they have given their enemies.

A mile beyond Gob-sorg is the Tibetan village of Galing-ka, where the praying-flags are as thick as masts in a dockyard, and streams of paper prayers are hung across the valley to prevent the entrance of evil spirits. Chubby little children run out and salute one with a cry of 'Backsheesh!' the first alien word in their infant vocabulary.

A mile further a sudden turn in the valley brings one to a level plain--a phenomenally flat piece of ground where one can race two miles along the straight. No one passes it without remarking that it is the best site for a hill-station in Northern India. Where else can one find a racecourse, polo-ground, fishing, and shooting, and a rainfall that is little more than a third of that of Darjeeling? Three hundred feet above the stream on the west bank is a plateau, apparently intended for building sites. The plain in the valley was naturally designed for the training of mounted infantry, and is now, probably for the first time, being turned to its proper use.

LINGMATHANG, March 18.

I have left the discomforts of Phari, and am camping now on the Lingmathang Plain. I am writing in a natural cave in the rock. The opening is walled in by a sangar of stones 5 feet high, from which pine-branches support a projecting roof. On fine days the space between the roof and wall is left open, and called the window; but when it snows, gunny-bags are let down as purdahs, and the den becomes very warm and comfortable. There is a natural hearth, a natural chimney-piece, and a natural chimney that draws excellently. The place is sheltered by high cliffs, and it is very pleasant to look out from this snugness on a wintry landscape, and ground covered deep with snow.

Outside, seventy shaggy Tibetan ponies, rough and unshod, averaging 12? hands, are tethered under the shelter of a rocky cliff. They are being trained according to the most approved methods of modern warfare. The Mounted Infantry Corps, mostly volunteers from the 23rd and 32nd Pioneers and 8th Gurkhas, are under the command of Captain Ottley of the 23rd. The corps was raised at Gnatong in December, and though many of the men had not ridden before, after two months' training they cut a very respectable figure in the saddle. A few years ago a proposal was made to the military authorities that the Pioneers, like other regiments, should go in for a course of mounted infantry training. The reply caused much amusement at the time. The suggestion was not adopted, but orders were issued that 'every available opportunity should be taken of teaching the Pioneers to ride in carts.' A wag in the force naturally suggests that the new Ekka Corps, now running between Phari and Tuna, should be utilized to carry out the spirit of this order. Certainly on the road beyond the Tangla the ekkas would require some sitting.

The present mission is the third 'show' on which the 23rd and 32nd have been together during the last nine years. In Chitral and Waziristan they fought side by side. It is no exaggeration to say that these regiments have been on active service three years out of five since they were raised in 1857. The original draft of the 32nd, it will be remembered, was the unarmed volunteer corps of Mazbi Sikhs, who offered themselves as an escort to the convoy from Lahore to Delhi during the siege. The Mazbis were the most lawless and refractory folk in the Punjab, and had long been the despair of Government. On arrival at Delhi they were employed in the trenches, rushing in to fill up the places of the killed and wounded as fast as they fell. It will be remembered that they formed the fatigue party who carried the powder-bags to blow up the Cashmere Gate. A hundred and fifty-seven of them were killed during the siege. With this brilliant opening it is no wonder that they have been on active service almost continually since.

A frontier campaign would be incomplete without the 32nd or 23rd. It was the 32nd who cut their way through 5 feet of snow, and carried the battery guns to the relief of Chitral. The 23rd Pioneers were also raised from the Mazbi Sikhs in the same year of the Mutiny, 1857. The history of the two regiments is very similar. The 23rd distinguished themselves in China, Abyssinia, Afghanistan, and numerous frontier campaigns. One of the most brilliant exploits was when, with the Gordon Highlanders under Major (now Sir George) White, they captured the Afghan guns at Kandahar. To-day the men of the two regiments meet again as members of the same corps on the Lingmathang Plain. Naturally the most cordial relations exist between the men, and one can hear them discussing old campaigns as they sit round their pinewood fires in the evenings. They and the twenty men of the 8th Gurkhas (of Manipur fame) turn out together every morning for exercise on their diminutive steeds. They ride without saddle or stirrups, and though they have only been horsemen for two months, they seldom fall off at the jumps. The other day, when a Mazbi Sikh took a voluntary into the hedge, a genial Gurkha reminded him of the eccentric order 'to practise riding in carts.'

At Lingmathang we have had a fair amount of sport of a desultory kind. The neighbouring forests are the home of that very rare and little-known animal, the shao, or Sikkim stag. The first animal of the species to fall to a European gun was shot by Major Wallace Dunlop on the Lingmathang Hills in January. A month later Captain Ottley wounded a buck which he was not able to follow up on account of a heavy fall of snow. Lately one or two shao--does in all cases--have come down to visit the plain. While we were breakfasting on the morning of the 16th, we heard a great deal of shouting and halloaing, and a Gurkha jemadar ran up to tell us that a female shao, pursued by village dogs, had broken through the jungle on the hillside and emerged on the plain a hundred yards from our camp. We mounted at once, and Ottley deployed the mounted infantry, who were ready for parade, to head the beast from the hills. The shao jinked like a hare, and crossed and recrossed the stream several times, but the poor beast was exhausted, and, after twenty minutes' exciting chase, we surrounded it. Captain Ottley threw himself on the animal's neck and held it down until a sepoy arrived with ropes to bind its hind-legs. The chase was certainly a unique incident in the history of sport--a field of seventy in the Himalayas, a clear spurt in the open, no dogs, and the quarry the rarest zoological specimen in the world. The beast stood nearly 14 hands, and was remarkable for its long ears and elongated jaw. The sequel was sad. Besides the fright and exhaustion, the captured shao sustained an injury in the loin; it pined, barely nibbled at its food, and, after ten days, died.

Sikkim stags are sometimes shot by native shikaris, and there is great rivalry among members of the mission force in buying their heads. They are shy, inaccessible beasts, and they are not met with beyond the wood limit.

The shooting in the Chumbi Valley is interesting to anyone fond of natural history, though it is a little disappointing from the sportsman's point of view. When officers go out for a day's shooting, they think they have done well if they bring home a brace of pheasants. When the sappers and miners began to work on the road below Gautsa, the blood-pheasants used to come down to the stream to watch the operations, but now one sees very few game-birds in the valley. The minal is occasionally shot. The cock-bird, as all sportsmen know, is, with the exception of the Argus-eye, the most beautiful pheasant in the world. There is a lamasery in the neighbourhood, where the birds are almost tame. The monks who feed them think that they are inhabited by the spirits of the blest. Where the snow melts in the pine-forests and leaves soft patches and moist earth, you will find the blood-pheasant. When you disturb them they will run up the hillside and call vociferously from their new hiding-place, so that you may get another shot. Pheasant-shooting here is not sport; the birds seldom rise, and when they do it is almost impossible to get a shot at them in the thick jungle. One must shoot them running for the pot. Ten or a dozen is not a bad bag for one gun later in the year, when more snow has fallen.

At a distance the blood-pheasant appears a dowdy bird. The hen is quite insignificant, but, on a closer acquaintance, the cock shows a delicate colour-scheme of mauve, pink, and green, which is quite different from the plumage of any other bird I have seen. The skins fetch a good price at home, as fishermen find them useful for making flies. A sportsman who has shot in the Yatung Valley regularly for four years tells me that the cock-bird of this species is very much more numerous than the hen. Another Chumbi pheasant is the tracopan, a smaller bird than the minal, and very beautifully marked. I have not heard of a tracopan being shot this season; the bird is not at all common anywhere on this side of the Himalayas.

Snow-partridge sometimes come down to the Lingmathang hills; in the adjacent Kongbu Valley they are plentiful. These birds are gregarious, and are found among the large, loose boulders on the hill-tops. In appearance they are a cross between the British grouse and the red-legged partridge, having red feet and legs uncovered with feathers, and a red bill and chocolate breast. The feathers of the back and rump are white, with broad, defined bars of rich black.

Another common bird is the snow-pigeon. Large flocks of them may be seen circling about the valley anywhere between Phari and Chumbi. Sometimes, when we are sitting in our cave after dinner, we hear the tweek of solitary snipe flying overhead, but we have never flushed any. Every morning before breakfast I stroll along the river bank with a gun, and often put up a stray duck. I have frequently seen goosanders on the river, but not more than two or three in a party. They never leave the Himalayas. The only migratory duck I have observed are the common teal and Brahminy or ruddy sheldrake, and these only in pairs. The latter, though despised on the plains, are quite edible up here. I discredit the statement that they feed on carrion, as I have never seen one near the carcasses of the dead transport animals that are only too plentiful in the valley just now. After comparing notes with other sportsmen, I conclude that the Ammo Chu Valley is not a regular route for migratory duck. The odd teal that I shot in February were probably loiterers that were not strong enough to join in the flight southwards.

Near Lingmathang I shot the ibis bill (Ibidorhynchus Struthersi), a bird which is allied to the oyster catchers. This was the first Central Asian species I met.

GAUTSA, February.

Gautsa, which lies five miles north of Lingmathang, nearly half-way between Chumbi and Phari, must be added to the map. A week or two ago the place was deserted and unnamed; it did not boast a single cowherd's hut. Now it is a busy camp, and likely to be a permanent halting-place on the road to Phari. The camp lies in a deep, moss-carpeted hollow, with no apparent egress. On three sides it is flanked by rocky cliffs, densely forested with pine and silver birch; on the fourth rises an abrupt wall of rock, which is suffused with a glow of amber light an hour before sunset. The Ammo Chu, which is here nothing but a 20-foot stream frozen over at night, bisects the camp. The valley is warm and sheltered, and escapes much of the bitter wind that never spares Chumbi. After dinner one prefers the open-air and a camp fire. Officers who have been up the line before turn into their tents regretfully, for they know that they are saying good-bye to comfort, and will not enjoy the genial warmth of a good fire again until they have crossed the bleak Tibetan tablelands and reached the sparsely-wooded Valley of Gyantse.

CHAPTER IV

PHARI JONG

February 15.

Icy winds and suffocating smoke are not conducive to a literary style, though they sometimes inspire a rude eloquence that is quite unfit for publication. As

I write we are huddling over the mess-room brazier--our youngest optimist would not call it a fire. Men drop in now and then from fatigue duty, and utter an incisive phrase that expresses the general feeling, while we who write for an enlightened public must sacrifice force for euphemism. A week at Phari dispels all illusions; only a bargee could adequately describe the place. Yet the elements, which 'feelingly persuade us' what we are, sometimes inspire us with the eloquence of discomfort.

At Gautsa the air was scented with the fragrance of warm pine-trees, and there was no indication of winter save the ice on the Ammo Chu. The torrent roared boisterously beneath its frozen surface, and threw up little tentacles of frozen spray, which glistened fantastically in the sun. Three miles further up the stream the wood-belt ends abruptly; then, after another three miles, one passes the last stunted bush; after that there is nothing but brown earth and yellow withered grass.

Five miles above Gautsa is Dotah, the most cheerless camp on the march. The wind blows through the gorge unceasingly, and penetrates to the bone. On the left bank of the stream is the frozen waterfall, which might be worshipped by the fanciful and superstitious as embodying the genius of the place, hard and resistless, a crystallized monument of the implacable spirit of Nature in these high places.

At Kamparab, where we camped, two miles higher up the stream, the thermometer fell to 14?below zero. Close by is the meeting-place of the sources of the Ammo Chu. All the plain is undermined with the warrens of the long-haired marmots and voles, who sit on their thresholds like a thousand little spies, and curiously watch our approach, then dive down into their burrows to tell their wives of the strange bearded invaders. They are the despair of their rivals, the sappers and miners, who are trying to make a level road for the new light ekkas. One envies them their warmth and snugness as one rides against the bitter penetrating winds.

Twelve miles from Gautsa a turn in the valley brings one into view of Phari Jong. At first sight it might be a huge isolated rock, but as one approaches the bastions and battlements become more distinct. Distances are deceptive in this rarefied air, and objects that one imagines to be quite close are sometimes found to be several miles distant.

The fort is built on a natural mound in the plain. It is a huge rambling building six stories high, surrounded by a courtyard, where mules and ponies are stabled. As a military fortification Phari Jong is by no means contemptible. The walls are of massive stonework which would take heavy guns to demolish. The angles are protected from attacking parties by machicolated galleries, and three enormous bastions project from each flank. These are crumbling in places, and the Pioneers might destroy the bastion and breach the wall with a bag or two of guncotton. On the eastern side there is a square courtyard like an Arab caravanserai, where cattle are penned. The fortress would hold the whole Tibetan army, with provisions for a year. It was evacuated the night before we reconnoitred the valley.

The interior of the Jong is a warren of stairs, landings, and dark cavernous rooms, which would take a whole day to explore. The walls are built of stone and mud, and coated with century-old smoke. There are no chimneys or adequate windows, and the filth is indescribable. When Phari was first occupied, eighty coolies were employed a whole week clearing away refuse. Judging by the accretion of dirt, a new-comer might class the building as medieval; but filth is no criterion of age, for everything left in the same place becomes quickly coated with grime an inch thick. The dust that invades one's tent at Chumbi is clean and wholesome compared to the Phari dirt, which is the filth of human habitation, the secretion of centuries of foul living. It falls from the roof on one's head, sticks to one's clothes as one brushes against the wall, and is blown up into one's eyes and throat from the floor.

The fort is most insanitary, but a military occupation is necessary. The hacking coughs which are prevalent among officers and men are due to impurities of the air which affect the lungs. Cartloads of dirt are being scraped away every day, but gusts of wind from the lower stories blow up more dust, which penetrates every nook and cranny of the draughty rooms, so that there is a fresh layer by nightfall. To clear the lower stories and cellars would be a hopeless task; even now rooms are found in unexpected places which emit clouds of dust whenever the wind eddies round the basement.

I explored the ground-floor with a lantern, and was completely lost in the maze of passages and dark chambers. When we first occupied the fort, they were filled with straw, gunpowder, and old arms. A hundred and forty maunds of inferior gunpowder was destroyed, and the arms now litter the courtyard. These the Tibetans themselves abandoned as rubbish. The rusty helmets, shields, and breastplates are made of the thinnest iron plates interlaced with leathern thongs, and would not stop an arrow. The old bell-mouthed matchlocks, with their wooden ground-rests, would be more dangerous to the Tibetan marksmen than the enemy. The slings and bows and arrows are reckoned obsolete even by these primitive warriors. Perhaps they attribute more efficacy to the praying-wheels which one encounters at every corner of the fort. The largest are in niches in the wall to left and right of the gateway; rows of smaller ones are attached to the banisters on the landings and to the battlements of the roof. The wheels are covered with grime--the grime of Lamas' hands. Dirt and religion are inseparable in Tibet. The Lamas themselves are the most filthy and malodorous folk I have met in the country. From this it must not be inferred that one class is more cleanly in its habits than another, for nobody ever thinks of washing. Soap is not included in the list of sundries that pass the Customs House at Yatung. If the Lamas are dirtier than the yak-herds and itinerant merchants it is because they lead an indoor life, whereas the pastoral folk are continually exposed to the purifying winds of the tablelands, which are the nearest equivalent in Tibet to a cold bath.

I once read of a Tibetan saint, one of the pupils of Naropa, who was credited with a hundred miraculous gifts, one of which was that he could dive into the water like a fish. Wherein the miracle lay had often puzzled me, but when I met the Lamas of the Kanjut Gompa I understood at once that it was the holy man's contact with the water.

Phari is eloquent of piety, as it is understood in Tibet. The better rooms are frescoed with Buddhistic paintings, and on the third floor is a library, now used as a hospital, where xylograph editions of the Lamaist scriptures and lives of the saints are pigeon-holed in lockers in the wall. The books are printed on thin oblong sheets of Chinese paper, enclosed in boards, and illuminated with quaint coloured tailpieces of holy men in devotional attitudes. Phari fort, with its casual blending of East and West, is full of incongruous effects, but the oddest and most pathetic incongruity is the chorten on the roof, from which, amidst praying-flags and pious offerings of coloured raiment, flutters the Union Jack.

February 18.

The troops are so busy making roads that they have very little time for amusements. The 8th Gurkhas have already constructed some eight miles of road on each side of Phari for the ekka transport. Companies of the 23rd Pioneers are repairing the road at Dotah, Chumbi, and Rinchengong. The 32nd are working at Rinchengong, and the sappers and miners on the Nathula and at Gautsa.

We have started football, and the Gurkhas have a very good idea of the game. One loses one's wind completely at this elevation after every spurt of twenty yards, but recovers it again in a wonderfully short time. Other amusements are sliding and tobogganing, which are a little disappointing to enthusiasts. The ice is lumpy and broken, and the streamlets that run down to the plain are so tortuous that fifty yards without a spill is considered a good run for a toboggan. The funniest sight is to see the Gurkha soldiers trying to drag the toboggan uphill, slipping and tumbling and sprawling on the ice, and immensely enjoying one another's discomfiture.

To clear the dust from one's throat and shake off the depression caused by weeks of waiting in the same place, there is nothing like a day's shooting or exploring in the neighbourhood of Phari. I get up sometimes before daybreak, and spend the whole day reconnoitring with a small party of mounted infantry. Yesterday we crossed a pass which looked down into the Kongbu Valley--a likely camping-ground for the Tibetan troops. The valley is connected to the north with the Tuna plateau, and is almost as fertile in its lower stretches as Chumbi. A gray fortress hangs over the cliff on the western side of the valley, and above it tower the glaciers of Shudu-Tsenpa and the Gora Pass into Sikkim. On the eastern side, at a creditable distance from the fort, we could see the Kongbu nunnery, which looked from where we stood like an old Roman viaduct. The nuns, I was told, are rarely celibate; they shave the head and wear no ornaments.

Riding back we saw some burrhel on the opposite hills, too far off to make a successful stalk possible. The valley is full of them, and a week later some officers from Phari on a yak-collecting expedition got several good heads. The Tibetan gazelle, or goa (Gazella hirticaudata), is very common on the Phari plateau, and we bagged two that afternoon. When the force first occupied the Jong, they were so tame that a sportsman could walk up to within 100 yards of a herd, and it was not an uncommon thing for three buck to fall to the same gun in a morning. Now one has to manoeuvre a great deal to get within 300 yards of them.

Sportsmen who have travelled in other parts of Tibet say the goa are very shy and inaccessible. Perhaps their comparative tameness near Phari may be accounted for by the fact that the old trade route crosses the plateau, and they have never been molested by the itinerant merchants and carriers. Gazelle meat is excellent. It has been a great resource for the garrison. No epicure could wish for anything better.

Another unfamiliar beast that one meets in the neighbourhood of Phari is the kyang, or Tibetan wild ass (Equus hemionus), one or two of which have been shot for specimens. The kyang is more like a zebra than a horse or donkey. Its flesh, I believe, is scorned even by camp-followers. Hare are fairly plentiful, but they are quite flavourless. A huge solitary gray wolf (Canis laniger) was shot the other day, the only one of its kind I have seen. Occasionally one puts up a fox. The Tibetan species has a very fine brush that fetches a fancy price in the bazaar. At present there is too much ice on the plain to hunt them, but they ought to give good sport in the spring.

It was dark when we rode into the Jong. After a long day in the saddle, dinner is good, even though it is of yak's flesh, and it is good to sit in front of a fire even though the smoke chokes you. I went so far as to pity the cave-dwellers at Chumbi. Phari is certainly very much colder, but it has its diversions and interests. There is still some shooting to be had, and the place has a quaint old-world individuality of its own, which seasons the monotony of life to a contemplative man. One is on the borderland, and one has a Micawber-like feeling that something may turn up. After dinner there is bridge, which fleets the time considerably, but at Chumbi there were no diversions of any kind--nothing but dull, blank, uninterrupted monotony.

February 20.

For two days half a blizzard has been blowing, and expeditions have been impossible. Everything one eats and drinks has the same taste of argol smoke. At breakfast this morning we had to put our chapatties in our pockets to keep them clean, and kept our meat covered with a soup-plate, making surreptitious dives at it with a fork. After a few seconds' exposure it was covered with grime. Sausages and bully beef, which had just been boiled, were found to be frozen inside. The smoke in the mess-room was suffocating. So to bed, wrapped in sheepskins and a sleeping-bag. Under these depressing conditions I have been reading the narratives of Bogle and Manning, old English worthies who have left on record the most vivid impressions of the dirt and cold and misery of Phari.

It is ninety years since Thomas Manning passed through Phari on his way to Lhasa. Previously to his visit we only know of two Englishmen who have set foot in Phari--Bogle in 1774, and Turner in 1783, both emissaries of Warren Hastings. Manning's journal is mostly taken up with complaints of his Chinese servant, who seems to have gained some mysterious ascendancy over him, and to have exercised it most unhandsomely. As a traveller Manning had a genius for missing effects; it is characteristic of him that he spent sixteen days at Phari, yet except for a casual footnote, evidently inserted in his journal after his return, he makes no mention of the Jong. Were it not for Bogle's account of thirty years before, we might conclude that the building was not then in existence.

On October 21, 1811, Manning writes in his diary: 'We arrived at Phari Jong. Frost. Frost also two days before. I was lodged in a strange place, but so were the natives.' On the 27th he summarized his impressions of Phari:--'Dirt, dirt, grease, smoke, misery, but good mutton.'

Manning's journal is expressive, if monosyllabic. He was of the class of subjective travellers, who visit the ends of the earth to record their own personal discomforts. Sensitive, neurotic, ever on the look-out for slights, he could not have been a happy vagabond. A dozen lines record the impressions of his first week at Phari. He was cheated; he was treated civilly; he slighted the magistrates, mistaking them for idle fellows; he was turned out of his room to make way for Chinese soldiers; he quarrelled with his servant. A single extract portrays the man to the life, as if he were sitting dejectedly by his yak-dung fire at this hour brooding over his wrongs:--

"The Chinaman was cross again." Says I, "Was that a bird at the magistrate's that flapped so loud?" Answer: "What signifies whether it was a bird or not?"

Where he sat I thought he might see; and I was curious to know if such large birds frequented the building. These are the answers I get. He is always discontented and grumbling, and takes no trouble off my hands. Being younger, and, like all Asiatics, able to stoop and crouch without pain or difficulty, he might assist me in many things without trouble to himself. A younger brother or any English young gentleman would in his place of course lay the cloth, and do other little services when I am tired; but he does not seem to have much of the generous about him, nor does he in any way serve me, or behave to me with any show of affection or goodwill: consequently I grow no more attached to him than the first day I saw him. I could not have thought it possible for me to have lived so long with anyone without either disliking him or caring sixpence for him. He has good qualities, too. The strangeness of his situation may partly excuse him. (I am more attached to my guide, with all his faults, who has been with me but a few days.) My guide has behaved so damnably ill since I wrote that, that I wish it had not come into my mind.'

I give the extract at length, not only as an illuminating portrait of Manning, but as an incidental proof that he visited the Jong, and that it was very much the same building then as it is to-day. But had it not been for the flapping of the bird which occasioned the quarrel with his Chinese servant, Manning would have left Phari without a reference to the wonderful old fortress which is the most romantic feature on the road from India to Gyantse. Appended to the journal is this footnote to the word building, which I have italicized in the extract: 'The building is immensely large, six or more stories high, a sort of fortress. At a distance it appears to be all Phari Jong. Indeed, most of it consists of miserable galleries and holes.'

Members of the mission force who have visited Phari will no doubt attribute Manning's evident ill-humour and depression during his stay there to the environments of the place, which have not changed much in the last ninety years. But his spirits improved as he continued his journey to Gyantse and Lhasa, and he reveals himself the kindly, eccentric, and affectionate soul who was the friend and intimate of Charles Lamb.

Bogle arrived at Phari on October 23, 1774. He and Turner and Manning all entered Tibet through Bhutan. 'As we advanced,' he wrote in his journal, 'we came in sight of the castle of Phari Jong, which cuts a good figure from without. It rises into several towers with the balconies, and, having few windows, has the look of strength; it is surrounded by the town.' The only other reference he makes to the Jong shows us that the fortress was in bad repair so long ago as 1774. 'The two Lhasa officers who have the government of Phari Jong sent me some butter, tea, etc., the day after my arrival; and letting me know that they expected a visit from me, I went. The inside of the castle did not answer the notion I had formed of it. The stairs are ladders worn to the bone, and the rooms are little better than garrets.'

The origin of the fort is unknown. Some of the inhabitants of Phari say that it was built more than a hundred years ago, when the Nepalese were overrunning Sikkim. But this is obviously incorrect, as the Tibetan-Nepalese War, in which the Chinese drove the Gurkhas out of Tibet, and defeated their army within a day's march of Khatmandu, took place in 1788-1792, whereas Bogle's description of the Jong was written fourteen years earlier. A more general impression is that centuries ago orders came from Lhasa to collect stones on the hillsides, and the building was constructed by forced labour in a few months. That is a tale of endurance and suffering that might very likely be passed from father to son for generations.

Bogle's description of the town might have been written by an officer of the garrison to-day, only he wrote from the inmate's point of view. He noticed the houses 'so huddled together that one may chance to overlook them,' and the flat roofs covered with bundles of straw. He knocked his head against the low ceilings, and ran against the pillars that supported the beams. 'In the middle of the roof,' he wrote, 'is a hole to let out smoke, which, however, departs not without making the whole room as black as a chimney. The opening serves also to let in the light; the doors are full of holes and crevices, through which the women and children keep peeping.' Needless to say nothing has changed in the last hundred and thirty years, unless it is that the women are bolder. I looked down from the roof this morning on Phari town, lying like a rabbit-warren beneath the fort. All one can see from the battlement are the flat roofs of low black houses, from which smoke issues in dense fumes. The roofs are stacked with straw, and connected by a web of coloured praying-flags running from house to house, and sometimes over the narrow alleys that serve as streets. Enormous fat ravens perch on the wall, and innumerable flocks of twittering sparrows. For warmth's sake most of the rooms are underground, and in these subterranean dens Tibetans, black as coal-heavers, huddle together with yaks and mules. Tibetan women, equally dirty, go about, their faces smeared and blotched with caoutchouc, wearing a red, hoop-like head-dress, ornamented with alternate turquoises and ruby-coloured stones.

In the fort the first thing one meets of a morning is a troop of these grimy sirens, climbing the stairs, burdened with buckets of chopped ice and sacks of yak-dung, the two necessaries of life. The Tibetan coolie women are merry folk; they laugh and chatter over their work all day long, and do not in the least resist the familiarities of the Gurkha soldiers. Sometimes as they pass one they giggle coyly, and put out the tongue, which is their way of showing respect to those in high places; but when one hears their laughter echoing down the stairs it is difficult to believe that it is not intended for saucy impudence. Their merriment sounds unnatural in all this filth and cold and discomfort. Certainly if Bogle returned to Phari he would find the women very much bolder, though, I am afraid, not any cleaner. Could he see the Englishmen in Phari to-day, he might not recognise his compatriots.

Often in civilized places I shall think of the group at Phari in the mess-room after dinner--a group of ruffianly-looking bandits in a blackened, smut-begrimed room, clad in wool and fur from head to foot, bearded like wild men of the woods, and sitting round a yak-dung fire, drinking rum. After a week at Phari the best-groomed man might qualify for a caricature of Bill Sikes. Perhaps one day in Piccadilly one may encounter a half-remembered face, and something familiar in walk or gait may reveal an old friend of the Jong. Then in 'Jimmy's,' memories of argol-smoke and frozen moustaches will give a zest to a bottle of beaune or chablis, which one had almost forgotten was once dreamed of among the unattainable luxuries of life.

March 26-28.

Orders have come to advance from Phari Jong. It seems impossible, unnatural, that we are going on. After a week or two the place becomes part of one's existence; one feels incarcerated there. It is difficult to imagine life anywhere else. One feels as if one could never again be cold or dirty, or miserably uncomfortable, without thinking of that gray fortress with its strange unknown history, standing alone in the desolate plain. For my own part, speaking figuratively--and unfigurative language is impotent on an occasion like this--the place will leave an indelible black streak--very black indeed--on a kaleidoscopic past. There can be no faint impressions in one's memories of Phari Jong. The dirt and smoke and dust are elemental, and the cold is the cold of the Lamas' frigid hell.

All the while I was in Phari I forgot the mystery of Tibet. I have felt it elsewhere, but in the Jong I only wondered that the inscrutable folk who had lived in the rooms where we slept, and fled in the night, were content with their smut-begrimed walls, blackened ceilings, and chimneyless roofs, and still more how amidst these murky environments any spiritual instincts could survive to inspire the religious frescoings on the wall. Yet every figure in this intricate blending of designs is significant and symbolical. One's first impression is that these allegories and metaphysical abstractions must have been meaningless to the inmates of the Jong; for we in Europe cannot dissociate the artistic expression of religious feeling from cleanliness and refinement, or at least pious care. One feels that they must be the relics of a decayed spirituality, preserved not insincerely, but in ignorant superstition, like other fetishes all over the world. Yet this feeling of scepticism is not so strong after a month or two in Tibet. At first one is apt to think of these dirty people as merely animal and sensual, and to attribute their religious observances to the fear of demons who will punish the most trivial omission in ritual.

Next one begins to wonder if they really believe in the efficacy of mechanical prayer, if they take the trouble to square their conscience with their inclinations, and if they have any sincere desire to be absorbed in the universal spirit. Then there may come a suspicion that the better classes, though not given to inquiry, have a settled dogma and definite convictions about things spiritual and natural that are not easily upset. Perhaps before we turn our backs on the mystery of Tibet we will realize that the Lamas despise us as gross materialists and philistines--we who are always groping and grasping after the particular, while they are absorbed in the sublime and universal.

After all, devious and unscrupulous as their policy may have been, the Tibetans have had one definite aim in view for centuries--the preservation of their Church and State by the exclusion of all foreign and heretical influences. When we know that the Mongol cannot conceive of the separation of the spiritual and temporal Government, it is only natural to infer that the first mission, spiritual or otherwise, to a foreign Court should introduce the first elements of dissolution in a system of Government that has held the country intact for centuries. And let it be remarked that Great Britain is not responsible for this deviation in a hitherto inveterate policy.

But to return to Phari. My last impression of the place as I passed out of its narrow alleys was a very dirty old man, seated on a heap of yak-dung over the gutter. He was turning his prayer-wheel, and muttering the sacred formula that was to release him from all rebirth in this suffering world. The wish seemed natural enough.

It was a bright, clear morning when we turned our backs on the old fort and started once more on the road to Lhasa. Five miles from Phari we passed the miserable little village of Chuggya, which is apparently inhabited by ravens and sparrows, and a diminutive mountain-finch that looks like a half-starved robin. A mile to the right before entering the village is the monastery of the Red Lamas, which was the lodging-place of the Bhutanese Envoy during his stay at Phari. The building, which is a landmark for miles, is stone-built, and coated over with red earth, which gives it the appearance of brick. Its overhanging gables, mullioned windows without glass, that look like dominoes in the distance, the pendent bells, and the gay decorations of Chinese paper, look quaint and mystical, and are in keeping with the sacred character of the place. Bogle stopped here on October 27, 1774, and drank tea with the Abbot. It is very improbable that any other white man has set foot in the monastery since, until the other day, when some of the garrison paid it a visit and took photographs of the interior. The Lamas were a little deprecatory, but evidently amused. I did not expect them to be so tolerant of intrusion, and their clamour for backsheesh on our departure dispelled one more illusion.

At Chuggya we were at the very foot of Chumulari (23,930 feet), which seems to rise sheer from the plain. The western flank is an abrupt wall of rock, but, as far as one can see, the eastern side is a gradual ascent of snow, which would present no difficulties to the trained mountaineer. One could ride up to 17,000 feet, and start the climb from a base 2,000 feet higher than Mont Blanc. Chumulari is the most sacred mountain in Tibet, and it is usual for devout Buddhists to stop and offer a sacrifice as they pass. Bogle gives a detailed account of the service, the rites of which are very similar to some I witnessed at Galingka on the Tibetan New Year, February 16.

'Here we halted,' he wrote in his journal, 'and the servants gathering together a parcel of dried cow-dung, one of them struck fire with his tinder-box and lighted it. When the fire was well kindled, Parma took out a book of prayers, one brought a copper cup, another filled it with a kind of fermented liquor out of a new-killed sheep's paunch, mixing in some rice and flour; and after throwing some dried herbs and flour into the flame, they began their rites. Parma acted as chaplain. He chanted the prayers in a loud voice, the others accompanying him, and every now and then the little cup was emptied towards the rock, about eight or ten of these libations being poured forth. The ceremony was finished by placing upon the heap of stones the little ensign which my fond imagination had before offered up to my own vanity.'

Most of the flags and banners one sees to-day on the chortens and roofs of houses, and cairns on the mountain-tops, must be planted with some such inaugural ceremony.

Facing Chumulari on the west, and apparently only a few miles distant, are the two Sikkim peaks of Powhunri (23,210 feet) and Shudu-Tsenpa (22,960 feet). From Chuggya the Tangla is reached by a succession of gradual rises and depressions. The pass is not impressive, like the Jelap, as a passage won through a great natural barrier. One might cross it without noticing the summit, were it not for the customary cairns and praying-flags which the Lamas raise in all high places.

From a slight rise on the east of the pass one can look down across the plateau on Tuna, an irregular black line like a caterpillar, dotted with white spots, which glasses reveal to be tents. The Bamtso lake lies shimmering to the east beneath brown and yellow hills. At noon objects dance elusively in the mirage. Distances are deceptive. Yaks grazing are like black Bedouin tents. Here, then, is the forbidden land. The approach is as it should be. One's eyes explore the road to Lhasa dimly through a haze. One would not have it laid out with the precision of a diagram.

CHAPTER V

THE ROAD AND TRANSPORT

To write of any completed phase of the expedition at this stage, when I have carried my readers only as far as Tuna, is a lapse in continuity that requires an apology. My excuse is that to all transport officers, and everyone who was in touch with them, the Tuna and Phari plains will be remembered as the very backbone of resistance, the most implacable barriers to our advance.

The expedition was essentially a transport 'show.' It is true that the Tibetans proved themselves brave enemies, but their acquired military resources are insignificant when compared with the obstacles Nature has planted in the path of their enemies. The difficulty of the passes, the severity of the climate, the sterility of the mountains and tablelands, make the interior of the country almost inaccessible to an invading army. That we went through these obstacles and reached Lhasa itself was a matter of surprise not only to the Tibetans, but to many members of the expeditionary force.

To appreciate the difficulties the mission force had to contend with, one must first realize the extraordinary changes of climate that are experienced in the journey from Siliguri to Tuna. Choose the coldest day in the year at Kew Gardens, expose yourself freely to the wind, and then spend five minutes in the tropical house, and you may gather some idea of the sensation of sleeping in the Rungpo Valley the night after crossing the Jelapla.

When I first made the journey in early January, even the Rungpo Valley was chilly, and the vicissitudes were not so marked; but I felt the change very keenly in March, when I made a hurried rush into Darjeeling for equipment and supplies. Our camp at Lingmathang was in the pine-forest at an elevation of 10,500 feet. It was warm and sunny in the daytime, in places where there was shelter from the wind. Leaf-buds were beginning to open, frozen waterfalls to thaw, migratory duck were coming up the valley in twos and threes from the plains of India--even a few vultures had arrived to fatten on the carcasses of the dead transport animals. The morning after leaving Lingmathang I left the pine-forest at 13,000 feet, and entered a treeless waste of shale and rock. When I crossed the Jelapla half a hurricane was blowing. The path was a sheet of ice, and I had to use hands and knees, and take advantage of every protuberance in the rock to prevent myself from being blown over the khud. The road was impassable for mules and ponies.

The cold was numbing. The next evening, in a valley 13,000 feet beneath, I was suffering from the extreme of heat. The change in scenery and vegetation is equally striking--from glaciers and moraines to tropical forests brilliant with the scarlet cotton-flower and purple Baleria. In Tibet I had not seen an insect of any kind for two months, but in the Sikkim valleys the most gorgeous butterflies were abundant, and the rest-house at Rungpo was invested by a plague of flies. In the hot weather the climate of the Sikkim valleys is more trying than that of most stations in the plains of India. The valleys are close and shut in, and the heat is intensified by the radiation from the rocks, cliffs, and boulders. In the rains the climate is relaxing and malarious. The Supply and Transport Corps, who were left behind at stages like Rungpo through the hot weather, had, to my mind, a much harder time on the whole than the half-frozen troops at the front, and they were left out of all the fun.

Besides the natural difficulties of the road, the severity of climate, and the scarcity of fodder and fuel, the Transport Corps had to contend with every description of disease and misfortune--anthrax, rinderpest, foot and mouth disease, aconite and rhododendron poisoning, falling over precipices, exhaustion from overwork and underfeeding. The worst fatalities occurred on the Khamba Jong side in 1903. The experiments with the transport were singularly unsuccessful. Out of two hundred buffaloes employed at low elevations, only three survived, and the seven camels that were tried on the road between Siliguri and Gantok all died by way of protest. Later on in the year the yak corps raised in Nepal was practically exterminated. From four to five thousand were originally purchased, of which more than a thousand died from anthrax before they reached the frontier. All the drinking-water on the route was infected; the Nepalese did not believe the disease was contagious, and took no precautions. The disease spread almost universally among the cattle, and at the worst time twenty or thirty died a day. The beasts were massed on the Nepal frontier. Segregation camps were formed, and ultimately, after much patient care, the disease was stamped out.

Then began the historic march through Sikkim, which, as a protracted struggle against natural calamities, might be compared to the retreat of the Ten Thousand, or the flight of the Kalmuck Tartars. Superstitious natives might well think that a curse had fallen on us and our cattle. As soon as they were immune from anthrax, the reduced corps were attacked by rinderpest, which carried off seventy. When the herds left the Singli-la range and descended into the valley, the sudden change in climate overwhelmed hundreds. No real yak survived the heat of the Sikkim valleys. All that were now left were the zooms, or halfbreeds from the bull-yaks and the cow, and the cross from the bull and female yaks. In Sikkim, which is always a hotbed of contagious cattle diseases, the wretched survivors were infected with foot and mouth disease. The epidemic is not often fatal, but visiting an exhausted herd, fever-stricken, and weakened by every vicissitude of climate, it carried off scores. Then, to avoid spreading contagion, the yaks were driven through trackless, unfrequented country, up and down precipitous mountain-sides, and through dense forests. Again segregation camps were formed, and the dead cattle were burnt, twenty and thirty at a time. Every day there was a holocaust. Then followed the ascent into high altitudes, where a more insidious evil awaited the luckless corps. The few survivors were exterminated by pleuro-pneumonia. When, on January 23, the 3rd Yak Corps reached Chumbi, it numbered 437; two months afterwards all but 70 had died. On March 21, 80 exhausted beasts straggled into Chumbi; they were the remainder of the 1st and 2nd Yak Corps, which originally numbered 2,300 heads. The officers, who, bearded and weather-beaten, deserted by many of their followers, after months of wandering, reached our camp with the remnants of the corps, told a story of hardship and endurance that would provide a theme for an epic.

The epic of the yaks does not comprise the whole tale of disaster. Rinderpest carried off 77 pack-bullocks out of 500, and a whole corps was segregated for two months with foot and mouth disease. Amongst other casualties there were heavy losses among the Cashmere pony corps, and the Tibet pony corps raised locally. The animals were hastily mobilized and incompletely equipped, overworked and underfed. Cheap and inferior saddlery was issued, which gave the animals sore backs within a week. The transport officer was in a constant dilemma. He had to overwork his animals or delay the provisions, fodder, and warm clothing so urgently needed at the front. Ponies and mules had no rest, but worked till they dropped. Of the original draft of mules that were employed on the line to Khamba Jong, fully 50 per cent. died. It is no good trying to blink the fact that the expedition was unpopular, and that at the start many economical shifts were attempted which proved much more expensive in the end. Our party system is to blame. The Opposition must be appeased, expenses kept down, and the business is entered into half-heartedly. In the usual case a few companies are grudgingly sent to the front, and then, when something like a disaster falls or threatens, John Bull jumps at the sting, scenting a national insult. A brigade follows, and Government wakes to the necessity of grappling with the situation seriously.

But to return to the spot where the evil effects of the system were felt, and not merely girded at. To replace and supplement the local drafts of animals that were dying, trained Government mule corps were sent up from the plains, properly equipped and under experienced officers. These did excellent work, and 2,600 mules arrived in Lhasa on August 3 in as good condition as one could wish. Of all transport animals, the mule is the hardiest and most enduring. He does not complain when he is overloaded, but will go on all day, and when he drops there is no doubt that he has had enough. Nine times out of ten when he gives up he dies. No beast is more indifferent to extremes of heat and cold. On the road from Kamparab to Phari one day, three mules fell over a cliff into a snowdrift, and were almost totally submerged. Their drivers could not pull them out, and, to solve the dilemma, went on and reported them dead. The next day an officer found them and extricated them alive. They had been exposed to 46?of frost. They still survive.

Nothing can beat the Sircar mule when he is in good condition, unless it is the Balti and Ladaki coolie. Several hundred of these hardy mountaineers were imported from the North-West frontier to work on the most dangerous and difficult sections of the road. They can bear cold and fatigue and exposure better than any transport animal on the line, and they are surer-footed. Mules were first employed over the Jelap, but were afterwards abandoned for coolies. The Baltis are excellent workers at high altitudes, and sing cheerily as they toil up the mountains with their loads. I have seen them throw down their packs when they reached the summit of a pass, make a rush for the shelter of a rock, and cheer lustily like school-boys. But the coolies were not all equally satisfactory. Those indented from the Nepal durbar were practically an impressed gang. Twelve rupees a month with rations and warm clothing did not seem to reconcile them to hard work, and after a month or two they became discontented and refractory. Their officers, however, were men of tact and decision, and they were able to prevent what might have been a serious mutiny. The discontented ones were gradually replaced by Baltis, Ladakis, and Garwhalis, and the coolies became the most reliable transport corps on the line.

Thus, the whole menagerie, to use the expression current at the time, was got into working order, and a system was gradually developed by which the right animal, man, or conveyance was working in the right place, and supplies were sent through at a pace that was very creditable considering the country traversed.

From the railway base at Siliguri to Gantok, a distance of sixty miles, the ascent in the road is scarcely perceptible. With the exception of a few contractors' ponies, the entire carrying along this section of the line was worked by bullock-carts. Government carts are built to carry 11 maunds (880 pounds), but contractors often load theirs with 15 or 16 maunds. As the carrying power of mules, ponies, and pack-bullocks is only 2 maunds, it will be seen at once that transport in a mountainous country, where there can be no road for vehicles, is nearly five times as difficult and complicated as in the plains. And this is without making any allowance for the inevitable mortality among transport animals at high elevations, or taking into account the inevitable congestion on mountain-paths, often blocked by snow, carried away by the rains, and always too narrow to admit of any large volume of traffic.

In the beginning of March, when the line was in its best working order, from 1,500 to 2,000 maunds were poured into Rungpo daily. Of these, only 400 or 500 maunds reached Phari; the rest was stored at Gantok or consumed on the road. Later, when the line was extended to Gyantse, not more than 100 maunds a day reached the front.

In the first advance on Gyantse, our column was practically launched into the unknown. As far as we knew, no local food or forage could be obtained. It was too early in the season for the spring pasturage. We could not live on the country. The ever-lengthening line of communication behind us was an artery, the severing of which would be fatal to our advance.

One can best realize the difficulties grappled with by imagining the extreme case of an army entering an entirely desert country. A mule, it must be remembered, can only carry its own food for ten days. That is to say, in a country where there is no grain or fodder, a convoy can make at the most nine marches. On the ninth day beasts and drivers will have consumed all the supplies taken with them. Supposing on the tenth day no supply-base has been reached, the convoy is stranded, and can neither advance nor retire. Nor must we forget that our imaginary convoy, which has perished in the desert, has contributed nothing to the advance of the army. Food and clothing for the troops, tents, bedding, guns, ammunition, field-hospital, treasury, still await transport at the base.

Fortunately, the country between our frontier and Lhasa is not all desert. Yet it is barren enough to make it a matter of wonder that, with such short preparation, we were able to push through troops to Gyantse in April, when there was no grazing on the road, and to arrive in Lhasa in August with a force of more than 4,000 fighting men and followers.

Before the second advance to Gyantse the spring crops had begun to appear. Without them we could not have advanced. All other local produce on the road was exhausted. That is to say, for 160 miles, with the important exception of wayside fodder, we subsisted entirely on our own supplies. The mules carried their own grain, and no more. Gyantse once reached, the Tibetan Government granaries and stores from the monasteries produced enough to carry us on. But besides the transport mules, there were 100 Maxim and battery mules, as well as some 200 mounted infantry ponies, and at least 100 officers' mounts, to be fed, and these carried nothing--contributed nothing to the stomach of the army.

How were these beasts to be fed, and how was the whole apparatus of an army to be carried along, when every additional transport animal was a tax on the resources of the transport? There were two possible solutions, each at first sight equally absurd and impracticable:--wheeled transport in Tibet, or animals that did not require feeding. The Supply and Transport men were resourceful and fortunate enough to provide both. It was due to the light ekka and that providentially ascetic beast, the yak, that we were able to reach Lhasa.

The ekkas were constructed in the plains, and carried by coolies from the cart-road at Rungpo eighty miles over the snow passes to Kamparab on the Phari Plain. The carrying capacity of these light carts is 400 pounds, two and a half times that of a mule, and there is only one mouth to feed. They were the first vehicles ever seen in Tibet, and they saved the situation.

The ekkas worked over the Phari and Tuna plains, and down the Nyang Chu Valley as far as Kangma. They were supplemented by the yaks.

The yak is the most extraordinary animal Nature has provided the transport officer in his need. He carries 160 pounds, and consumes nothing. He subsists solely on stray blades of grass, tamarisk, and tufts of lichen, that he picks up on the road. He moves slowly, and wears a look of ineffable resignation. He is the most melancholy disillusioned beast I have seen, and dies on the slightest provocation. The red and white tassels and favours of cowrie-shells the Tibetans hang about his neck are as incongruous on the poor beast as gauds and frippery on the heroine of a tragedy.

If only he were dependable, our transport difficulties would be reduced to a minimum. But he is not. We have seen how the four thousand died in their passage across Sikkim without doing a day's work. Local drafts did better. Yet I have often passed the Lieutenant in command of the corps lamenting their lack of grit. 'Two more of my cows died this morning. Look, there goes another! D--n the beasts! I believe they do it out of spite!' And the chief Supply and Transport officer, always a humorist in adversity, when asked why they were dying off every day, said: 'I think it must be due to overfeeding.' But we owe much to the yak.

The final advance from Gyantse to Lhasa was a comparatively easy matter. Crops were plentiful, and large supplies of grain were obtained from the monasteries and jongs on the road. We found, contrary to anticipation, that the produce in this part of Tibet was much greater than the consumption. In many places we found stores that would last a village three or four years. Our transport animals lived on the country. We arrived at Lhasa with 2,600 mules and 400 coolies. The yak and donkey corps were left at the river for convoy work. It would have been impossible to have pushed through in the winter.

All the produce we consumed on the road was paid for. In this way the expense of the army's keep fell on the Lhasa Government, who had to pay the indemnity, and our presence in the country was not directly, at any rate, a burden on the agricultural population of the villages through which we passed.

Looking back on the splendid work accomplished by the transport, it is difficult to select any special phase more memorable than another. The complete success of the organization and the endurance and grit displayed by officers and men are equally admirable. I could cite the coolness of a single officer in a mob of armed and mutinous coolies, when the compelling will of one man and a few blows straight from the shoulder kept the discontented harnessed to their work and quelled a revolt; or the case of another who drove his diseased yaks over the snow passes into Chumbi, and after two days' rest started with a fresh corps on ten months of the most tedious labour the mind of man can imagine, rising every day before daybreak in an almost Arctic cold, traversing the same featureless tablelands, and camping out at night cheerfully in the open plain with his escort of thirty rifles. There was always the chance of a night attack, but no other excitement to break the eternal monotony. But it was all in the day's work, and the subaltern took it like a picnic. Another supreme test of endurance in man and beast were the convoys between Chumbi and Tuna in the early part of the year, which for hardships endured remind me of Skobeleff's dash through the Balkans on Adrianople. Only our labours were protracted, Skobeleff's the struggle of a few days. Even in mid-March a convoy of the 12th Mule Corps, escorted by two companies of the 23rd Pioneers, were overtaken by a blizzard on their march between Phari and Tuna, and camped in two feet of snow with the thermometer 18?below zero. A driving hurricane made it impossible to light a fire or cook food. The officers were reduced to frozen bully beef and neat spirits, while the sepoys went without food for thirty-six hours. The fodder for the mules was buried deep in snow. The frozen flakes blowing through the tents cut like a knife. While the detachment was crossing a stream, the mules fell through the ice, and were only extricated with great difficulty. The drivers arrived at Tuna frozen to the waist. Twenty men of the 12th Mule Corps were frostbitten, and thirty men of the 23rd Pioneers were so incapacitated that they had to be carried in on mules. On the same day there were seventy cases of snow-blindness among the 8th Gurkhas.

Until late in April all the plain was intersected by frozen streams. Blankets were stripped from the mules to make a pathway for them over the ice. Often they went without water at night, and at mid-day, when the surface of the ice was melted, their thirst was so great that many died from overdrinking.

Had the Tibetans attacked us in January, they would have taken us at a great disadvantage. The bolts of our rifles jammed with frozen oil. Oil froze in the Maxims, and threw them out of gear. More often than not the mounted infantry found the butts of their rifles frozen in the buckets, and had to dismount and use both hands to extricate them.

I think these men who took the convoys through to Tuna; the 23rd, who wintered there and supplied most of the escort; and the 8th Gurkhas, who cut a road in the frost-bound plain, may be said to have broken the back of the resistance to our advance. They were the pioneers, and the troops who followed in spring and summer little realized what they owed to them.

The great difficulties we experienced in pushing through supplies to Tuna, which is less than 150 miles from our base railway-station at Siliguri, show the absurdity of the idea of a Russian advance on Lhasa. The nearest Russian outpost is over 1,000 miles distant, and the country to be traversed is even more barren and inhospitable than on our frontier.

Up to the present the route to Chumbi has been vi?Siliguri and the Jelap and Nathu Passes, but the natural outlet of the valley is by the Ammo Chu, which flows through Bhutan into the Dooars, where it becomes the Torsa. The Bengal-Dooars Railway now extends to Madhari Hat, fifteen miles from the point where the Torsa crosses the frontier, whence it is only forty-eight miles as the crow flies to Rinchengong in the Chumbi Valley. When the projected Ammo Chu cart-road is completed, all the difficulty of carrying stores into Chumbi will be obviated. Engineers are already engaged on the first trace, and the road will be in working order within a few months. It avoids all snow passes, and nowhere reaches an elevation of more than 9,000 feet. The direct route will shorten the journey to Chumbi by several days, bring Lhasa within a month's journey of Calcutta, and considerably improve trade facilities between Tibet and India.

CHAPTER VI

THE ACTION AT THE HOT SPRINGS

The village of Tuna, which lies at the foot of bare yellow hills, consists of a few deserted houses. The place is used mainly as a halting-stage by the

Tibetans. The country around is sterile and unproductive, and wood is a luxury that must be carried from a distance of nearly fifty miles.

It was in these dismal surroundings that Colonel Younghusband's mission spent the months of January, February, and March. The small garrison suffered all the discomforts of Phari. The dirt and grime of the squalid little houses became so depressing that they pitched their tents in an open courtyard, preferring the numbing cold to the filth of the Tibetan hovels. Many of the sepoys fell victims to frost-bite and pneumonia, and nearly every case of pneumonia proved fatal, the patient dying of suffocation owing to the rarefied air.

Colonel Younghusband had not been at Tuna many days before it became clear that there could be no hope of a peaceful solution. The Tibetans began to gather in large numbers at Guru, eight miles to the east, on the road to Lhasa. The Depon, or Lhasa General, whom Colonel Younghusband met on two occasions, repeated that he was only empowered to treat on condition that we withdrew to Yatung. Messages were sent from the Tibetan camp to Tuna almost daily asking us to retire, and negotiations again came to a deadlock. After a month the tone of the Tibetans became minatory. They threatened to invest our camp, and an attack was expected on March 1, the Tibetan New Year. The Lamas, however, thought better of it. They held a Commination Service instead, and cursed us solemnly for five days, hoping, no doubt, that the British force would dwindle away by the act of God. Nobody was 'one penny the worse.'

Though we made no progress with the Tibetans during this time, Colonel Younghusband utilized the halt at Tuna in cementing a friendship with Bhutan. The neutrality of the Bhutanese in the case of a war with Tibet was a matter of the utmost importance. Were these people unfriendly or disposed to throw in their lot with their co-religionists, the Tibetans, our line of communications would be exposed to a flank attack along the whole of the Tuna Plain, which is conterminous with the Bhutan frontier, as well as a rear attack anywhere in the Chumbi Valley as far south as Rinchengong. The Bhutanese are men of splendid physique, brave, warlike, and given to pillage. Their hostility would have involved the despatch of a second force, as large as that sent to Tibet, and might have landed us, if unprepared, in a serious reverse. The complete success of Colonel Younghusband's diplomacy was a great relief to the Indian Government, who were waiting with some anxiety to see what attitude the Bhutanese would adopt. Having secured from them assurances of their good will, Colonel Younghusband put their friendship to immediate test by broaching the subject of the Ammo Chu route to Chumbi through Bhutanese territory. Very little time was lost before the concession was obtained from the Tongsa Penlop, ruler of Bhutan, who himself accompanied the mission as far as Lhasa in the character of mediator between the Dalai Lama and the British Government. The importance of the Ammo Chu route in our future relations with Tibet I have emphasized elsewhere.

I doubt if ever an advance was more welcome to waiting troops than that which led to the engagement at the Hot Springs.

For months, let it be remembered, we had been marking time. When a move had to be made to escort a convoy, it was along narrow mountain-paths, where the troops had to march in single file. There was no possibility of an attack this side of Phari. The ground covered was familiar and monotonous. One felt cooped in, and was thoroughly bored and tired of the delay, so that when General Macdonald marched out of Phari with his little army in three columns, a feeling of exhilaration communicated itself to the troops.

Here was elbow-room at last, and an open plain, where all the army corps of Europe might manoeuvre. At Tuna, on the evening of the 29th, it was given out in orders that a reconnaissance in force was to be made the next morning, and two companies of the 32nd Pioneers would be left at Guru. The Tibetan camp at the Hot Springs lay right across our line of march, and the hill that flanked it was lined with their sangars. They must either fight or retire. Most of us thought that the Tibetans would fade away in the mysterious manner they have, and build another futile wall further on. The extraordinary affair that followed must be a unique event in military history.

The morning of the 30th was bitterly cold. An icy wind was blowing, and snow was lying on the ground. I put on my thick sheepskin for the first time for two months, and I owe my life to it.

About an hour after leaving Tuna, two or three Tibetan messengers rode out from their camp to interview Colonel Younghusband. They got down from their ponies and began chattering in a very excited manner, like a flock of frightened parrots. It was evident to us, not understanding the language, that they were entreating us to go back, and the constant reference to Yatung told us that they were repeating the message that had been sent into the Tuna camp almost daily during the past few months--that if we retired to Yatung the Dalai Lama would send an accredited envoy to treat with us. Being met with the usual answer, they mounted dejectedly and rode off at a gallop to their camp.

Soon after they had disappeared another group of horsemen were seen riding towards us. These proved to be the Lhasa Depon, accompanied by an influential Lama and a small escort armed with modern rifles. The rifles were naturally inspected with great interest. They were of different patterns--Martini-Henri, Lee-Metford, Snider--but the clumsily-painted stocks alone were enough to show that they were shoddy weapons of native manufacture. They left no mark on our troops.

According to Tibetan custom, a rug was spread on the ground for the interview between Colonel Younghusband and the Lhasa Depon, who conferred sitting down. Captain O'Connor, the secretary of the mission, interpreted. The Lhasa Depon repeated the entreaty of the messengers, and said that there would be trouble if we proceeded. Colonel Younghusband's reply was terse and to the point.

'Tell him,' he said to Captain O'Connor, 'that we have been negotiating with Tibet for fifteen years; that I myself have been waiting for eight months to meet responsible representatives from Lhasa, and that the mission is now going on to Gyantse. Tell him that we have no wish to fight, and that he would be well advised if he ordered his soldiers to retire. Should they remain blocking our path, I will ask General Macdonald to remove them.'

The Lhasa Depon was greatly perturbed. He said that he had no wish to fight, and would try and stop his men firing upon us. But before he left he again tried to induce Colonel Younghusband to turn back. Then he rode away to join his men. What orders he gave them will never be known.

I do not think the Tibetans ever believed in our serious intention to advance.

No doubt they attributed our evacuation of Khamba Jong and our long delay in Chumbi to weakness and vacillation. And our forbearance since the negociations of 1890 must have lent itself to the same interpretation.

As we advanced we could see the Tibetans running up the hill to the left to occupy the sangars. To turn their position, General Macdonald deployed the 8th Gurkhas to the crest of the ridge; at the same time the Pioneers, the Maxim detachment of the Norfolks, and Mountain Battery were deployed on the right until the Tibetan position was surrounded.

The manoeuvre was completely successful. The Tibetans on the hill, finding themselves outflanked by the Gurkhas, ran down to the cover of the wall by the main camp, and the whole mob was encircled by our troops.

It was on this occasion that the Sikhs and Gurkhas displayed that coolness and discipline which won them a European reputation. They had orders not to fire unless they were fired upon, and they walked right up to the walls of the sangars until the muzzles and prongs of the Tibetan matchlocks were almost touching their chests. The Tibetans stared at our men for a moment across the wall, and then turned and shambled down sulkily to join their comrades in the redan.

No one dreamed of the sanguinary action that was impending. I dismounted, and hastily scribbled a despatch on my saddle to the effect that the Tibetan position had been taken without a shot being fired. The mounted orderly who carried the despatch bore a similar message from the mission to the Foreign Office. Then the disarming began. The Tibetans were told that if they gave up their arms they would be allowed to go off unmolested. But they did not wish to give up their arms. It was a ridiculous position, Sikh and Mongol swaying backwards and forwards as they wrestled for the possession of swords and matchlocks. Perhaps the humour of it made one careless of the underlying danger. Accounts differ as to how this wrestling match developed into war, how, to the delight of the troops, the toy show became the 'real thing.' Of one thing I am certain, that a rush was made in the south-east corner before a shot was fired. If there had been any firing, I would not have been wandering about by the Tibetan flank without a revolver in my hand. As it was, my revolver was buried in the breast pocket of my Norfolk jacket under my poshteen.

I have no excuse for this folly except a misplaced contempt for Tibetan arms and courage--a contempt which accounted for our only serious casualty in the affair of 1888.[12] Also I think there was in the margin of my consciousness a feeling that one individual by an act of rashness might make himself responsible for the lives of hundreds. Hemmed in as the Tibetans were, no one gave them credit for the spirit they showed, or imagined that they would have the folly to resist. But we had to deal with the most ignorant and benighted people on earth, most of whom must have thought our magazine rifles and Maxims as harmless as their own obsolete matchlocks, and believed that they bore charms by which they were immune from death.

[12] When Colonel Bromhead pursued a Tibetan unarmed. Called upon to surrender, the Tibetan turned on Colonel Bromhead, cut off his right arm, and badly mutilated the left.

The attack on the south-east corner was so sudden that the first man was on me before I had time to draw my revolver.[13] He came at me with his sword lifted in both hands over his head. He had a clear run of ten yards, and if I had not ducked and caught him by the knees he must have smashed my skull open. I threw him, and he dragged me to the ground. Trying to rise, I was struck on the temple by a second swordsman, and the blade glanced off my skull. I received the rest of my wounds, save one or two, on my hands--as I lay on my face I used them to protect my head. After a time the blows ceased; my assailants were all shot down or had fled. I lay absolutely still for a while until I thought it safe to raise my head. Then I looked round, and, seeing no Tibetans near in an erect position, I got up and walked out of the ring between the rifles of the Sikhs. The firing line had been formed in the meantime on a mound about thirty yards behind me, and I had been exposed to the bullets of our own men from two sides, as well as the promiscuous fire of the Tibetans.

[13] The reports sent home at the time of the Hot Springs affair were inaccurate as to the manner in which I was wounded, and also Major Wallace Dunlop, who was the only European anywhere near me at the time. Major Dunlop shot his own man, but at such close quarters that the Tibetan's sword slipped down the barrel of his rifle and cut off two fingers of his left hand. General Macdonald and Captain Bignell, who shot several men with their

revolvers, were standing at the corner where the wall joined the ruined house, and did not see the attack on myself and Dunlop.

The Tibetans could not have chosen a spot more fatal for their stand--a bluff hill to the north, a marsh and stream on the east, and to the west a stone wall built across the path, which they had to scale in their attempted assault on General Macdonald and his escort. Only one man got over. Inside there was barely an acre of ground, packed so thickly with seething humanity that the cross-fire which the Pioneers poured in offered little danger to their own men.

The Lhasa General must have fired off his revolver after I was struck down. I cannot credit the rumour that his action was a signal for a general attack, and that the Tibetans allowed themselves to be herded together as a ruse to get us at close quarters. To begin with, the demand that they should give up their arms, and the assurance that they might go off unmolested, must have been quite unexpected by them, and I doubt if they realized the advantage of an attack at close quarters.

My own impression is that the shot was the act of a desperate man, ignorant and regardless of what might ensue. To return to Lhasa with his army disarmed and disbanded, and without a shot having been fired, must have meant ruin to him, and probably death. When we reached Gyantse we heard that his property had been confiscated from his family on account of his failure to prevent our advance.

The Depon was a man of fine presence and bearing. I only saw him once, in his last interview with Colonel Younghusband, but I cannot dissociate from him a personal courage and a pride that must have rankled at the indignity of his position. Probably he knew that his shot was suicidal.

The action has been described as one of extreme folly. But what was left him if he lived except shame and humiliation? And what Englishman with the same prospect to face, caught in this dark eddy of circumstance, would not have done the same thing? He could only fire, and let his men take their chance, God help them!

And the rabble? They have been called treacherous. Why, I don't know. They were mostly impressed peasants. They did not wish to give up their arms. Why should they? They knew nothing of the awful odds against them. They were being hustled by white men who did not draw knives or fire guns. Amid that babel of 1,500 men, many of them may not have heard the command; they may not have believed that their lives would have been spared.

Looking back on the affair with all the sanity of experience, nothing is more natural than what happened. It was folly and suicide, no doubt; but it was human nature. They were not going to give in without having a fling. I hope I shall not be considered a pro-Tibetan when I say that I admire their gallantry and dash.

As my wounds were being dressed I peered over the mound at the rout. They were walking away! Why, in the name of all their Bodhisats and Munis, did they not run? There was cover behind a bend in the hill a few hundred yards distant, and they were exposed to a devastating hail of bullets from the Maxims and rifles, that seemed to mow down every third or fourth man. Yet they walked!

It was the most extraordinary procession I have ever seen. My friends have tried to explain the phenomenon as due to obstinacy or ignorance, or Spartan contempt for life. But I think I have the solution. They were bewildered. The impossible had happened.

Prayers, and charms, and mantras, and the holiest of their holy men, had failed them. I believe they were obsessed with that one thought. They walked with bowed heads, as if they had been disillusioned in their gods.

After the last of the retiring Tibetans had disappeared round the corner of the Guru road, the 8th Gurkhas descended from the low range of hills on the right of the position, and crossed the Guru Plain in extended order with the 2nd Mounted Infantry on their extreme left. Orders were then received by Major Row, commanding the detachment, to take the left of the two houses which were situated under the hills at the further side of the plain. This movement was carried out in conjunction with the mounted infantry. The advance was covered by the 7-pounder guns of the Gurkhas under Captain Luke, R.A. The attacking force advanced in extended order by a series of small rushes. Cover was scanty, but the Tibetans, though firing vigorously, fired high, and there were no casualties. At last the force reached the outer wall of the house, and regained breath under cover of it. A few men of the Gurkhas then climbed on to the roof and descended into the house, making prisoners of the inmates, who numbered forty or fifty. Shortly afterwards the door, which was strongly barricaded, was broken in, and the remainder of the force entered the house.

During the advance a number of the Tibetans attempted to escape on mules and ponies, but the greater number of these were followed up and killed. The Tibetan casualties were at least 700.

Perhaps no British victory has been greeted with less enthusiasm than the action at the Hot Springs. Certainly the officers, who did their duty so thoroughly, had no heart in the business at all. After the first futile rush the Tibetans made no further resistance. There was no more fighting, only the slaughter of helpless men.

It is easy to criticise after the event, but it seems to me that the only way to have avoided the lamentable affair at the Hot Springs would have been to have drawn up more troops round the redan, and, when the Tibetans were hemmed in with the cliff in their rear, to have given them at least twenty minutes to lay down their arms. In the interval the situation might have been made clear to everyone. If after the time-limit they still hesitated, two shots might have brought them to reason. Then, if they were mad enough to decide on resistance, their suicide would be on their own heads. But to send two dozen sepoys into that sullen mob to take away their arms was to invite disaster. Given the same circumstances, and any mob in the world of men, women, or children, civilized or savage, and there would be found at least one rash spirit to explode the mine and set a spark to a general conflagration.

It was thought at the time that the lesson would save much future bloodshed. But the Tibetan is so stubborn and convinced of his self-sufficiency that it took many lessons to teach him the disparity between his armed rabble and the resources of the British Raj. In the light of after-events it is clear that we could have made no progress without inflicting terrible punishment. The slaughter at Guru only forestalled the inevitable. We were drawn into the vortex of war by the Tibetans' own folly. There was no hope of their regarding the British as a formidable Power, and a force to be reckoned with, until we had killed several thousand of their men.

After the action the Tibetan wounded were brought into Tuna, and an abandoned dwelling-house was fitted up as a hospital. An empty cowshed outside served as an operating-theatre. The patients showed extraordinary hardihood and stoicism. After the Dzama Tang engagement many of the wounded came in riding on yaks from a distance of fifty or sixty miles. They were consistently cheerful, and always ready to appreciate a joke. One man, who lost both legs, said: 'In my next battle I must be a hero, as I cannot run away.' Some of the wounded were terribly mutilated by shell. Two men who were shot through the brain, and two who were shot through the lungs, survived. For two days Lieutenant Davys, Indian Medical Service, was operating nearly all day. I think the Tibetans were really impressed with our humanity, and looked upon Davys as some incarnation of a medicine Buddha. They never hesitated to undergo operations, did not flinch at pain, and took chloroform without fear. Their recuperative power was marvellous. Of the 168 who were received in hospital, only 20 died; 148 were sent to their homes on hired yaks cured. Everyone who visited the hospital at Tuna left it with an increased respect for the Tibetans.

* * * * *

Three months after the action I found the Tibetans still lying where they fell. One shot through the shoulder in retreat had spun as he fell facing our rifles. Another tore at the grass with futile fingers through which a delicate pink primula was now blossoming. Shrunk arms and shanks looked hideously dwarfish. By the stream the bodies lay in heaps with parched skin, like mummies, rusty brown. A knot of coarse black hair, detached from a skull, was circling round in an eddy of wind. Everything had been stripped from the corpses save here and there a wisp of cloth, looking more grim than the nakedness it covered, or round the neck some inexpensive charm, which no one had thought worth taking for its occult powers. Nature, more kindly, had strewn round them beautiful spring flowers--primulas, buttercups, potentils. The stream 'bubbled oilily,' and in the ruined house bees were swarming.

Ten miles beyond the Springs an officer was watering his horse in the Bamtso Lake. The beast swung round trembling, with eyes astare. Among the weeds lay the last victim.

CHAPTER VII

A HUMAN MISCELLANY

The Tibetans stood on the roofs of their houses like a row of cormorants, and watched the doolie pass underneath. At a little distance it was hard to distinguish the children, so motionless were they, from the squat praying-flags wrapped in black skin and projecting from the parapets of the roof. The very babes were impassive and inscrutable. Beside them perched ravens of an ebony blackness, sleek and well groomed, and so consequential that they seemed the most human element of the group.

My Tibetan bearers stopped to converse with a woman on the roof who wore a huge red hoop in her hair, which was matted and touzled like a negress's. A child behind was searching it, with apparent success. The woman asked a question, and the bearers jerked out a few guttural monosyllables, which she received with indifference. She was not visibly elated when she heard that the doolie contained the first victim of the Tibetan arms. I should like to have heard her views on the political situation and the question of a settlement. Some of her relatives, perhaps, were killed in the m 阬閑 at the Hot Springs. Others who had been taken prisoners might be enlisted in the new doolie corps, and receiving an unexpected wage; others, perhaps, were wounded and being treated in our hospitals with all the skill and resources of modern science; or they were bringing in food-stuffs for our troops, or setting booby-traps for them, and lying in wait behind sangars to snipe them in the Red Idol Gorge.

The bearers started again; the hot sun and the continued exertion made them stink intolerably. Every now and then they put down the doolie, and began discussing their loot--ear-rings and charms, rough turquoises and ruby-coloured stones, torn from the bodies of the dead and wounded. For the moment I was tired of Tibet.

I remembered another exodus when I was disgusted with the country. I had been allured across the Himalayas by the dazzling purity of the snows. I had escaped the Avernus of the plains, and I might have been content, but there was the seduction of the snows. I had gained an upper story, but I must climb on to the roof. Every morning the Sun-god threw open the magnificent portals of his domain, dazzling rifts and spires, black cliffs glacier-bitten, the flawless vaulted roof of Kinchenjunga--

'Myriads of topaz lights and jacinth work Of subtlest jewellery.'

One morning the roof of the Sun-god's palace was clear and cloudless, but about its base hung little clouds of snow-dust, as though the Olympians had been holding tourney, and the dust had risen in the tracks of their chariots. All this was seen over galvanized iron roofs. The Sun-god had thrown open his palace, and we were playing pitch and toss on the steps. While I was so engrossed I looked up. Columns of white cloud were rising to obscure the entrance. Then a sudden shaft of sunlight broke the fumes. There was a vivid flash, a dazzle of jewel-work, and the portals closed. I was covered with bashfulness and shame. It was a direct invitation. I made some excuse to my companion, said I had an engagement, went straight to my rooms, and packed.

But while the aroma of my carriers insulted the pure air, and their chatter over their tawdry spoil profaned the silent precincts of Chumulari, their mountain goddess, I thought more of the disenchantment of that earlier visit. I remembered sitting on a hillside near a lamasery, which was surrounded by a small village of Lamas' houses. Outside the temple a priest was operating on a yak for vaccine. He had bored a large hole in the shoulder, into which he alternately buried his forearm and squirted hot water copiously. A hideous yellow trickle beneath indicated that the poor beast was entirely perforated. A crowd of admiring little boys and girls looked on with relish. The smell of the poor yak was distressing, but the smell of the Lama was worse. I turned away in disgust--turned my back contentedly and without regret on the mysterious land and the road to the Forbidden City. At that moment, if the Dalai Lama himself had sent me a chaise with a dozen outriders and implored me to come, I would not have visited him, not for a thousand yaks. The scales of vagabondage fell from my eyes; the spirit of unrest died within me. I had a longing for fragrant soap, snowy white linen, fresh-complexioned ladies and clean-shaven, well-groomed men.

And here again I was returning very slowly to civilization; but I was coming back with half an army corps to shake the Dalai Lama on his throne--or if there were no throne or Dalai Lama, to do what? I wondered if the gentlemen sitting snugly in Downing Street had any idea.

At Phari I was snow-bound for a week, and there were no doolie-bearers. The Darjeeling dandy-wallahs were no doubt at the front, where they were most wanted, as the trained army doolie corps are plainsmen, who can barely breathe, much less work, at these high elevations. At last we secured some Bhutias who were returning to the front.

The Bhutia is a type I have long known, though not in the capacity of bearer. These men regarded the doolie with the invalid inside as a piece of baggage that had to be conveyed from one camp to another, no matter how. Of the art of their craft they knew nothing, but they battled with the elements so stoutly that one forgave them their awkwardness. They carried me along mountain-paths so slippery that a mule could find no foothold, through snow so deep and clogging that with all their toil they could make barely half a mile an hour; and they took shelter once from a hailstorm in which exposure without thick head-covering might have been fatal. Often they dropped the doolie, sometimes on the edge of a precipice, in places where one perspired with fright; they collided quite unnecessarily with stones and rocks; but they got through, and that was the main point. Men who have carried a doolie over a difficult mountain-pass (14,350 feet), slipping and stumbling through snow and ice in the face of a hurricane of wind, deserve well of the great Raj which they serve.

On the road into Darjeeling, owing to the absence of trained doolie-bearers, I met a human miscellany that I am not likely to forget. Eight miles beyond the Jelap lies the fort of Gnatong, whence there is a continual descent to the plains of India. The neighbouring hills and valleys had been searched for men; high wages were offered, and at last from some remote village in Sikkim came a dozen weedy Lepchas, simian in appearance, and of uncouth speech, who understood no civilized tongue. They had never seen a doolie, but in default of better they were employed. It was nobody's fault; bearers must be had, and the profession was unpopular. I was their 'first job.' I settled myself comfortably, all unconscious of my impending fate. They started off with a wild whoop, threw the doolie up in the air, caught it on their shoulders, and played cup and ball with the contents until they were tired. I swore at them in Spanish, English, and Hindustani, but it was small relief, as they didn't take the slightest notice, and I had neither hands to beat them nor feet to kick them over the khud. My orderly followed and told them in a mild North-Country accent that they would be punished if they did it again; there is some absurd army regulation about British soldiers striking followers. For all they knew, he was addressing the stars. They dropped the thing a dozen times in ten miles, and thought it the hugest joke in the world. I shall shy at a hospital doolie for the rest of my natural life.

There is a certain Mongol smell which is the most unpleasant human odour I know. It is common to Lepchas, Bhutanese, and Tibetans, but it is found in its purest essence in these low-country, cross-bred Lepchas, who were my close companions for two days. When we reached the heat of the valley, they jumped into the stream and bathed, but they emerged more unsavoury than ever. It was a relief to pass a dead mule. At the next village they got drunk, after which they developed an amazing surefootedness, and carried me in without mishap.

After two days with my Lepchas we reached Rungli (2,000 feet), whence the road to the plains is almost level. Here a friend introduced me to a Jemadar in a Gurkha regiment.

'He writes all about our soldiers and the fighting in Tibet,' he said. 'It all goes home to England on the telegraph-wire, and people at home are reading what he says an hour or two after he has given khubber to the office here.'

'Oh yes,' said the Jemadar in Hindustani, 'and if things are well the people in England will be very glad; and if we are ill and die, and there is too much cold, they will be very sorry.'

The Jemadar smiled. He was most sincere and sympathetic. If an Englishman had said the same thing, he would have been thought half-witted, but Orientals have a way of talking platitudes as if they were epigrams.

The Jemadar's speech was so much to the point that it called up a little picture in my mind of the London Underground and a liveried official dealing out Daily Mails to crowds of inquirers anxious for news of Tibet. Only the sun blazed overhead and the stream made music at our feet.

I left the little rest-hut in the morning, resigned to the inevitable jolting, and expecting another promiscuous collection of humanity to do duty as kahars. But, to my great joy, I found twelve Lucknow doolie-wallahs waiting by the veranda, lithe and erect, and part of a drilled corps. Drill discipline is good, but in the art of their trade these men needed no teaching. For centuries their ancestors had carried palanquins in the plains, bearing Rajas and ladies of high estate, perhaps even the Great Mogul himself. The running step to their strange rhythmic chants must be an instinct to them. That morning I knew my troubles were at an end. They started off with steps of velvet, improvising as they went a kind of plaintive song like an intoned litany.

The leading man chanted a dimeter line, generally with an iambus in the first foot; but when the road was difficult or the ascent toilsome, the metre became trochaic, in accordance with the best traditions of classical poetry. The hind-men responded with a sing-song trochaic dimeter which sounded like a long-drawn-out monosyllable. They never initiated anything. It was not custom; it had never been done. The laws of Nature are not so immutable as the ritual of a Hindu guild.

We sped on smoothly for eight miles, and when I asked the kahars if they were tired, they said they would not rest, as relays were waiting on the road. All the way they chanted their hymn of the obvious:--

'Mountains are steep; Chorus: Yes, they are. The road is narrow; Yes, it is. The sahib is wounded; That is so. With many wounds; They are many. The road goes down; Yes, it does. Now we are hurrying; Yes, we are.'

Here they ran swiftly till the next rise in the hill.

Waiting in the shade for relays, I heard two Englishmen meet on the road. One had evidently been attached, and was going down to join his regiment; the other was coming up on special service. I caught fragments of our crisp expressive argot.

Officer going down (apparently disillusioned): 'Oh, it's the same old bald-headed maidan we usually muddle into.'

Officer coming up: '... Up above Phari ideal country for native cavalry, isn't it?... A few men with lances prodding those fellows in the back would soon put the fear of God into them. Why don't they send up the --th Light Cavalry?'

Officer going down: 'They've Walers, and you can't feed 'em, and the --th are all Jats. They're no good; can't do without a devil of a lot of milk. They want bucketsful of it. Well, bye-bye; you'll soon get fed up with it.'

The doolie was hitched up, and the kahars resumed their chant:

'A sahib goes up; Yes, he does. A sahib goes down; That is so.'

The heat and the monotonous cadence induced drowsiness, and one fell to thinking of this odd motley of men, all of one genus, descended from the anthropoid ape, and exhibiting various phases of evolution--the primitive Lepcha, advanced little further than his domestic dog; the Tibetan kahar caught in the wheel of civilization, and forming part of the mechanism used to bring his own people into line; the Lucknow doolie-bearer and the Jemadar Sahib, products of a hoary civilization that have escaped complexity and nerves; and lord of all these, by virtue of his race, the most evolved, the English subaltern. All these folk are brought together because the people on the other side of the hills will insist on being obsolete anachronisms, who have been asleep for hundreds of years while we have been developing the sense of our duty towards our neighbour. They must come into line; it is the will of the most evolved.

The next day I was carried for miles through a tropical forest. The damp earth sweated in the sun after last night's thunder-storm, and the vegetation seemed to grow visibly in the steaming moisture. Gorgeous butterflies, the epicures of a season, came out to indulge a love of sunshine and suck nectar from all this profusion. Overhead, birds shrieked and whistled and beat metal, and did everything but sing. The cicadas raised a deafening din in praise of their Maker, seeming to think, in their natural egoism, that He had made the forest, oak, and gossamer for their sakes. We were not a thousand feet above the sea. Thousands of feet above us, where we were camping a day or two ago, our troops were marching through snow.

The next morning we crossed the Tista River, and the road led up through sal forests to a tea-garden at 3,500 feet. Here we entered the most perfect climate in the world, and I enjoyed genial hospitality and a foretaste of civilization: a bed, sheets, a warm bath, clean linen, fruit, sparkling soda, a roomy veranda with easy-chairs, and outside roses and trellis-work, and a garden bright with orchids and wild-turmeric and a profusion of semi-tropical and English flowers--all the things which the spoilt children of civilization take as a matter of course, because they have never slept under the stars, or known what it is to be hungry and cold, or exhausted by struggling against the forces of untamed Nature.

At noon next day, in the cantonments at Jelapahar, an officer saw a strange sight--a field-hospital doolie with the red cross, and twelve kahars, Lucknow men, whose plaintive chant must have recalled old days on the North-West frontier. Behind on a mule rode a British orderly of the King's Own Scottish Borderers, bearded and weather-stained, and without a trace of the spick-and-spanness of cantonments. I saw the officer's face lighten; he became visibly excited; he could not restrain himself--he swung round, rode after my orderly, and began to question him without shame. Here was civilization longing for the wilderness, and over there, beyond the mist, under that snow-clad peak, were men in the wilderness longing for civilization.

A cloud swept down and obscured the Jelap, as if the chapter were closed. But it is not. That implacable barrier must be crossed again, and then, when we have won the most secret places of the earth, we may cry with Burton and his Arabs, 'Voyaging is victory!'

CHAPTER VIII

THE ADVANCE OF THE MISSION OPPOSED

The intention of the Tibetans at the Hot Springs has not been made clear. They say that their orders were to oppose our advance, but to avoid a battle, just as our orders were to take away their arms, if possible, without firing a shot. The muddle that ensued lends itself to several interpretations, and the Tibetans ascribe their loss to British treachery. They say that we ordered them to destroy the fuses of their matchlocks, and then fired on them. This story was taken to Lhasa, with the result that the new levies from the capital were not deterred by the terrible punishment inflicted on their comrades. Orders were given to oppose us on the road to Gyantse, and an armed force, which included many of the fugitives from Guru, gathered about Kangma.

The peace delegates always averred that we fired the first shot at Guru. But even if we give the Tibetans the benefit of the doubt, and admit that the action grew out of the natural excitement of two forces struggling for arms, both of whom were originally anxious to avoid a conflict, there is still no doubt that the responsibility of continuing the hostilities lies with the Tibetans.

On the morning of April 7 ten scouts of the 2nd Mounted Infantry, under Captain Peterson, found the Tibetans occupying the village of Samando, seventeen miles beyond Kalatso. As our men had orders not to fire or provoke an attack, they sent a messenger up to the walls to ask one of the Tibetans to come out and parley. They said they would send for a man, and invited us to come nearer. When we had ridden up to within a hundred yards of the village, they opened a heavy fire on us with their matchlocks. Our scouts spread out, rode back a few hundred yards, and took cover behind stones. Not a man or pony was hit. Before retiring, the mounted infantry fired a few volleys at the Tibetans who were lining the roofs of two large houses and a wall that connected them, their heads only appearing above the low turf parapets. Twice the Tibetans sent off a mounted man for reinforcements, but our shooting was so good that each time the horse returned riderless. The next morning we found the village unoccupied, and discovered six dead left on the roofs, most of whom were wounded about the chest. Our bullets had penetrated the two feet of turf and killed the man behind. Putting aside the question of Guru, the Samando affair was the first overt act of hostility directed against the mission.

After Samando there was no longer any doubt that the Tibetans intended to oppose our advance. On the 8th the mounted infantry discovered a wall built across the valley and up the hills just this side of Kangma, which they reported as occupied by about 1,000 men. As it was too late to attack that night, we formed camp. The next morning we found the wall evacuated, and the villagers reported that the Tibetans had retired to the gorge below. This habit of building formidable barriers across a valley, stretching from crest to crest of the flanking hills, is a well-known trait of Tibetan warfare. The wall is often built in the night and abandoned the next morning. One would imagine that, after toiling all night to make a strong position, the Tibetans would hold their wall if they intended to make a stand anywhere. But they do not grudge the labour. Wall-building is an instinct with them. When a Tibetan sees two stones by the roadside, he cannot resist placing one on the top of the other. So wherever one goes the whole countryside is studded with these monuments of wasted labour, erected to propitiate the genii of the place, or from mere force of habit to while away an idle hour. During the campaign of 1888 it was this practice of strengthening and abandoning positions more than anything else which gained the Tibetans the reputation of cowardice, which they have since shown to be totally undeserved.

On April 8, owing to the delay in reconnoitring the wall, we made only about eight miles, and camped. The next morning we had marched about two miles, when we found the high ridge on the left flank occupied by the enemy, and the mounted infantry reported them in the gorge beyond. Two companies of the 8th Gurkhas under Major Row were sent up to the hill on the left to turn the enemy's right flank, and the mountain battery (No. 7) came into action on the right at over 3,000 yards. The enemy kept up a continuous but ineffectual fire from the ridge, none of their jingal bullets falling anywhere near us. The Gurkhas had a very difficult climb. The hill was quite 2,000 feet above the valley; the lower and a good deal of the other slopes were of coarse sand mixed with shale, and the rest nothing but slippery rock. The summit of the hill was approached by a number of step-like shale terraces covered with snow. When only a short way up, a snowstorm came on and obscured the Gurkhas from view. The cold was intense, and the troops in the valley began to collect the sparse brushwood, and made fires to keep themselves warm.

On account of the nature of the hillside and the high altitude, the progress of the Gurkhas was very slow, and it took them nearly three hours to reach the ridge held by the enemy. When about two-thirds of the way up, they came under fire from the ridge, but all the shots went high. The jingals carried well over them at about 1,200 yards. The enemy also sent a detachment to meet them on the top, but these did not fire long, and retired as the Gurkhas advanced. When the 8th reached the summit, the Tibetans were in full flight down the opposite slope, which was also snow-covered. Thirty were shot down in the rout, and fifty-four who were hiding in the caves were made prisoners.

In the meanwhile the battery had been making very good practice at 3,000 yards. Seven men were found dead on the summit, and four wounded, evidently by their fire.

But to return to the main action in the gorge. The Tibetans held a very strong position among some loose boulders on the right, two miles beyond the gully which the Gurkhas had ascended to make their flank attack. The rocks extended from the bluff cliff to the path which skirted the stream. No one could ask for better cover; it was most difficult to distinguish the drab-coated Tibetans who lay concealed there. To attack this strong position General Macdonald sent Captain Bethune with one company of the 32nd Pioneers, placing Lieutenant Cook with his Maxim on a mound at 500 yards to cover Bethune's advance. Bethune led a frontal attack. The Tibetans fired wildly until the Sikhs were within eighty yards, and then fled up the valley. Not a single man of the 32nd was hit during the attack, though one sepoy was wounded in the pursuit by a bullet in the hand from a man who lay concealed behind a rock within a few yards of him. While the 32nd were dislodging the Tibetans from the path and the rocks above it, the mounted infantry galloped through them to reconnoitre ahead and cut off the fugitives in the valley. They also came through the enemy's fire at very close quarters without a casualty. On emerging from the gorge the mounted infantry discovered that the ridge the Tibetans had held was shaped like the letter S, so that by doubling back along an almost parallel valley they were able to intercept the enemy whom the Gurkhas had driven down the cliffs. The unfortunate Tibetans were now hemmed in between two fires, and hardly a man of them escaped.

The Tibetan casualties, as returned at the time, were much exaggerated. The killed amounted to 100, and, on the principle that the proportion of wounded must be at least two to one, it was estimated that their losses were 300. But, as a matter of fact, the wounded could not have numbered more than two dozen.

The prisoners taken by the Gurkhas on the top of the ridge turned out to be impressed peasants, who had been compelled to fight us by the Lamas. They were not soldiers by inclination or instinct, and I believe their greatest fear was that they might be released and driven on to fight us again.

The action at the Red Idol Gorge may be regarded as the end of the first phase of the Tibetan opposition. We reached Gyantse on April 11, and the fort was surrendered without resistance. Nothing had occurred on the march up to disturb our estimate of the enemy. Since the campaign of 1888 no one had given the Tibetans any credit for martial instincts, and until the Karo la action and the attack on Gyantse they certainly displayed none. It would be hard to exaggerate the strategical difficulties of the country through which we had to pass. The progress of the mission and its escort under similar conditions would have been impossible on the North-West frontier or in any country inhabited by a people with the rudiments of sense or spirit. The difficulties of transport were so great that the escort had to be cut down to the finest possible figure. There were barely enough men for pickets, and many of the ordinary precautions of field manoeuvres were out of the question. But the Tibetan failed to realize his opportunities. He avoided the narrow forest-clad ravines of Sikkim and Chumbi, and made his first stand on the open plateau at Guru. Fortunately for us, he never learnt what transport means to a civilized army. A bag of barley-meal, some weighty degchies, and a massive copper teapot slung over the saddle are all he needs; evening may produce a sheep or a yak. His movements are not hampered by supplies. If the importance of the transport question had ever entered his head, he would have avoided the Tuna camp, with its Maxims and mounted infantry, and made a dash upon the line of communications. A band of hardy mountaineers in their own country might very easily surprise and annihilate an ill-guarded convoy in a narrow valley thickly forested and flanked by steep hills. To furtively cut an artery in your enemy's arm and let out the blood is just as effective as to knock him on the head from in front. But in this first phase of the operations the Tibetans showed no strategy; they were badly led, badly armed, and apparently devoid of all soldier-like qualities. Only on one or two occasions they displayed a desperate and fatal courage, and this new aspect of their character was the first indication that we might have to revise the views we had formed sixteen years ago of an enemy who has seemed to us since a unique exception to the rule that a hardy mountain people are never deficient in courage and the instinct of self-defence.

The most extraordinary aspect of the fighting up to our arrival at Gyantse was that we had only one casualty from a gunshot wound--the Sikh who was shot in the hand at the Dzama Tang affair by a Tibetan whose jezail was almost touching him. Yet at the Hot Springs the Tibetans fired off their matchlocks and rifles into the thick of us, and at Guru an hour afterwards the

Gurkhas walked right up to a house held by the enemy, under heavy fire, and took it without a casualty. The mounted infantry were exposed to a volley at Samando at 100 yards, and again in the Red Idol Gorge they rode through the enemy's fire at an even shorter range. In the same action the 32nd made a frontal attack on a strong position which was held until they were within eighty yards, and not a man was hit. No wonder we had a contempt for the Tibetan arms. Their matchlocks, weapons of the rudest description, must have been as dangerous to their own marksmen as to the enemy; their artillery fire, to judge by our one experience of it at Dzama Tang, was harmless and erratic; and their modern Lhasa-made rifles had not left a mark on our men. The Tibetans' only chance seemed to be a rush at close quarters, but they had not proved themselves competent swordsmen. My own individual case was sufficient to show that they were bunglers. Besides the twelve wounds I received at the Hot Springs, I found seven sword-cuts on my poshteen, none of which were driven home. During the whole campaign we had only one death from sword-wounds.

Arrived at Gyantse, we settled down with some sense of security. A bazaar was held outside the camp. The people seemed friendly, and brought in large quantities of supplies. Colonel Younghusband, in a despatch to the Foreign Office, reported that with the surrender of Gyantse Fort on April 12 resistance in that part of Tibet was ended. A letter was received from the Amban stating that he would certainly reach Gyantse within the next three weeks, and that competent and trustworthy Tibetan representatives would accompany him. The Lhasa officials, it was said, were in a state of panic, and had begged the Amban to visit the British camp and effect a settlement.

On April 20 General Macdonald's staff, with the 10-pounder guns, three companies of the 23rd Pioneers, and one and a half companies of the 8th Gurkhas, returned to Chumbi to relieve the strain on the transport and strengthen the line of communications. Gyantse Jong was evacuated, and we occupied a position in a group of houses, as we thought, well out of range of fire from the fort.

Everything was quiet until the end of April, when we heard that the Tibetans were occupying a wall in some strength near the Karo la, forty-two miles from Gyantse, on the road to Lhasa. Colonel Brander, of the 32nd Pioneers, who was left in command at Gyantse, sent a small party of mounted infantry and pioneers to reconnoitre the position. They discovered 2,000 of the enemy behind a strong loopholed wall stretching across the valley, a distance of nearly 600 yards. As the party explored the ravine they had a narrow escape from a booby-trap, a formidable device of Tibetan warfare, which was only employed against our troops on this occasion. An artificial avalanche of rocks and stones is so cunningly contrived that the removal of one stone sends the whole engine of destruction thundering down the hillside. Luckily, the Tibetans did not wait for our main body, but loosed the machine on an advance guard of mounted infantry, who were in extended order and able to take shelter behind rocks.

On the return of the reconnaissance Colonel Brander decided to attack, as he considered the gathering threatened the safety of the mission. The Karo Pass is an important strategical position, lying as it does at the junction of the two roads to India, one of which leads to Kangma, the other to Gyantse. A strong force holding the pass might at any moment pour troops down the valley to Kangma, cut us off in the rear, and destroy our line of communications. When Colonel Brander led his small force to take the pass, it was not with the object of clearing the road to Lhasa. The measure was purely defensive: the action was undertaken to keep the road open for convoys and reinforcements, and to protect isolated posts on the line. The force with the mission was still an 'escort,' and so far its operations had been confined to dispersing the armed levies that blocked the road.

On May 3 Colonel Brander left Gyantse with his column of 400 rifles, comprising three companies of the 32nd Pioneers, under Captains Bethune and Cullen and Lieutenant Hodgson; one company of the 8th, under Major Row and Lieutenant Coleridge, with two 7-pounder guns; the Maxim detachment of the Norfolks, under Lieutenant Hadow; and forty-five of the 1st Mounted Infantry, under Captain Ottley. On the first day the column marched eighteen miles, and halted at Gobshi. On the second day they reached Ralung, eleven miles further, and on the third marched up the pass and encamped on an open spot about two miles from where the Tibetans had built their wall. A reconnaissance that afternoon estimated the enemy at 2,000, and they were holding the strongest position on the road to Lhasa. They had built a wall the whole length of a narrow spur and up the hill on the other side of the stream, and in addition held detached sangars high up the steep hills, and well thrown forward. Their flanks rested on very high and nearly precipitous rocks. It was only possible to climb the ridge on our right from a mile behind, and on the left from nearly three-quarters of a mile. Colonel Brander at first considered the practicability of delaying the attack on the main wall until the Gurkhas had completed their flanking movements, cleared the Tibetans out of the sangars that enfiladed our advance in the valley, and reached a position on the hills beyond the wall, whence they could fire into the enemy's rear. But the cliffs were so sheer that the ascent was deemed impracticable, and the next morning it was decided to make a frontal attack without waiting for the Gurkhas to turn the flank. No one for a moment thought it could be done.

The troops marched out of camp at ten o'clock. One company of the 32nd Pioneers, under Captain Cullen, was detailed to attack on the right, and a second company, under Captain Bethune, to follow the river-bed, where they were under cover of the high bank until within 400 yards of the wall, and then rush the centre of the position. The 1st Mounted Infantry, under Captain Ottley, were to follow this company along the valley. The guns, Maxims, and one company of the 32nd in reserve, occupied a small plateau in the centre. Half a company of the 8th Gurkhas were left behind to guard the camp. A second half-company, under Major Row, were sent along the hillside on the left to attack the enemy's extreme right sangar, but their progress over the shifting shale slopes and jagged rocks was so slow that the front attack did not wait for them.

The fire from the wall was very heavy, and the advance of Cullen's and Bethune's companies was checked. Bethune sent half a company back, and signalled to the mounted infantry to retire. Then, compelled by some fatal impulse, he changed his mind, and with half a company left the cover of the river-bed and rushed out into the open within forty yards of the main wall, exposed to a withering fire from three sides. His half-company held back, and Bethune fell shot through the head with only four men by his side--a bugler, a store-office babu, and two devoted Sikhs. What the clerk was doing there no one knows, but evidently the soldier in the man had smouldered in suppression among the office files and triumphed splendidly. It was a gallant reckless charge against uncounted odds. Poor Bethune had learnt to despise the Tibetans' fire, and his contempt was not unnatural. On the march to Gyantse the enemy might have been firing blank cartridges for all the effect they had left on our men. At Dzama Tang Bethune had made a frontal attack on a strong position, and carried it without losing a man. Against a similar rabble it might have been possible to rush the wall with his handful of Sikhs, but these new Kham levies who held the Karo la were a very different type of soldier.

The frontal attack was a terrible mistake, as was shown four hours afterwards, when the enemy were driven from their position without further loss to ourselves by a flanking movement on the right.

At twelve o'clock Major Row, after a laborious climb, reached a point on a hillside level with the sangars, which were strongly held on a narrow ledge 200 yards in front of him. Here he sent up a section of his men under cover of projecting rocks to get above the sangars and fire down into them. In the meanwhile some of the enemy scrambled on to the rocks above, and began throwing down boulders at the Gurkhas, but these either broke up or fell harmless on the shale slopes above. After waiting an hour, Major Row went back himself and found his section checked half-way by the stone-throwing and shots from above; they had tried another way, but found it impracticable.

Keeping a few men back to fire on any stone-throwers who showed themselves, Row dribbled his men across the difficult place, and in half an hour reached the rocky ledge above the sangars and looked right down on the enemy. At the first few shots from the Gurkhas they began to bolt, and, coming into the fire of the men below, who now rushed forward, nearly every man--forty in all--was killed. One or two who escaped the fire found their flight cut off by a precipice, and in an abandonment of terror hurled themselves down on the rocks below. After clearing the sangar, the Gurkhas had only to surmount the natural difficulties of the rocky and steep hill; for though the enemy fired on them from the wall, their shooting was most erratic. When at last they reached a small spur that overlooked the Tibetan main position, they found, to their disgust, that each man was protected from their fire by a high stone traverse, on the right-hand of which he lay secure, and fired through loopholes barely a foot from the ground.

The Gurkhas had accomplished a most difficult mountaineering feat under a heavy fire; they had turned the enemy out of their sangars, and after four hours' climbing they had scaled the heights everyone thought inaccessible. But their further progress was barred by a sheer cliff; they had reached a cul-de-sac. Looking up from the valley, it appeared that the spot where they stood commanded the enemy's position, but we had not reckoned on the traverses. This amazing advance in the enemy's defensive tactics had rendered their position unassailable from the left, and made the Gurkhas' flanking movement a splendid failure.

It was now two o'clock, and, except for the capture of the enemy's right sangars, we had done nothing to weaken their opposition. The frontal and flanking attacks had failed. Bethune was killed, and seventeen men. Our guns had made no impression on their wall. Looking down from the spur which overlooked the Tibetan camp and the valley beyond, the Gurkhas could see a large reinforcement of at least 500 men coming up to join the enemy. The situation was critical. In four hours we had done nothing, and we knew that if we could not take the place by dusk we would have to abandon the attack or attempt to rush the camp at night. That would have been a desperate undertaking--400 men against 3,000, a rush at close quarters with the bayonet, in which the superiority of our modern rifles would be greatly discounted.

Matters were at this crisis, when we saw the Tibetans running out of their extreme left sangars. At twelve o'clock, when the front attack had failed and the left attack was apparently making no progress, fifteen men of the 32nd who were held in reserve were sent up the hill on the right. They had reached a point above the enemy's left forward sangar, and were firing into it with great effect. Twice the Tibetans rushed out, and, coming under a heavy Maxim fire, bolted back again. The third time they fled in a mass, and the Maxims mowed down about thirty. The capture of the sangars was a signal for a general stampede. From the position they had won the Sikhs could enfilade the main wall itself. The Tibetans only waited a few shots; then they turned and fled in three huge bodies down the valley. Thus the fifteen Sikhs on the right saved the situation. The tension had been great. In no other action during the campaign, if we except Palla, did the success of our arms stand so long in doubt. Had we failed to take the wall by daylight, Colonel Brander's column would have been in a most precarious position. We could not afford to retire, and a night attack could only have been pushed home with heavy loss.

Directly the flight began, the 1st Mounted Infantry--forty-two men, under

Captain Ottley--rode up to the wall. They were ten minutes making a breach. Then they poured into the valley and harassed the flying masses, riding on their flanks and pursuing them for ten miles to within sight of the Yamdok Tso. It showed extraordinary courage on the part of this little band of Masbis and Gurkhas that they did not hesitate to hurl themselves on the flanks of this enormous body of men, like terriers on the heels of a flock of cattle, though they had had experience of their stubborn resistance the whole day long, and rode through the bodies of their fallen comrades. Not a man drew rein. The Tibetans were caught in a trap. The hills that sloped down to the valley afforded them little cover. Their fate was only a question of time and ammunition. The mounted infantry returned at night with only three casualties, having killed over 300 men.

The sortie to the Karo la was one of the most brilliant episodes of the campaign. We risked more then than on any other occasion. But the safety of the mission and many isolated posts on the line was imperilled by this large force at the cross-roads, which might have increased until it had doubled or trebled if we had not gone out to disperse it. A weak commander might have faltered and weighed the odds, but Colonel Brander saw that it was a moment to strike, and struck home. His action was criticised at the time as too adventurous. But the sortie is one of the many instances that our interests are best cared for by men who are beyond the telegraph-poles, and can act on their own initiative without reference to Government offices in Simla.

As the column advanced to the Karo la, a message was received that the mission camp at Gyantse had been attacked in the early morning of the 5th, and that Major Murray's men--150 odd rifles--had not only beaten the enemy off, but had made three sorties from different points and killed 200.

With the action at the Karo la and the attack on the mission at Gyantse began the second phase of the operations, during which we were practically besieged in our own camp, and for nine weeks compelled to act on the defensive. The courage of the Tibetans was now proved beyond a doubt. The new levies from Kham and Shigatze were composed of very different men from those we herded like sheep at Guru. They were also better armed than our previous assailants, and many of them knew how to shoot. At the same time they were better led. The primitive ideas of strategy hitherto displayed by the Tibetans gave place to more advanced tactics. The usual story got wind that the Tibetans were being led by trained Russian Buriats. But there was no truth in it. The altered conditions of the campaign, as we may call it, after it became necessary to begin active operations, were due to the force of circumstances--the arrival of stouter levies from the east, the great numerical superiority of the enemy, and their strongly fortified positions.

The operations at Gyantse are fully dealt with in another chapter, and I will conclude this account of the opposition to our advance with a description of the attack on the Kangma post, the only attempt on the part of the enemy to cut off our line of communications. Its complete failure seems to have deterred the Tibetans from subsequent ventures of the kind.

From Ralung, ten miles this side of the Karo la, two roads branch off to India. The road leading to Kangma is the shortest route; the other road makes a d闰our of thirty miles to include Gyantse. Ralung lies at the apex of the triangle, as shown in this rough diagram. Gyantse and Kangma form the two base angles.

If it had been possible, a strong post would have been left at the Karo la after the action of May 6. But our small force was barely sufficient to garrison Gyantse, and we had to leave the alternative approach to Kangma unguarded. An attack was expected there; the post was strongly fortified, and garrisoned by two companies of the 23rd Pioneers, under Captain Pearson.

The attack, which was made on June 7, was unexpectedly dramatic. We have learnt that the Tibetan has courage, but in other respects he is still an unknown quantity. In motive and action he is as mysterious and unaccountable as his paradoxical associations would lead us to imagine. In dealing with the Tibetans one must expect the unexpected. They will try to achieve the impossible, and shut their eyes to the obvious. They have a genius for doing the wrong thing at the wrong time. Their dogged courage, their undoubted heroism, their occasional acuteness, their more general imbecile folly and vacillation and inability to grasp a situation, make it impossible to say what they will do in any given circumstances. A few dozen men will hurl themselves against hopeless odds, and die to a man fighting desperately; a handful of impressed peasants will devote themselves to death in the defence of a village, like the old Roman patriots. At other times they will forsake a strongly sangared position at the first shot, and thousands will prowl round a camp at night, shouting grotesquely, but too timid to make a determined attack on a vastly outnumbered enemy.

The uncertainty of the enemy may be accounted for to some extent by the fact that we are not often opposed by the same levies, which would imply that theirs is greatly the courage of ignorance. Yet in the face of the fighting at Palla, Naini, and Gyantse Jong, this is evidently no fair estimate of the Tibetan spirit. The men who stood in the breach at Gyantse in that hell of shrapnel and Maxim and rifle fire, and dropped down stones on our Gurkhas as they climbed the wall, met death knowingly, and were unterrified by the resources of modern science in war, the magic, the demons, the unseen, unimagined messengers of death.

But the men who attacked the Kangma post, what parallel in history have we for these? They came by night many miles over steep mountain cliffs and rocky ravines, perhaps silently, with determined purpose, weighing the odds; or, as I like to think, boastfully, with song and jest, saying, 'We will steal in upon these English at dawn before they wake, and slay them in their beds. Then we will hold the fort, and kill all who come near.'

They came in the gray before dawn, and hid in a gully beside our camp. At five the reveillé sounded and the sentry left the bastions. Then they sprang up and rushed, sword in hand, their rifles slung behind their backs, to the wall. The whole attack was directed on the south-east front, an unscalable wall of solid masonry, with bastions at each corner four feet thick and ten feet high. They directed their attack on the bastions, the only point on that side they could scramble over. They knew nothing of the fort and its tracing. Perhaps they had expected to find us encamped in tents on the open ground. But from the shallow nullah where they lay concealed, not 200 yards distant, and watched our sentry, they could survey the uncompromising front which they had set themselves to attack with the naked sword. They had no artillery or guncotton or materials for a siege, but they hoped to scale the wall and annihilate the garrison that held it. They had come from Lhasa to take Kangma, and they were not going to turn back. They came on undismayed, like men flushed with victory. The sepoys said they must be drunk or drugged. They rushed to the bottom of the wall, tore out stones, and flung them up at our sepoys; they leapt up to seize the muzzles of our rifles, and scrambled to gain a foothold and lift themselves on to the parapet; they fell bullet-pierced, and some turned savagely on the wall again. It was only a question of time, of minutes, and the cool mechanical fire of the 23rd Pioneers would have dropped every man. One hundred and six bodies were left under the wall, and sixty more were killed in the pursuit. Never was there such a hopeless, helpless struggle, such desperate and ineffectual gallantry.

Almost before it was light the yak corps with their small escort of thirty rifles of the 2nd Gurkhas were starting on the road to Kalatso. They had passed the hiding-place of the Tibetans without noticing the 500 men in rusty-coloured cloaks breathing quietly among the brown stones. Then the Tibetans made their charge, just as the transport had passed, and a party of them made for the yaks. Two Tibetan drivers in our service stood directly in their path. 'Who are you?' cried one of the enemy. 'Only yak-drivers,' was the frightened answer. 'Then, take that,' the Tibetan said, slashing at his arm with no intent to kill. The Gurkha escort took up a position behind a sangar and opened fire--all save one man, who stood by his yak and refused to come under cover, despite the shouts and warnings of his comrades. He killed several, but fell himself, hacked to pieces with swords. The Tibetans were driven off, and joined the rout from the fort. The whole affair lasted less than ten minutes.

Our casualties were: the isolated Gurkha killed, two men in the fort wounded by stones, and three of the 2nd Gurkhas severely wounded--two by sword-cuts, one by a bullet in the neck.

But what was the flame that smouldered in these men and lighted them to action? They might have been Paladins or Crusaders. But the Buddhists are not fanatics. They do not stake eternity on a single existence. They have no Mahdis or Juggernaut cars. The Tibetans, we are told, are not patriots. Politicians say that they want us in their country, that they are priest-ridden, and hate and fear their Lamas. What, then, drove them on? It was certainly not fear. No people on earth have shown a greater contempt for death. Their Lamas were with them until the final assault. Twenty shaven polls were found hiding in the nullah down which the Tibetans had crept in the dark, and were immediately despatched. What promises and cajoleries and threats the holy men used no one will ever know. But whatever the alternative, their simple followers preferred death.

The second phase of the operations, in which we had to act on the defensive in Gyantse, and the beginning of the third phase, which saw the arrival of reinforcements and the collapse of the Tibetan opposition, are described by an eye-witness in the next two chapters. During the whole of these operations I was invalided in Darjeeling, owing to a second operation which had to be performed on my amputation wound.

CHAPTER IX

GYANTSE

[BY HENRY NEWMAN]

Gyantse Plain lies at the intersection of four great valleys running almost at right angles to one another. In the north-eastern corner there emerge two gigantic ridges of sandstone. On one is built the jong, and on the other the monastery. The town fringes the base of the jong, and creeps into the hollow between the two ridges. The plain, about six miles by ten, is cultivated almost to the last inch, if we except a few stony patches here and there. There are, I believe, thirty-three villages in the plain. These are built in the midst of groves of poplar and willow. At one time, no doubt, the waters from the four valleys united to form a lake. Now they have found an outlet, and flow peacefully down Shigatze way. High up on the cold mountains one sees the cold bleached walls of the Seven Monasteries, some of them perched on almost inaccessible cliffs, whence they look sternly down on the warmth and prosperity below.

For centuries the Gyantse folk had lived self-contained and happy, practising their simple arts of agriculture, and but dimly aware of any world outside their own. Then one day there marched into their midst a column of British troops--white-faced Englishmen, dark, lithe Gurkhas, great, solemn, bearded Sikhs--and it was borne in upon the wondering Gyantse men that beyond their frontiers there existed great nations--so great, indeed, that they ventured to dispute on equal terms with the awful personage who ruled from Lhasa. It is true that from time to time there must have passed through Gyantse rumours of war on the distant frontier. The armies that we defeated at Guru and in the Red Idol Gorge had camped at Gyantse on their way to and fro. Gyantse saw and wondered at the haste of Lhasa despatch-riders. But I question whether any Gyantse man realized that events, great and shattering in his world, were impending when the British column rounded the corner of Naini Valley.

At first we were received without hostility, or even suspicion. The ruined jong, uninhabited save for a few droning Lamas, was surrendered as soon as we asked for it. A clump of buildings in a large grove near the river was rented without demur--though at a price--to the Commission. And when the country-people found that there was a sale for their produce, they flocked to the camp to sell. The entry of the British troops made no difference to the peace of Gyantse till the Lamas of Lhasa embarked on the fatal policy of levying more troops in Lhasa, Shigatze, and far-away Kham, and sending them down to fight. Then there entered the peaceful valley all the horrors of war--dead and maimed men in the streets and houses, burning villages, death and destruction of all kinds. Gyantse Plain and the town became scenes of desolation. To the British army in India war, unfortunately, is nothing new, but one can imagine what an upheaval this business of which I am about to write meant to people who for generations had lived in peace.

The incidents connected with the arrival of the mission with its escort at Gyantse need not be described in detail. On the day of arrival we camped in the midst of some fallow fields about two miles from the jong. The same afternoon a Chinese official, who called himself 'General' Ma, came into camp with the news that the jong was unoccupied, and that the local Tibetans did not propose to offer any resistance. The next morning we took quiet possession of the jong, placing two companies of Pioneers in garrison. The General with a small escort visited the monastery behind the fort, and was received with friendliness by the venerable Abbot. Neither the villagers nor the towns-people showed any signs of resentment at our presence. The Jongpen actively interested himself in the question of procuring an official residence for Colonel Younghusband and the members of the mission. There were reports of the Dalai Lama's representatives coming in haste to treat. Altogether the outlook was so promising that nobody was surprised when, after a stay of a week, General Macdonald, bearing in mind the difficulty of procuring supplies for the whole force, announced his intention of returning to Chumbi with the larger portion of the escort, leaving a sufficient guard with the mission.

The guard left behind consisted of four companies of the 32nd Pioneers, under Colonel Brander; four companies of the 8th Gurkhas, under Major Row; the 1st Mounted Infantry, under Captain Ottley; and the machine-gun section of the Norfolks, under Lieutenant Hadow. Mention should also be made of the two 7-pounder mountain-guns attached to the 8th Gurkhas, under the command of Captain Luke.

Before the General left for Chumbi he decided to evacuate the jong. The grounds on which this decision was come to were that the whole place was in a ruinous and dangerous condition, the surroundings were insanitary, there was only one building fit for human habitation, the water-supply was bad and deficient, and there seemed to be no prospect of further hostilities. Besides, from the military point of view there was some risk in splitting up the small guard to be left behind between the jong and the mission post. However, the precaution was taken of further dismantling the jong. The gateways and such portions as seemed capable of lending themselves to defence were blown up.

The house, or, rather, group of houses, rented by Colonel Younghusband for the mission was situated about 100 yards from a well-made stone bridge over the river. A beautiful grove, mostly of willow, extended behind the post along the banks of the river to a distance of about 500 yards. The jong lay about 1,800 yards to the right front. There were two houses in the intervening space, built amongst fields of iris and barley. Small groups of trees were dotted here and there. Altogether, the post was located in a spot as pleasant as one could hope to find in Tibet.

For some days before the General left, all the troops were engaged in putting the post in a state of defence. It was found that the force to be left behind could be easily located within the perimeter of a wall built round the group of houses. There was no room, however, for 200 mules and their drivers, needed for convoy purposes. These were placed in a kind of hornwork thrown out to the right front.

After the departure of the General we resigned ourselves to what we conceived would be a monotonous stay at Gyantse of two or three months, pending the signing of the treaty. The people continued to be perfectly friendly. A market was established outside the post, to which practically the whole bazaar from Gyantse town was removed. We were able to buy in the market, very cheap, the famous Gyantse carpets, for which enormous prices are demanded at Darjeeling and elsewhere in India. Unarmed officers wandered freely about Gyantse town, and the monks of Palkhor Choide, the monastery behind the fort, willingly conducted parties over the most sacred spots. They even readily sold some of the images before the altars, and the silk screens which shrouded the forms of the gigantic Buddhas. I mention these facts about the carpets and images because, when hereafter they adorned Simla and Darjeeling drawing-rooms, unkind people began to say that British officers had wantonly looted Palkhor Choide, one of the most famous monasteries in Tibet.

A little shooting was to be had, and officers wandered about the plain, gun in hand, bringing home mountain-hare--a queer little beast with a blue rump--duck, and pigeon. Occasionally an excursion up one of the side valleys would result in the shooting of a burhel or of a Tibetan gazelle. The country-people met with were all perfectly friendly.

Another feature of those first few peaceful days at Gyantse was the eagerness with which the Tibetans availed themselves of the skilled medical attendance with the mission. At first only one or two men wounded at the Red Idol Gorge were brought in, but the skill of Captain Walton, Indian Medical Service, soon began to be noised abroad, and every morning the little outdoor dispensary was crowded with sufferers of all kinds.

But during the last week in May reports began to reach Colonel Younghusband that, so far from attempting to enter into negociations, the Lhasa Government was levying an army in Kham, and that already five or six hundred men were camped on the other side of the Karo la, and were busily engaged in building a wall. Lieutenant Hodgson with a small force was sent to reconnoitre. He came back with the news that the wall was already built, stretching from one side of the valley to the other, and that there were several thousand well-armed men behind it. Both Colonel Younghusband and Colonel Brander considered it highly necessary that this gathering should be immediately dispersed, for it is a principle in Indian frontier warfare to strike quickly at any tribal assembly, in order to prevent it growing into dangerous proportions. The possibly exciting effect the force on the Karo la might have on the inhabitants of Gyantse had particularly to be considered. Accordingly, on May 3 Colonel Brander led the major portion of the Gyantse garrison towards the Karo la, leaving behind as a guard to the post two companies of Gurkhas, a company of the 32nd Pioneers, and a few mounted infantry, all under the command of Major Murray.

I accompanied the Karo la column, and must rely on hearsay as to my facts with regard to the attack on the mission. We heard about the attack the night before Colonel Brander drove the Tibetans from their wall on the Karo la, after a long fight which altered all our previous conceptions of the fighting qualities of the Tibetans. The courage shown by the enemy naturally excited apprehension about the safety of the mission. Colonel Brander did not stay to rest his troops after their day of arduous fighting, but began his return march next morning, arriving at Gyantse on the 9th.

The column had been warned that it was likely to be fired on from the jong if it entered camp by the direct Lhasa road. Accordingly, we marched in by a circuitous route, moving in under cover of the grove previously mentioned. The Maxims and guns came into action at the edge of the grove to cover the baggage. But, though numbers of Tibetans were seen on the walls of the jong, not a shot was fired.

We then learnt the story of the attack on the post. It appears that the day after Colonel Brander left for the Karo la (May 3) certain wounded and sick Tibetans that we had been attending informed the mission that about 1,000 armed men had come down towards Gyantse from Shigatze, and were building a wall about twelve miles away. It was added that they might possibly attack the post if they got to know that the garrison had been largely depleted. This news seemed to be worth inquiring into, and, accordingly, next day Major Murray sent some mounted infantry to reconnoitre up the Shigatze road. The latter returned with the information that they had gone up the valley some seven or eight miles, but had found no signs of any enemy.

The very next morning the post was attacked at dawn. It appears that the Shigatze force, about 1,000 strong, was really engaged in building a wall twelve miles away. Hearing that very few troops were guarding the mission, its commander--who, I hear, was none other than Khomba Bombu, the very man who arrested Sven Hedin's dash to Lhasa--determined to make a sudden attack on the post. He marched his men during the night, and about an hour before sunrise had them crouching behind trees and inside ditches all round the post.

The attack was sudden and simultaneous. A Gurkha sentry had just time to fire off his rifle before the Tibetans rushed to our walls and had their muskets through our loopholes. The enemy did not for the moment attempt to scale, but contented themselves with firing into the post through the loopholes they had taken. This delay proved fatal to their plans, for it gave the small garrison time to rise and arm. The brunt of the Tibetan fire was directed on the courtyard of the house where the tents of the members of the mission were pitched. Major Murray, who had rushed out of bed half clad, first directed his attention to this spot. The Sikhs, emerging from their tents with bandolier and rifle, in extraordinary costumes, were directed towards the loopholes. Some were sent on the roof of the mission-house, whence they could enfilade the attackers. Elsewhere various junior officers had taken command. Captain Luke, who, owing to sickness, had not gone on with the Karo la column, took charge of the Gurkhas on the south and west fronts. Lieutenant Franklin, the medical officer of the 8th Gurkhas, rallied Gurkhas and Pioneers to the loopholes on the east and north. Lieutenant Lynch, the treasure-chest officer, who had a guard of about twenty Gurkhas, took his men to the main gate to the south. There were at this time in hospital about a dozen Sikhs, who had been badly burnt in a lamentable gunpowder explosion a few days previously. These men, bandaged and crippled as they were, rose from their couches, made their painful way to the tops of the houses, and fired into the enemy below. About a dozen Tibetans had just begun to scramble over the wall by the time the defenders had manned the whole position, which was now not only held by fighting men, but by various members of the mission, including Colonel Younghusband, who had emerged with revolvers and sporting guns. A few of the enemy got inside the defences, and were immediately shot down.

Our fire was so heavy and so well directed that it is supposed that not more than ten minutes elapsed from the time the first shot was fired to the time the enemy began to withdraw. The withdrawal, however, was only to the shelter of trees and ditches a few hundred yards away, whence a long but almost harmless fusillade was kept up on the post. After about twenty minutes of this firing, Major Murray determined on a rally. Lieutenant Lynch with his treasure guard dashed out from the south gate. Some five-and-twenty Tibetans were discovered hiding in a small refuse hut about fifteen yards from the gate. The furious Gurkhas rushed in upon them and killed them all, and then dashed on through the long grove, clearing the enemy in front of them. Returning along the banks of the river, the same party discovered another body of Tibetans hiding under the arches of the bridge. Twenty or thirty were shot down, and about fifteen made prisoners. Similar success attended a rally from the north-east gate made by Major Murray and Lieutenant Franklin. The enemy fled howling from their hiding-places towards the town and jong as soon as they saw our men issue. They were pursued almost to the very walls of the fort. Indeed, but for the fringe of houses and narrow streets at the base of the jong, Major Murray would have gone on. The Tibetans, however, turned as soon as they reached the shelter of walls, and it would have been madness to attack five or six hundred determined men in a maze of alleys and passages with only a weak company. Major Murray accordingly made his way back to the post, picking up a dozen prisoners en route.

In this affair our casualties only amounted to five wounded and two killed. One hundred and forty dead of the enemy were counted outside the camp.

During the course of the day Major Murray sent a flag of truce to the jong with an intimation to the effect that the Tibetans could come out and bury their dead without fear of molestation. The reply was that we could bury the dead ourselves without fear of molestation. As it was impossible to leave all the bodies in the vicinity of the camp, a heavy and disagreeable task was thrown on the garrison.

Towards sundown the enemy in the jong began to fire into the camp, and our troops became aware of the unpleasant fact that the Tibetans possessed jingals, which could easily range from 1,800 to 2,000 yards. It was also realized that the jong entirely dominated the post; that our walls and stockades, protection enough against a direct assault from the plain, were no protection against bullets dropped from a height. So for the next four days, pending the return of the Karo la column, the little garrison toiled unceasingly at improving the defences. Traverses were built, the walls raised in height, the gates strengthened. It was discovered that the Tibetan fire was heaviest when we attempted to return it by sniping at figures seen on the jong. Accordingly, pending the completion of the traverses and other new protective works, Major Murray forbade any return fire.

Such was the position of affairs when the Karo la column returned. One of Colonel Brander's first acts, after his weary troops had rested for an hour or two, was to turn the Maxim on the groups who could be seen wandering about the jong. They quickly disappeared under cover, but only to man their jingals. Then began the bombardment of the post, which we had to endure for nearly seven weeks.

This is the place to speak of the bombardment generally, for it would be tedious to recapitulate in the form of a diary incidents which, however exciting at the time, now seem remarkable only for their monotony. It may be said at once that the bombardment was singularly ineffective. From first to last only fifteen men in the post were hit. Of these twelve were either killed or died of the wound. Of course, I exclude the casualties in the fighting, of which I will presently speak, outside the post. But the futility of the bombardment must not be entirely put down to bad marksmanship on the part of the Tibetans. That our losses were not heavier is largely due to the fact that the garrison laboured daily--and at first at night also--in erecting protecting walls and traverses. Practically every tent had a traverse built in front of it. It was found that the hornwork in which the mules were located came particularly under fire of the jong. This was pulled down one dark night, and the mules transferred to a fresh enclosure at the back of the post. Strong parapets of sand-bags were built on the roofs of the houses. Every window facing the jong was securely blocked with mud bricks. It will be realized how considerable was the labour involved in building the traverses when it is remembered that the jong looked down into the post. The majority of the walls had to be considerably higher than the tents themselves. They were mostly built of stakes cut from the grove, with two feet of earth rammed in between. After the first week or so the enemy brought to bear on the post several brass cannon, throwing balls weighing four or five pounds, and travelling with a velocity which enabled them to penetrate our traverses-- when they struck them, for the majority of shots from the cannon whistled harmlessly over our heads.

Practically, we did not return the fire from the jong. All that was done in this direction was to place one of Lieutenant Hadow's Maxims on the roof of the house occupied by the mission, and thence to snipe during the daylight hours at any warriors who showed themselves above the walls of the jong. Hadow was very patient and persistent with his gun, and quickly made it clear to the Tibetans that, if we were obliged to keep under cover, so were they. But our fire from the post was probably as ineffective as that of the enemy from the jong, for the Tibetans build walls with extraordinary rapidity. Working mostly at night in order to avoid the malignant Maxim, the enemy within a few days almost altered the face of the jong. New walls, traverses, and covered ways seemed to spring up with the rapidity of mushrooms.

Our life during the siege, if so the bombardment can be called, was hardly as unpleasant as people might imagine. To begin with, we were never short of food--that is to say, of Tibetan barley and meat. The commissariat stock of tea--a necessity in Tibet--also never gave out. From time to time also convoys and parcel-posts with little luxuries came through. Again, the longest period for which we were without a letter-post was eight days. Socially, the relations of the officers with one another and with the members of the Commission were most harmonious. I make a point of mentioning this fact, because all those who have had any experience of sieges, or of similar conditions where small communities are shut up together in circumstances of hardship and danger, know how apt the temper is to get on edge, how often small differences are likely to give rise to bitter animosities. But we had in the Gyantse garrison men of such vast experience and geniality as Colonel Brander, of such high culture and attainment as Colonel Younghusband, Captain O'Connor, and Mr. Perceval Landon--the correspondent of The Times; men whose spirits never failed, and who found humour in everything, such as Major Row, Captain Luke, Captain Coleridge, Lieutenant Franklin. Amongst the besieged was Colonel Waddell, I.M.S., an Orientalist and Sinologist of European fame. Hence, in some of its aspects the Gyantse siege was almost a delightful episode. In the later days, when all the outpost fighting occurred, our spirits were somewhat damped, for we had to mourn brave men killed and sympathize with others dangerously wounded.

Of course, one of the first questions for consideration when the Karo la column returned to Gyantse was whether the enemy could or could not be turned out of the jong. To make a frontal attack on the frowning face overlooking the post would have been foolhardy, but Colonel Brander decided to make a reconnaissance to a monastery on the high hills to our right, whence the jong itself could be overlooked. A subsidiary reason for visiting this monastery was that it was known to have afforded shelter to a number of those who had fled from the attack on the post. The hill was climbed with every military precaution, but only a few old monks were found in occupation of the buildings. More disappointing was the fact that an examination through telescopes of the rear of the jong showed that the Tibetans had been also building indefatigably there. A strong loopholed wall ran zigzagging up the side of the rock. It was clear that nothing could be done till the General returned from Chumbi with more troops and guns.

For more than two weeks our rear remained absolutely open. The post, carried by mounted infantry, came in and went out regularly. Two large convoys reached us unopposed. The only danger lay in the fact that people seen entering or leaving the post came under a heavy fire from the jong. To minimize risks, departures from the post were always made before dawn.

During the two weeks streams of men could be seen entering the jong from both the Shigatze and Lhasa roads. Emboldened by numbers, and also by our non-aggressive attitude, the enemy began to cast about for means of taking the post. One of the first steps taken by the Tibetan General in pursuance of this policy was to occupy during the night a small house surrounded by trees, lying to our left front, almost midway between the jong and the post. On the morning of the 18th bullets from a new direction were whizzing in amongst us, and partly enfilading our traverses. This was not to be tolerated, and the same night arrangements were made for the capture of the position.

Five companies stole out during the hours of darkness and surrounded the house. The rush, delivered at dawn, was left to the Gurkhas. But the entrance was found blocked with stones, and the enemy was thoroughly awake by the time the Gurkhas were under the wall. Luckily, the loopholes were not so constructed as to allow the Tibetans to fire their jingals down upon our men, who had only to bear the brunt of showers of stones thrown upon them from the roof. The shower was well directed enough to bruise a good many Gurkhas. Three officers were struck-- Major Murray, Lieutenant Lynch, and Lieutenant Franklin, I.M.S. Whilst the Gurkhas were striving to effect an entrance, the Pioneer companies deployed on the flanks came under a heavy fire from the jong. We had three men hit. One fell on a bit of very exposed ground, and was gallantly dragged under cover by Colonel Brander and Captain Minogue, Staff officer.

It was soon evident that the Gurkhas would never get in without explosives. Accordingly, Lieutenant Gurdon, 32nd Pioneers, was sent to join them with a box of guncotton. Gurdon speedily blew a hole through the wall, and the Gurkhas dashed in yelling. The Tibetans on the roof could easily at this time have jumped off and escaped towards the jong. But they chose a braver part. They slid down into the middle of the courtyard, and, drawing their swords, awaited the Gurkha onset. I must not describe the pitiful struggle that followed. The Tibetans--about fifty in number--herded themselves together as if to meet a bayonet charge, but our troops, rushing through the door, extended themselves along the edges of the courtyard, and emptied their magazines into the mob. Within a minute all the fifty were either dead or mortally wounded.

The house was hereafter held by a company of Gurkhas all through the bombardment, and proved a great thorn in the side of the enemy; for the Gurkhas often used to sally out at night and ambuscade parties of men and convoys on the Shigatze road.

CHAPTER X

GYANTSE--continued

[BY HENRY NEWMAN]

On the afternoon of the day on which the house was taken we were provided with a new excitement--continuous firing was heard to the rear of the post about a mile away. Captain Ottley galloped out with his mounted infantry, and was only just in time to save a party of his men who were coming up from Kangma with the letter-bags. These Sikhs--eight in number--were riding along the edge of the river, when they were met by a fusillade from a number of the enemy concealed amongst sedges on the opposite bank. Before the Sikhs could take cover, one man was killed, three wounded, and seven out of the eight horses shot down. The remaining men showed rare courage. They carried their wounded comrades under cover of a ditch, untied and brought to the same place the letter-bags, and then lay down and returned the fire of the enemy. The Tibetans, however, were beginning to creep round, and the ammunition of the Sikhs was running low, when Captain Ottley dashed up to the rescue. Without waiting to consider how many of the enemy might be hiding in the sedge, Ottley took his twenty men splashing through the river. Nearly 300 Tibetans bolted out in all directions like rabbits from a cover. The mounted infantry, shooting and smiting, chased them to the very edge of the plain. On reaching hilly ground the enemy, who must have lost about fifty of their number, began to turn, having doubtless realized that they were running before a handful of men. At the same time shots were fired from villages, previously thought unoccupied, on Ottley's left, and a body of matchlock men were seen running up to reinforce from a large village on the Lhasa road. Under these conditions it would have been madness to continue the fight, and Ottley cleverly and skilfully withdrew without having lost a single man. In the meanwhile a company of Pioneers had brought in the men wounded in the attack on the postal riders.

This affair was even more significant than the occupation by the enemy of the position taken by the Gurkhas in the early morning. It showed that the Tibetan General had at last conceived a plan for cutting off our line of communications. This was a rude shock. It implied that the enemy had received reinforcements which were to be utilized for offensive warfare of the kind most to be feared by an invader. We knew that so long as our ammunition lasted there was absolutely no danger of the post being captured. But an enemy on the lines would certainly cause the greatest annoyance to, and might even cut off, our convoys. As it would be very difficult to get messages through, apprehensions as to our safety would be excited in the outer world. Further, General Macdonald's arrangements for the relief of the mission would have to be considerably modified if he were obliged to fight his way through to us.

With the same prompt decision that marked his action with regard to the gathering on the Karo la, Colonel Brander determined on the very next day to clear the villages found occupied by the mounted infantry. As far as could be discovered, the villages were five in number, all on the right bank of the river, and occupying a position which could be roughly outlined as an equilateral triangle. Captain Ottley was sent round to the rear of the villages to cut off the retreat of the enemy; Captain Luke took his two mountain-guns, under cover of the right bank of the river, to a position whence he could support the infantry attack, if necessary, by shell fire. Two companies of Pioneers with one in reserve were sent forward to the attack.

The first objective was two villages forming the base of the triangle of which I have spoken. The troops advanced cautiously, widely extended, but both villages were found deserted. They were set on fire. Then Captain Hodgson with a company went forward to the village forming the apex of the triangle. He came under a flanking fire from the villages on the left, and had one man severely wounded. The houses in front seemed to be unoccupied, and our right might have been swung round to face this fire; but Colonel Brander was determined to do the work thoroughly, and Hodgson was directed to move on and burn the village ahead of him before changing front. The troops accordingly took no notice of the flanking fire, and moved on till they were under the walls of the two houses of which the village was composed.

Suddenly fire was opened on our soldiers from the upper windows of the two houses. All the doors were found blocked with bricks and stones. Two Sikhs dropped, and for the moment it seemed as if we would lose heavily. But Lieutenant Gurdon with half a dozen men rushed up with a box of explosives, and blew a breach in the wall. Two of the party helping to lay the fuse were killed by shots fired from a loophole a few feet above. Captain Hodgson was the first man through the breach. He was confronted by a swordsman, who cut hard just as Hodgson fired his revolver. The man fell dead, but Hodgson received a severe wound on the wrist. But this was the only man who stood after the explosion. About thirty others in the village rushed to the roofs of the houses, jumped off, and fled to the left. They came, however, under a very heavy fire as they were running away, and the majority dropped.

Preparations were now made for taking the remaining village. This was protected by a high loopholed embankment, which sheltered about five or six hundred of the enemy. The Pioneers had just extended, and were advancing, when someone who happened to be looking at the jong through his glasses suddenly uttered a loud exclamation. Turning round, we all saw a dense stream of men, several thousands in number, forming up at the base of the rock, evidently with the intention of rushing the mission post whilst the majority of the garrison and the guns were engaged elsewhere. Colonel Brander immediately gave the order for the whole force to retire into the post at the double. The withdrawal was effected before the Tibetans made their contemplated rush, but we all felt that it was rather a narrow shave.

Troops were to have gone out again the next day to clear the village we had left untaken, but the mounted infantry reconnoitring in the morning reported that the enemy had fled, and that the lines of communication were again clear.

On the succeeding day a large convoy and reinforcements under Major Peterson, 32nd Pioneers, came safely through. The additional troops included a section of No. 7 (British) Mountain Battery, under Captain Easton; one and a half companies of Sappers and Miners, under Captain Shepherd and Lieutenant Garstin; and another company of the 32nd Pioneers. Major Peterson reported that his convoy had come under a heavy fire from the village and monastery of Naini. This monastery lies about seven miles from Gyantse in an opening of the valley just before the road turns into Gyantse Plain. It holds about 5,000 monks. When the column first passed by it, the monks were extremely friendly, bringing out presents of butter and eggs, and readily selling flour and meat. The monastery is surrounded by a wall thirty feet high, and at least ten feet thick. The buildings inside are also solidly built of stone. Altogether the position was a very difficult one to tackle, but Colonel Brander, following his usual policy, decided that the enemy must be turned out of it at all costs. Accordingly, on the 24th a column, which included Captain Easton's two guns, marched out to Naini. But the monastery and the group of buildings outside it were found absolutely deserted. The walls were far too heavy and strong to be destroyed by a small force, which had to return before nightfall, but Captain Shepherd blew up the four towers at the corners and a portion of the hall in which the Buddhas were enthroned.

The 27th provided a new excitement. About 1,000 yards to the right of the post stood what was known as the Palla House, the residence of a Tibetan nobleman of great wealth. The building consisted of a large double-storied house, surrounded by a series of smaller buildings, each within a courtyard of its own. During the night the Tibetans in the jong built a covered way extending about half the distance between the jong and Palla. In the morning the latter place was seen to be swarming with men, busily occupied in erecting defences, making loopholes, and generally engaged in work of a menacing character. The enemy could less be tolerated in Palla than in the Gurkha outpost, for fire from the former would have taken us absolutely in the flank, and the garrison was not strong enough to provide the labour necessary for building an entirely new series of traverses.

That very night Colonel Brander detailed the troops that were to take Palla by assault at dawn. The storming-party was composed of three companies of the 32nd under Major Peterson, assisted by the Sappers and Miners with explosives under Captain Shepherd. Our four mountain-guns, the 7-pounders under Captain Luke, and the 10-pounders under Captain Easton, escorted by a company of Gurkhas, were detailed to occupy a position on a ridge which overlooked Palla. The troops fell in at two in the morning. The night was pitch-dark, but with such care were the operations conducted that the troops had made a long d閨our, and got into their respective positions before dawn, without an alarm being raised.

Daylight was just breaking when Captain Shepherd crept up to the wall of the house on the extreme left, where it was believed the majority of the enemy were located, and laid his explosives. A tremendous explosion followed, the whole side of the house falling in. A minute afterwards, and Palla was alarmed and firing furiously all round, and even up in the air. The jong also awoke, and from that time till the village was finally ours poured a continuous storm of bullets into Palla, regardless whether friend or foe was hit. Our guns on the ridge did their best to quiet the jong, but without much effect. Against Tibetan walls, provided as they are with head cover, our experience showed shrapnel to be almost entirely useless.

A company of Pioneers followed Captain Shepherd into the breach he had made. But they found themselves only in a small courtyard, with no means of entering the rest of the village, except over or through high walls lined by the enemy. All that could be done was to blow in another breach. The preparations for doing this were attended with a good deal of danger. Of three men who attempted to rush across the courtyard, two were killed and the third mortally wounded. However, by creeping along under cover of the wall, Captain Shepherd and Lieutenant Garstin were able to lay the guncotton and light the fuse for another explosion. They were fired at from a distance of a few yards, but escaped being hit by a miracle. But the second explosion only led into another courtyard, from which there was also no exit. There was the same fire to be faced from the next house whilst the needful preparations were being made for making a third breach.

During the time Shepherd with his gallant lieutenants and equally gallant sepoys was working his way in from the left, the companies of Pioneers lining ditches and banks outside Palla were exposed to a persistent fire from about a hundred of the enemy inside the big two-storied house mentioned above. The men in this house--all Kham warriors--seemed to be filled with an extraordinary fury. Many exposed themselves boldly at the windows, calling to our men to come on. A dozen or so even climbed to the roof of the house, and danced about thereon in what seemed frantic derision. There was a Maxim on the ridge with the mountain-guns, the fire from which put an end to the fantastic display. Our rifle fire, however, seemed totally unable to check the Tibetan warriors in the loopholed windows. They kept up a fusillade which made a rush impossible. Major Peterson finally, with great daring, led a few men into the dwelling on the extreme right. The escalade was managed by means of a ruined tree which projected from the wall. But Peterson, like Shepherd, found himself in a courtyard with high walls which baffled further progress.

The fight now began to drag. Hours passed without any signal incident. The Tibetans were greatly elated at the failure of our troops to make progress. They shouted and yelled, and were encouraged by answering cheers from the jong. Then about mid-day the jong Commandant conceived the idea of reinforcing Palla. A dozen men mounted on black mules, followed by about fifty infantry, suddenly dashed out from the half-completed covered way mentioned above, and made for the village. This party was absolutely annihilated. As soon as it emerged from the covered way it came under the fire, not only of the troops round the village and on the hill, but of the Maxim on the roof of the mission-house. In three minutes every single man and mule was down, except one animal with a broken leg, gazing disconsolately at the body of its master.

This disaster evidently shook the Tibetans in Palla. Their fire slackened. Captain Luke on the ridge was then directed to put some common shell into the roof of the double-storied house. He dropped the shells exactly where they were wanted, and so disconcerted the enemy that Shepherd was able to resume his preparations for making a way into the Tibetan stronghold. But he still had to face an awkward fire, and the three further breaches he made were attended by the loss of several men, including Lieutenant Garstin, shot through the head. But the last explosion led our troops into the big house. Tibetan resistance then practically ceased. About twenty or thirty men made an attempt to get away to the jong, but the majority were shot down before they could reach the covered way.

In this affair our total casualties were twenty-three. In addition to Lieutenant Garstin, we had seven men killed. The wounded included Captain O'Connor, R.A., secretary to the mission, and Lieutenant Mitchell, 32nd Pioneers. The enemy must have lost quite 250 in killed and wounded. The position at Palla was too important to be abandoned, and for the rest of the bombardment it was held by a company of Sikhs. In order to provide free communication both day and night, Captain Shepherd, with his usual energy, dug a covered way from the post to the village.

The fight at Palla was the last affair of any importance in which the garrison was engaged pending the arrival of the relieving force. The Tibetans had received such a shock that in future they confined themselves practically to the defensive, if we except five half-hearted night attacks which were never anywhere near being pushed home. There were no more attempts to interrupt our lines of communication, though later on Naini was again occupied as part of the Tibetan scheme for resisting General Macdonald's advance. The jong Commandant devoted his energies chiefly to strengthening his already strong position.

The night attacks were all very similar in character, and may be summed up and dismissed in a paragraph. Generally about midnight, bands of Tibetans would issue from the jong and take up their position about four or five hundred yards from the post. Then they would shout wildly, and fire off their matchlocks and Martini rifles. The troops would immediately rush to their loopholes, clad in impossible garments, and wait shivering in the cold, finger on trigger, for the rush that never came. After shouting and firing for about an hour, the Tibetans would retire to the jong and our troops creep back to their beds. On no occasion did the enemy come close enough to be seen in the dark. We never fired a single shot from the post. Twice, however, the Gurkha outpost and the Sikhs at Palla were enabled to get in a few volleys at Tibetans as they slunk past. During the night attacks the jong remained silent, except on one occasion, when there was so much firing from the Gurkha outpost that the enemy thought we were about to make a counter-attack. Every jingal, musket, and rifle in the jong was then loosed off in any and every direction. We even heard firing in the rear of the monastery. Although no one was hit in this wild fire, the volume of it was ominously indicative of the strength in which the jong was held.

But even more ominous against the day when our troops should be called upon to take the jong were the defensive preparations mentioned above. Nearly every morning we found that during the night the enemy had built up a new wall or covered way somewhere on the jong or about the village that fringed the base of the rock. When the fortress was fortified as strongly as Tibetan wit could devise, the jong Commandant began to fortify and place in a position of defence the villages and monasteries on his right and left. It was calculated that, from the small monastery perched on the hills to his left to Tsechen Monastery on a ridge to his right, the Tibetan General had occupied and fortified a position with nearly seven miles of front.

Whilst the Tibetans were engaged in making these preparations, our garrison was busy collecting forage for the enormous number of animals coming up with the relief column. Our rear being absolutely open, small parties with mules were able to collect quantities of hay from villages within a radius of seven miles behind us. It was the fire opened on these parties when they attempted to push to the right or left of the jong which first revealed to us the full extent of the defensive position occupied by the enemy.

On June 6 Colonel Younghusband left the post with a returning convoy, in order to confer with the General at Chumbi. This convoy was attacked whilst halting at the entrenched post at Kangma. The enemy in this instance came down from the Karo la, and it is for this reason that I do not include the Kangma attack amongst the operations at and around Gyantse.

It was not till June 15 that we got definite news of the approaching advance of the relief column. Reinforcements had come up to Chumbi from India in the interval, and the General was accompanied by the 2nd Mounted Infantry under Captain Peterson, No. 7 British Mountain Battery under Major Fuller, a section of No. 30 Native Mountain Battery under Captain Marindin, four companies of the Royal Fusiliers under Colonel Cooper, four companies of the 40th Pathans under Colonel Burn, five companies of the 23rd Pioneers under Colonel Hogge, and the two remaining companies of the 8th Gurkhas under Colonel Kerr, together with the usual medical and other details.

The force arrived at Kangma on June 23. On the 25th a party of mounted infantry from Gyantse met Captain Peterson's mounted infantry reconnoitring at the monastery of Naini, previously mentioned. Whilst greetings were being exchanged a sudden fire was opened on our men from the monastery, which the enemy had apparently occupied and fortified during the night. The position was apparently held in strength, and the mounted infantry had no other course except to retire to their respective camps. Captain Peterson had one man mortally wounded.

On the evening of the 26th the sentries at the mission post saw about twenty mounted men, followed by two or three hundred infantry, issue from the rear of the jong and creep up the hills on our left in the direction of Naini. It was evident that a determined effort was to be made at the monastery to check the advance of the relief column, which was expected at Gyantse next day. Colonel Brander came to the conclusion that he had found an opportunity for catching the Tibetans in a trap. He determined to send out a force which would block the retreat of the enemy when they retired before the advance of the relief column. Accordingly, before dawn four companies of Pioneers, four guns, and the Maxim gun left the post, and ascended the hills overlooking the monastery. Captain Ottley's mounted infantry were directed to close the road leading directly from Gyantse to the monastery.

Colonel Brander's forces were in position some hours before the mounted infantry of the relief column appeared in sight. It was discovered that the enemy not only held the monastery, but some ruined towers on the hill above, and a cluster of one-storied dwellings in a grove below. Captain Peterson with his mounted infantry appeared in front of the monastery at eleven o'clock. He had with him a company of the 40th Pathans, and his orders were to clear the monastery with this small force, if the enemy made no signs of a stubborn resistance. Otherwise he was to await the arrival of more troops with the mountain-guns.

Peterson delivered his attack from the left, having dismounted his troopers, who, together with the 40th Pathans, were soon very hotly engaged. The troops came under a heavy fire both from the monastery and from a ruined tower above it, but advanced most gallantly. When under the walls of the monastery, they were checked for some time by the difficulty of finding a way in. In the meanwhile, hearing the heavy firing, the General and his Staff, followed by Major Fuller's battery and the rest of the 40th, had hastened up.

The battery came into action against the tower, and the 40th rushed up in support of their comrades. Colonel Brander's guns and Maxim on the top of the hill were also brought into play. For nearly an hour a furious cannonade and fusillade raged. Then the Pathans and Peterson's troopers, circling round the walls of the monastery, found a ramp up which they could climb. They swarmed up, and were quickly inside the building. But the Tibetans had realized that their retreat was cut off, and, instead of making a clean bolt for it, only retired slowly from room to room and passage to passage. Two companies of the 23rd were sent up to assist in clearing the monastery. It proved a perfect warren of dark cells and rooms. The Tibetan resistance lasted for over two hours. Bands of desperate swordsmen were found in knots under trap-doors and behind sharp turnings. They would not surrender, and had to be killed by rifle shots fired at a distance of a few feet.

While the monastery was being cleared, another fight had developed in the cluster of dwellings outside it to the right. From this spot Tibetan riflemen were enfilading our troops held in reserve. The remaining companies of the 23rd were sent to clear away the enemy. They took three houses, but could not effect an entrance into the fourth, which was very strongly barricaded. Lieutenant Turnbull, walking up to a window with a section, had three men hit in a few seconds. One man fell directly under the window. Turnbull carried him into safety in the most gallant fashion. Then the General ordered up the guns, which fired into the house at a range of a few hundred yards. But not till it was riddled with great gaping holes made by common shell did the fire from the house cease.

At about three o'clock the Tibetan resistance had completely died away, and the column resumed its march towards Gyantse, which was not reached till dark. But as the transport was making its slow way past Naini, about half a dozen Tibetans who had remained in hiding in the monastery and village opened fire on it. The Gurkha rearguard had a troublesome task in clearing these men out, and lost one man killed.

In this affair at Naini our casualties were six killed and nine wounded, including Major Lye, 23rd Pioneers, who received a severe sword-cut in the hand.

The General's camp was pitched about a mile from the mission post, well out of range of the jong, though our troops whilst crossing the river came under fire from some of the bigger jingals. The next day was one of rest, which the troops badly needed after their long march from Chumbi. The Tibetans in the jong also refrained from firing. On the 29th the General began the operations intended to culminate in the capture of the jong. His objective was Tsechen Monastery, on the extreme left. But before the monastery could be attacked, some twelve fortified villages between it and the river had to be cleared. It proved a difficult task, not so much on account of the resistance offered by the enemy--for after a few idle shots the Tibetans quickly retired on the monastery--as because of the nature of the ground that had to be traversed. The whole country was a network of deep irrigation channels and water-cuts, in the fording and crossing of which the troops got wet to the skin. However, by four in the afternoon all the villages had been cleared, and the Fusiliers were lying in a long grove under the right front of the monastery.

It was then discovered that not only was Tsechen very strongly held, but that masses of the enemy were lying behind the rocks on the top of the ridge, on the summit of which there was a ruined tower, also held by fifty or sixty men. The General sent two companies of Gurkhas to scale the ridge from the left, whilst the 40th Pathans were ordered to make a direct assault on the monastery. A hundred mounted infantry made their way to the rear to cut off the retreat of the enemy. Fuller and Marindin with their guns covered the advance of the infantry. Four Maxims were also brought into action. Our guns made splendid practice on the top of the ridge, and time and again we could see the enemy bolting from cover. But with magnificent bravery they would return to oppose the advance of the Gurkhas creeping round their flank. The guns had presently to cease fire to enable the Gurkhas to get nearer. A series of desperate little fights then took place on the top of the ridge, the Tibetans slinging and throwing stones when they found they could not load their muskets quickly enough. But as the Gurkhas would not be stopped, the Tibetans had to move. In the meanwhile the Pathans worked through the monastery below, only meeting with small resistance from a band of men in one house. The Tibetans fled in a mass over the right edge of the ridge into the jaws of the mounted infantry lying in wait below. Slaughter followed.

It was now quite dark, and the troops made their way back to camp. Next morning a party went up to Tsechen, found it entirely deserted, and set fire to it. The taking of the monastery cost us the lives of Captain Craster, 40th

Pathans, and two sepoys. Our wounded numbered ten, including Captains Bliss and Humphreys, 8th Gurkhas.

On July 1 the General intended assaulting the jong, but in the interval the jong Commandant sent in a flag of truce. He prayed for an armistice pending the arrival of three delegates who were posting down from Lhasa with instructions to make peace. As Colonel Younghusband had been directed to lose no opportunity of bringing affairs to an end at Gyantse, the armistice was granted, and two days afterwards the delegates, all Lamas, were received in open durbar in a large room in the mission post. Colonel Younghusband, after having satisfied himself that the delegates possessed proper credentials, made them a speech. He reviewed the history of the mission, pointing out that we had only come to Gyantse because of the obstinacy and evasion of the Tibetan officials, who could easily have treated with us at Khamba Jong and again at Tuna, had they cared to. We were perfectly willing to come to terms here, and it rested with the peace delegates whether we went on to Lhasa or not. Younghusband then informed the delegates that he was prepared to open negotiations on the next day. The delegates were due at eleven next morning, but they did not put in an appearance till three. They were then told that as a preliminary they must surrender the jong by noon on the succeeding day. They demurred a great deal, but the Commissioner was quite firm, and they went away downcast, with the assurance that if the jong was not surrendered we should take it by force. Younghusband, however, added that after the capture of the fort he was perfectly willing to open negotiations again.

Next day, shortly after noon, a signal gun was fired to indicate that the armistice was at an end, and the General forthwith began his preparations to storm the formidable hill fortress. The Tibetans had taken advantage of the armistice to build more walls and sangars. No one could look at the bristling jong without realizing how difficult was the task before our troops, and without anxiety as to the outcome of the assault in killed and wounded. But we all knew that the jong had to be taken, whatever the cost.

Operations began in the afternoon, the General making a demonstration against the left face of the jong and Palkhor Choide Monastery. Fuller's battery took up a position about 1,600 yards from the jong. Five companies of infantry were extended on either flank. Both the jong and monastery opened fire on our troops, and we had one man mortally wounded. The General's intention, however, was only to deceive the Tibetans into thinking that we intended to assault from that side. As soon as dusk fell, the troops were withdrawn and preparations made for the real assault.

The south-eastern face of the rock on which the jong is built is most precipitous, yet this was exactly the face which the General decided to storm. His reasons, I imagine, were that the fringe of houses at the base of the rock was thinnest on this side, and that the very multiplicity of sangars and walls that the enemy had built prevented their having the open field of fire necessary to stop a rush. Moreover, down the middle of the rock ran a deep fissure or cleft, which was commanded, the General noticed, by no tower or loopholed wall. At two points, however, the Tibetans had built walls across the fissure. The first of these the General believed could be breached by our artillery. Our troops through that could work their way round to either flank, and so into the heart of the jong.

The plan of operations was very simple. Before dawn three columns were to rush the fringe of houses at the base. Then was to follow a storm of artillery fire directed on all the salient points of the jong, after which our guns were to make a breach in the lower wall across the cleft up which the storming-party was later on to climb.

The action turned out exactly as was planned, with the exception that the fighting lasted much longer than was expected, for the Tibetans made a heroic resistance. The troops were astir shortly after midnight. The night was very dark, and the necessary deployment of the three columns took some hours. However, an hour before dawn the troops had begun their cautious advance, the General and his Staff taking up their position at Palla. The alarm was not given till our leading files were within twenty yards of the fringe of houses at the base of the rock. The storm of fire which then burst from the jong was an alarming indication of the strength in which it was held. The heavy jingals were all directed on Palla, and the General and his Staff had many narrow escapes. As on the previous occasion when the jong bombarded us at night, there were moments when every building in it seemed outlined in flame.

Of the three columns, only that on the extreme left, Gurkhas under Major

Murray, was able to get in at once. The other two columns were for the time being checked, so bullet-swept was the open space they had to cross. From time to time small parties of two or three dashed across in the dark, and gained the shelter of the walls of the houses in front. There were barely twenty men and half a dozen officers across when Captain Shepherd blew in the walls of the house most strongly held. The storming-party came under a most heavy fire from the jong above. Among those hit was Lieutenant Gurdon, of the 32nd. He was shot through the head, and died almost immediately. The breach made by Shepherd was the point to which most of the men of the centre and right columns made, but their progress became very slow when daylight appeared and the Tibetans could see what they were firing at. It was not till nearly nine o'clock that the whole fringe of houses at the base of the front face of the rock was in our possession.

Then followed several hours of cannonading and small-arms fire. The position the troops had now won was commanded almost absolutely from the jong. It was found impossible to return the Tibetan fire from the roofs of the houses we had occupied without exposing the troops in an unnecessary degree, but loopholes were hastily made in the walls of the rooms below, and the 40th Pathans were sent into a garden on the extreme right, where some cover was to be had. Colonel Campbell, commanding the first line, was able to show the enemy that our marksmen were still in a position to pick off such Tibetans as were rash enough to unduly expose themselves. In the meanwhile, Luke's guns on the extreme right, Fuller's battery at Palla, and Marindin's guns at the Gurkha outpost threw a stream of shrapnel on all parts of the jong.

But it was not till four o'clock in the afternoon that the General decided that the time had come to make the breach aforementioned. The reserve companies of Gurkhas and Fusiliers were sent across from Palla in the face of very heavy jingal and rifle fire, and took cover in the houses we had occupied. In the meanwhile Fuller was directed to make the breach. So magnificent was the shooting made by his guns that a dozen rounds of common shell, planted one below the other, had made a hole large enough for active men to clamber through. The enemy quickly saw the purport of the breach. Dozens of men could be distinctly seen hurrying to the wall above it.

Then the Gurkhas and Fusiliers began their perilous ascent. The nimble

Gurkhas, led by Lieutenant Grant, soon outpaced the Fusiliers, and in ten brief minutes forty or fifty of them were crouching under the breach. The Tibetans, finding their fire could not stop us, tore great stones from the walls and rolled them down the cleft. Dozens of men were hit and bruised. Presently Grant was through the breach, followed by fifteen or twenty flushed and shouting men. The breach won, the only thought of the enemy was flight. They made their way by the back of the jong into the monastery. By six o'clock every building in the great fortress was in our possession.

Our casualties in this affair were forty-three--Lieutenant Gurdon and seven men killed, and twelve officers, including the gallant Grant, and twenty-three men wounded. These casualties exclude a number of men cut and bruised with stones.

Next morning the monastery was found deserted. It was reported that the bulk of the enemy had fled to Dongtse, about ten miles up the Shigatze road. A column was sent thither, but found the place empty, except for a very humble and submissive monk.

On the 14th, having waited for over a week in the hope of the peace delegates putting in an appearance, the force started on its march to Lhasa.

CHAPTER XI

GOSSIP ON THE ROAD TO THE FRONT

ARI, SIKKIM, June 24.

I write in an old forest rest-house on the borders of British Bhutan.

The place is quiet and pastoral; climbing roses overhang the roof and invade the bedrooms; martins have built their nests in the eaves; cuckoos are calling among the chestnuts down the hill. Outside is a flower-garden, gay with geraniums and petunias and familiar English plants that have overrun their straggling borders and scattered themselves in the narrow plot of grass that fringes the forest. Some Government officer must have planted them years ago, and left them to fight it out with Nature and the caretaker.

The forest has encroached, and it is hard to say where Nature's hand or Art's begins and ends. Beside a rose-bush there has sprung up the solid pink club of the wild ginger, and from a bed of amaryllis a giant arum raises itself four feet in its dappled, snake-like sheath. Gardens have most charm in spots like this, where their mingled trimness and neglect contrast with the insolent unconcern of an encroaching forest.

At Ari I am fifty miles from Darjeeling, on the road to Lhasa.

On June 21 I set my face to Lhasa for the second time. I took another route to Chumbi, vi?Kalimpong and Pedong in British Bhutan. The road is no further, but it compasses some arduous ascents. On the other hand it avoids the low, malarious valleys of Sikkim, where the path is constantly carried away by slips. There is less chance of a block, and one is above the cholera zone. The Jelap route, which I strike to-morrow, is closed, owing to cholera and land-slips, so that I shall not touch the line of communications until within a few miles of Chumbi, in which time my wound will have had a week longer to heal before I risk a medical examination and the chance of being sent back. The relief column is due at Gyantse in a few days; it depends on the length of the operations there whether I catch the advance to Lhasa.

Through avoiding the Nathu-la route to Chumbi I had to arrange my own transport. In Darjeeling my coolies bolted without putting a pack on their backs. More were secured; these disappeared in the night at Kalimpong without waiting to be paid. Pack-ponies were hired to replace them, but these are now in a state of collapse. Arguing, and haggling, and hectoring, and blarneying, and persuading are wearisome at all times, but more especially in these close steamy valleys, where it is too much trouble to lift an eyelid, and the air induces an almost immoral state of lassitude, in which one is tempted to dole out silver indifferently to anyone who has it in his power to oil the wheels of life. I could fill a whole chapter with a jeremiad on transport, but it is enough to indicate, to those who go about in vehicles, that there are men on the road to Tibet now who would beggar themselves and their families for generations for a macadamized highway and two hansom cabs to carry them and their belongings smoothly to Lhasa. Before I reached Kalimpong I wished I had never left the 'radius.' No one should embark on Asiatic travel who is not thoroughly out of harmony with civilization.

The servant question is another difficulty. No native bearer wishes to join the field force. Why should he? He has to cook and pack and do the work of three men; he has to make long, exhausting marches; he is exposed to hunger, cold, and fatigue; he may be under fire every day; and he knows that if he falls into the hands of the Tibetans, like the unfortunate servants of Captain Parr at Gyantse, he will be brutally murdered and cut up into mincemeat. In return for which he is fed and clothed, and earns ten rupees more a month than he would in the security of his own home. After several unsuccessful trials, I have found one Jung Bir, a Nepali bearer, who is attached to me because I forget sometimes to ask for my bazaar account, and do not object to his being occasionally drunk. In Tibet the poor fellow will have little chance of drinking.

My first man lost his nerve altogether, and, when told to work, could only whine out that his father and mother were not with him. My next applicant was an opium-eater, prematurely bent and aged, with the dazed look of a toad that has been incarcerated for ages in a rock, and is at last restored to light and the world by the blow of a mason's hammer. He wanted money to buy more dreams, and for this he was willing to expose his poor old body to hardships that would have killed him in a month. Jung Bir was a Gurkha and more martial. His first care on being engaged was to buy a long and heavy chopper--'for making mince,' he said; but I knew it was for the Tibetans.

To reach Ari one has to descend twice, crossing the Teesta at 700 feet, and the Russett Chu at 1,500 feet. These valleys are hotter than the plains of India. The streams run east and west, and the cliffs on both sides catch the heat of the early morning sun and hold it all day. The closeness, the refraction from the rocks, and the evaporation of the water, make the atmosphere almost suffocating, and one feels the heat the more intensely by the change from the bracing air above. Crossing the Teesta, one enters British Bhutan, a strip of land of less than 300 square miles on the left bank of the river. It was ceded to us with other territories by the treaty of 1865; or, in plain words, it was annexed by us as a punishment for the outrage on Sir Ashley Eden, the British Envoy, who was captured and grossly insulted by the Bhutanese at Punakha in the previous year. The Bhutanese were as arrogant, exclusive, and impossible to deal with, in those days, as the Tibetans are to-day. Yet they have been brought into line, and are now our friends. Why should not the Tibetans, who are of the same stock, yield themselves to enlightenment?

Their evolution would be no stranger.

Nine miles above the Teesta bridge is Kalimpong, the capital of British Bhutan, and virtually the foreign mart for what trade passes out of Tibet. The Tomos of the Chumbi Valley, who have the monopoly of the carrying, do not go further south than this. At Kalimpong I found a horse-dealer with a good selection of 'Bhutia tats.' These excellent little beasts are now well known to be as strong and plucky a breed of mountain ponies as can be found anywhere. I discovered that their fame is not merely modern when I came across what must be the first reference to them in history in the narrative of Master Ralph Fitch, England's pioneer to India. 'These northern merchants,' says Fitch, speaking of the Bhutia, 'report that in their countrie they haue very good horses, but they be litle.' The Bhutias themselves, equally ubiquitous in the Sikkim Himalayas, but not equally indispensable, Fitch describes to the letter. At Kalimpong I found them dirty, lazy, good-natured, independent rascals, possessed, apparently, of wealth beyond their deserts, for hard work is as alien to their character as straight dealing. Even the drovers will pay a coolie good wages to cut grass for them rather than walk a mile downhill to fetch it themselves.

The main street of Kalimpong is laid out in the correct boulevard style, with young trees protected by tubs and iron railings. It is dominated by the church of the Scotch Mission, whose steeple is a landmark for miles. The place seems to be overrun with the healthiest-looking English children I have seen anywhere, whose parents are given over to very practical good works.

I took the Bhutan route chiefly to avoid running the gauntlet of the medicals; but another inducement was the prospect of meeting Father Desgodins, a French Roman Catholic, Vicar Apostolic of the Roman Catholic Mission to Western Tibet, who, after fifty years' intimacy with various Mongol types, is probably better acquainted with the Tibetans than any other living European.

I met Father Desgodins at Pedong. The rest-house here looks over the valley to his symmetrical French presbytery and chapel, perched on the hillside amid waving maize-fields, whose spring verdure is the greenest in the world. Scattered over the fields are thatched Lamas' houses and low-storied gompas, with overhanging eaves and praying-flags--'horses of the wind,' as the Tibetans picturesquely call them, imagining that the prayers inscribed on them are carried to the good god, whoever he may be, who watches their particular fold and fends off intruding spirits as well as material invaders.

Behind the presbytery are terraced rice-fields, irrigated by perennial streams, and bordered by thick artemisia scrub, which in the hot sun, after rain, sends out an aromatic scent, never to be dissociated in travellers' dreams and reveries from these great southern slopes of the Himalayas.

Desgodins is an erect old gentleman with quiet, steely gray eyes and a tawny beard now turning gray. He is known to few Englishmen, but his adventurous travels in Tibet and his devoted, strenuous life are known throughout Europe.

He was sent out from France to the Tibet Mission shortly after the murder of Krick and Bourry by the Mishmis. Failing to enter Tibet from the south through Sikkim, he made preparations for an entry by Ladak. His journey was arrested by the Indian Mutiny, when he was one of the besieged at Agra. He afterwards penetrated Western Tibet as far as Khanam, but was recalled to the Chinese side, where he spent twenty-two perilous and adventurous years in the establishment of the mission at Batang and Bonga. The mission was burnt down and the settlement expelled by the Lamas. In 1888 Father Desgodins was sent to Pedong, his present post, as Pro-vicar of the Mission to Western Tibet.

With regard to the present situation in Tibet, Father Desgodins expressed astonishment at our policy of folded arms.

'You have missed the occasion,' he said; 'you should have made your treaty with the Tibetans themselves in 1888. You could have forced them to treat then, when they were unprepared for a military invasion. You should have said to them'--here Desgodins took out his watch--'"It is now one o'clock. Sign that treaty by five, or we advance to-morrow." What could they have done? Now you are too late. They have been preparing for this for the last fifteen years.'

Father Desgodins was right. It is the old story of ill-advised conciliation and forbearance. We were afraid of the bugbear of China. The British Government says to her victim after the chastisement: 'You've had your lesson. Now run off and be good.' And the spoilt child of arrested civilization runs off with his tongue in his cheek and learns to make new arms and friends. The British Government in the meantime sleeps in smug complacency, and Exeter Hall is appeased.

'But why did you not treat with the Tibetans themselves?' Desgodins asked. 'China!'--here he made an expressive gesture--'I have known China for fifty years. She is not your friend.' Of course it is to the interest of China to keep the tea monopoly, and to close the market to British India. Travellers on the Chinese borders are given passports and promises of assistance, but the natives of the districts they traverse are ordered to turn them back and place every obstacle in their way. Nobody knows this better than Father Desgodins. China's policy is the same with nations as with individuals. She will always profess willingness to help, but protest that her subjects are unmanageable and out of hand. Why, then, deal with China at all? We can only answer that she had more authority in Lhasa in 1888. Moreover, we were more afraid of offending her susceptibilities. But that bubble has burst.

Others who hold different views from Desgodins say that this very unruliness of her vassal ought to make China welcome our intervention in Tibet, if we engage to respect her claims there when we have subdued the Lamas. This policy might certainly point a temporary way out of the muddle, whereby we could save our face and be rid of the Tibet incubus for perhaps a year. But the plan of leaving things to the suzerain Power has been tried too often.

As I rode down the Pedong street from the presbytery someone called me by name, and a little, smiling, gnome-like man stepped out of a whitewashed office. It was Phuntshog, a Tibetan friend whom I had known six years previously on the North-East frontier. I dismounted, expecting entertainment.

The office was bare of furniture save a new writing-table and two chairs, but heaped round the walls were piles of cast steel and iron plates and files and pipes for bellows. Phuntshog explained that he was frontier trade examiner, and that the steel had been purchased in Calcutta by a Lama last year, and was confiscated on the frontier as contraband. It was material for an armoury. The spoilt child was making new arms, like the schoolboy who exercises his muscle to avenge himself after a beating.

'Do you get much of this sort of thing?' I asked.

'Not now,' he said; 'they have given up trying to get it through this way.'

A few years ago eight Mohammedans, experts in rifle manufacture, had been decoyed from a Calcutta factory to Lhasa. Two had died there, and one I traced at Yatung. His wife had not been allowed to pass the barrier, but he was given a Tibetan helpmate. The wife lived some months at Yatung, and used to receive large instalments from her husband; once, I was told, as much as Rs. 1,400. But he never came back. The Tibetans have learned to make rifles for themselves now. Phuntshog had a story about another suspicious character, a mysterious Lama who arrived in Darjeeling in 1901 from Calcutta with 5,000 alms bowls for Tibet, which he said he had purchased in Germany. The man was detained in Darjeeling five months under police espionage, and finally sent back to Calcutta.

Our Intelligence Department on this frontier is more alert than it used to be. Dorjieff, Phuntshog told me, had been to Darjeeling twice, and stayed in a trader's house at Kalimpong several days. He wore the dress of a Lama. The ostensible object of his journey was to visit the sacred Chorten at Khatmandu and the shrines of Benares. He visited these, and was known to spend some time in Calcutta. On the occasion of the mission to St. Petersburg Dorjieff and his colleagues entered India through Nepal, took train to Bombay, and shipped thence to Odessa. The discovery of the Lamas' visit to India was almost simultaneous with their departure from Bombay.

Phuntshog is not an admirer of our Tibetan policy. We ought to have laid ourselves out, he said, to influence the Lamas by secret agents, as Russia did. There was no chance of a compromise now; they would fight to the death. Phuntshog said much more which I suspected was inspired by the daily newspapers, so I questioned him as to the feelings of the natives of the district.

'The feeling of patriotism is extinct,' he said; and he looked at his stomach, showing that he spoke the truth. 'We Tibetan British subjects are fed well and paid well by your Government. We want nothing more. My family are here. Now I have no trade to examine.' His eyes slowly surveyed the room, glanced over his office table, with its pen and ink and blank paper, lit on the 150 maunds of cast-steel, and finally rested on two volumes by his elbow.

'Do you read much?' I asked.

'Sometimes,' he said. 'I have learnt a good deal from these books.'

They were the Holy Bible and Miss Braddon's 'Dead Men's Shoes.'

'Phuntshog,' I said, 'you are a psychological enigma. Your mind is like that cast-iron huddled in the corner there, bought in an enlightened Western city and destined for your benighted Lhasa, but stuck halfway. Only it was going the other way. You don't understand? Neither do I.'

And here at Ari, as I look across the valley of the Russett Chu to Pedong, and hear the vesper bell, I cannot help thinking of that strange conflict of minds-- the devotee who, seeing further than most men, has cared nothing for the things of this incarnation, and Phuntshog, the strange hybrid product of restless Western energies, stirring and muddying the shallows of the Eastern mind. Or are they depths?

Who knows? I know nothing, only that these men are inscrutable, and one cannot see into their hearts.

CHAPTER XII

TO THE GREAT RIVER

I reached Gyantse on July 12. The advance to Lhasa began on the 14th. As might be expected from the tone of the delegates, peace negociations fell through. The Lhasa Government seemed to be chaotic and conveniently inaccessible. The Dalai Lama remained a great impersonality, and the four Shap 閣 or Councillors disclaimed all responsibility. The Tsong-du, or National Assembly, who virtually governed the country, had sent us no communication. The delegates' attitude of non possumus was not assumed. Though these men were the highest officials in Tibet, they could not guarantee that any settlement they might make with us would be faithfully observed. There seemed no hope of a solution to the deadlock except by absolute militarism. If the Tibetans had fought so stubbornly at Gyantse, what fanaticism might we not expect at Lhasa! Most of us thought that we could only reach the capital through the most awful carnage. We pictured the 40,000 monks of Lhasa hurling themselves defiantly on our camp. We saw them mown down by Maxims, lanes of dead. A hopeless struggle, and an ugly page in military history. Still, we must go on; there was no help for it. The blood of these people was on their own heads.

We left Gyantse on the 14th, and plunged into the unknown towards Lhasa, which we had reason to believe lay in some hidden valley 150 miles to the north, beyond the unexplored basin of the Tsangpo. Every position on the road was held. The Karo la had been enormously strengthened, and was occupied by 2,000 men. The enemy's cavalry, which we had never seen, were at Nagartse Jong. Gubshi, a dilapidated fort, only nineteen miles on the road, was held by several hundred. The Tibetans intended to dispute the passage of the Brahmaputra, and there were other strong positions where the path skirted the Kyi-chu for miles beneath overhanging rocks, which were carefully prepared for booby-traps. We had to launch ourselves into this intensely hostile region and compel some people--we did not know whom--to attach their signatures and seals to a certain parchment which was to bind them to good behaviour in the future, and a recognition of obligations they had hitherto disavowed.

Our force consisted of eight companies of the 8th Gurkhas, five companies of the 32nd Pioneers, four companies of the 40th Pathans, four companies of the Royal Fusiliers, two companies of Mounted Infantry, No. 30 British Mountain Battery, a section of No. 7 Native Mountain Battery, 1st Madras Sappers and Miners, machine-gun section of the Norfolks, and details.[14] The 23rd Pioneers, to their disgust, were left to garrison Gyantse. The transport included mule, yak, donkey, and coolie corps.

[14] Companies of Pathans and Gurkhas were left to garrison Ralung, Nagartse, Pehte, Chaksam, and Toilung Bridge.

The first three marches to Ralung were a repetition of the country between Kalatso and Gyantse--in the valley a strip of irrigated land, green and gold, with alternate barley and mustard fields between hillsides bare and verdureless save for tufts of larkspur, astragalus, and scattered yellow poppies. To Gyantse one descends 2,000 feet from a country entirely barren of trees to a valley of occasional willow and poplar groves; while from Gyantse, as one ascends, the clusters of trees become fewer, until one reaches the treeless zone again at Ralung (15,000 feet). The last grove is at Gubchi.

I quote some notes of the march from my diary:

'July 14.--The villages by the roadside are deserted save for old women and barking dogs. The Tibetans came down from the Karo la and impressed the villagers. Many have fled into the hills, and are hiding among the rocks and caves. Our pickets fired on some to-night. Seeing their heads bobbing up and down among the rocks, they thought they were surrounded. Many of the fugitives were women. Luckily, none were hit. They were brought into camp whimpering and salaaming, and became embarrassingly grateful when it was made clear to them that they were not to be tortured or killed, but set free. They were called back, however, to give information about grain, and thought their last hour had come.'

'July 16.--All the houses between Gubchi and Ralung are decorated with diagonal blue, red, and white stripes, characteristic of the Ning-ma sect of Buddhists. They remind me of the walls of Damascus after the visit of the German Emperor. Heavy rain falls every day. Last night we camped in a wet mustard-field. It is impossible to keep our bedding dry.'

From Ralung the valley widens out, and the country becomes more bleak. We enter a plateau frequented by gazelle. Cultivation ceases. The ascent to the Karo Pass is very gradual. The path takes a sudden turn to the east through a narrow gorge.

On the 17th we camped under the Karo la in the snow range of Noijin Kang Sang, at an elevation of 1,000 feet above Mont Blanc. The pass was free of snow, but a magnificent glacier descended within 500 feet of the camp. We lay within four miles of the enemy's position. Most of us expected heavy fighting the next morning, as we knew the Tibetans had been strengthening their defences at the Karo la for some days. Volleys were fired on our scouts on the 16th and 17th. The old wall had been extended east and west until it ended in vertical cliffs just beneath the snow-line. A second barrier had been built further on, and sangars constructed on every prominent point to meet flank attacks. The wall itself was massively strong, and it was approached by a steep cliff, up which it was impossible to make a sustained charge, as the rarefied air at this elevation (16,600 feet) leaves one breathless after the slightest exertion. The Karo la was the strongest position on the road to Lhasa. If the Tibetans intended to make another stand, here was their chance.

In the messes there was much discussion as to the seriousness of the opposition we were likely to meet with. The flanking parties had a long and difficult climb before them that would take them some hours, and the general feeling was that we should be lucky if we got the transport through by noon. But when one of us suggested that the Tibetans might fail to come up to the scratch, and abandon the position without firing a shot, we laughed at him; but his conjecture was very near the mark.

At 7 a.m. the troops forming the line of advance moved into position. The disposition of the enemy's sangars made a turning movement extremely difficult, but a frontal attack on the wall, if stubbornly resisted, could not be carried without severe loss. General Macdonald sent flanking parties of the 8th Gurkhas on both sides of the valley to scale the heights and turn the Tibetan position, and despatched the Royal Fusiliers along the centre of the valley to attack the wall when the opposition had been weakened.

Stretched on a grassy knoll on the left, enjoying the sunshine and the smell of the warm turf, we civilians watched the whole affair with our glasses. It might have been a picnic on the Surrey downs if it were not for the tap-tap of the Maxim, like a distant woodpecker, in the valley, and the occasional report of the 10-pounders by our side, which made the valleys and cliffs reverberate like thunder.

The Tibetans' ruse was to open fire from the wall directly our troops came into view, and then evacuate the position. They thus delayed the pursuit while we were waiting for the scaling-party to ascend the heights.

At nine o'clock the Gurkhas on the left signalled that no enemy were to be seen. At the same time Colonel Cooper, of the Royal Fusiliers, heliographed that the wall was unoccupied and the Tibetans in full retreat. The mounted infantry were at once called up for the pursuit. Meanwhile one or two jingals and some Tibetan marksmen kept up an intermittent fire on the right flanking party from clefts in the overhanging cliffs. A battery replied with shrapnel, covering our advance. These pickets on the left stayed behind and engaged our right flanking party until eleven o'clock. To turn the position the Gurkhas climbed a parallel ridge, and were for a long time under fire of their jingals. The last part of the ascent was along the edge of a glacier, and then on to the shoulder of the ridge by steps which the Gurkhas cut in the ice with their kukris, helping one another up with the butts of their rifles. They carried rope scaling-ladders, but these were for the descent. At 11.30 Major Murray and his two companies of Gurkhas appeared on the heights, and possession was taken of the pass. The ridge that the Tibetans had held was apparently deserted, but every now and then a man was seen crouching in a cave or behind a rock, and was shot down. One Kham man shot a Gurkha who was looking into the cave where he was hiding. He then ran out and held up his thumbs, expecting quarter. He was rightly cut down with kukris. The dying Gurkha's comrades rushed the cave, and drove six more over the precipice without using steel or powder. They fell sheer 300 feet. Another Gurkha cut off a Tibetan's head with his own sword. On several occasions they hesitated to soil their kukris when they could despatch their victims in any other way.

On a further ridge, a heart-breaking ascent of shale and boulders, we saw two or three hundred Tibetans ascending into the clouds. We had marked them at the beginning of the action, before we knew that the wall was unoccupied. Even then it was clear that the men were fugitives, and had no thought of holding the place. We could see them hours afterwards, with our glasses, crouching under the cliffs. We turned shrapnel and Maxims on them; the hillsides began to move. Then a company of Pathans was sent up, and despatched over forty. It was at this point I saw an act of heroism which quite changed my estimate of these men. A group of four were running up a cliff, under fire from the Pathans at a distance of about 500 yards. One was hit, and his comrade stayed behind to carry him. The two unimpeded Tibetans made their escape, but the rescuer could only shamble along with difficulty. He and his wounded comrade were both shot down.

The 18th was a disappointing day to our soldiers. But the action was of great interest, owing to the altitude in which our flanking parties had to operate. There is a saying on the Indian frontier: 'There is a hill; send up a Gurkha.' These sturdy little men are splendid mountaineers, and will climb up the face of a rock while the enemy are rolling down stones on them as coolly as they will rush a wall under heavy fire on the flat. Their arduous climb took three and a half hours, and was a real mountaineering feat. The cave fighting, in which they had three casualties, took place at 19,000 feet, and this is probably the highest elevation at which an action has been fought in history.

A few of the Tibetans fled by the highroad, along which the mounted infantry pursued, killing twenty and taking ten prisoners. I asked a native officer how he decided whom to spare or kill, and he said he killed the men who ran, and spared those who came towards him. The destiny that preserved the lives of our ten Kham prisoners when nearly the whole of the levy perished reminded me in its capriciousness of Caliban's whim in Setebos:

'Let twenty pass, and stone the twenty-first, Loving not, hating not, just choosing so.'

These Kham men were in our mounted infantry camp until the release of the prisoners in Lhasa, and made themselves useful in many ways--loading mules, carrying us over streams, fetching wood and water, and fodder for our horses. They were fed and cared for, and probably never fared better in their lives. When they had nothing to do, they would sit down in a circle and discuss things resignedly--the English, no doubt, and their ways, and their own distant country. Sometimes they would ask to go home; their mothers and wives did not know if they were alive or dead. But we had no guarantee that they would not fight us again. Now they knew the disparity of their arms they might shrink from further resistance, yet there was every chance that the Lamas would compel them to fight. They became quite popular in the camp, these wild, long-haired men, they were so good-humoured, gentle in manner, and ready to help.

I was sorry for these Tibetans. Their struggle was so hopeless. They were brave and simple, and none of us bore the slightest vindictiveness against them. Here was all the brutality of war, and none of the glory and incentive. These men were of the same race as the people I had been living amongst at Darjeeling--cheerful, jolly fellows--and I had seen their crops ruined, their houses burnt and shelled, the dead lying about the thresholds of what were their homes, and all for no fault of their own--only because their leaders were politically impossible, which, of course, the poor fellows did not know, and there was no one to tell them. They thought our advance an act of unprovoked aggression, and they were fighting for their homes.

Fortunately, however, this slaughter was beginning to put the fear of God into them. We never saw a Tibetan within five miles who did not carry a huge white flag. The second action at the Karo la was the end of the Tibetan resistance. The fall of Gyantse Jong, which they thought unassailable, seems to have broken their spirit altogether. At the Karo la they had evidently no serious intention of holding the position, but fought like men driven to the front against their will, with no confidence or heart in the business at all. The friendly Bhutanese told us that the Tibetans would not stand where they had once been defeated, and that levies who had once faced us were not easily brought into the field again. These were casual generalizations, no doubt, but they contained a great deal of truth. The Kham men who opposed us at the first Karo la action, the Shigatze men who attacked the mission in May, and the force from Lhasa who hurled themselves on Kangma, were all new levies. Many of our prisoners protested very strongly against being released, fearing to be exposed again to our bullets and their own Lamas.

On the 18th we reached Nagartse Jong, and found the Shap awaiting us. They met us in the same impracticable spirit. We were not to occupy the jong, and they were not empowered to treat with us unless we returned to Gyantse. It was a repetition of Khamba Jong and Tuna. In the afternoon a durbar was held in Colonel Younghusband's tent, when the Tibetans showed themselves appallingly futile and childish. They did not seem to realize that we were in a position to dictate terms, and Colonel Younghusband had to repeat that it was now too late for any compromise, and the settlement must be completed at Lhasa.

From Nagartse we held interviews with these tedious delegates at almost every camp. They exhausted everyone's patience except the Commissioner's. For days they did not yield a point, and refused even to discuss terms unless we returned to Gyantse. But their protests became more urgent as we went on, their tone less minatory. It was not until we were within fifty miles of Lhasa that the Tibetan Government deigned to enter into communication with the mission. At Tamalung Colonel Younghusband received the first communication from the National Assembly; at Chaksam arrived the first missive the British Government had ever received from the Dalai Lama. During the delay at the ferry the councillors practically threw themselves on

Colonel Younghusband's mercy. They said that their lives would be forfeited if we proceeded, and dwelt on the severe punishment they might incur if they failed to conclude negociations satisfactorily. But Colonel Younghusband was equal to every emergency. It would be impossible to find another man in the British Empire with a personality so calculated to impress the Tibetans. He sat through every durbar a monument of patience and inflexibility, impassive as one of their own Buddhas. Priests and councillors found that appeals to his mercy were hopeless. He, too, had orders from his King to go to Lhasa; if he faltered, his life also was at stake; decapitation would await him on his return. That was the impression he purposely gave them. It curtailed palaver. How in the name of all their Buddhas were they to stop such a man?

The whole progress of negociations put me in mind of the coercion of very naughty children. The Lamas tried every guile to reduce his demands. They would be cajoling him now if he had not given them an ultimatum, and if they had not learnt by six weeks' contact and intercourse with the man that shuffling was hopeless, that he never made a promise that was not fulfilled, or a threat that was not executed. The Tibetan treaty was the victory of a personality, the triumph of an impression on the least impressionable people in the world. But I anticipate.

While the Shap were holding Colonel Younghusband in conference at Nagartse, their cavalry were escorting a large convoy on the road to Lhasa. Our mounted infantry came upon them six miles beyond Nagartse, and as they were rounding them up the Tibetans foolishly fired on them. We captured eighty riding and baggage ponies and mules and fourteen prisoners, and killed several. They made no stand, though they were well armed with a medley of modern rifles and well mounted. This was actually the last shot fired on our side. The delegates had been full of assurances that the country was clear of the enemy, hoping that the convoy would get well away while they delayed us with fruitless protests and reiterated demands to go back. While they were palavering in the tent, they looked out and saw the Pathans go past with their rich yellow silks and personal baggage looted in the brush with the cavalry. Their consternation was amusing, and the situation had its element of humour. A servant rushed to the door of the tent and delivered the whole tale of woe. A mounted infantry officer arrived and explained that our scouts had been fired on. After this, of course, there was no talk of anything except the restitution of the loot. The Shap 閣 deserved to lose their kit. I do not remember what was arranged, but if any readers of this record see a gorgeous yellow cloak of silk and brocade at a fancy-dress ball in London, I advise them to ask its history.

This last encounter with the Tibetans is especially interesting, as they were the best-armed body of men we had met. The weapons we captured included a Winchester rifle, several Lhasa-made Martinis, a bolt rifle of an old Austrian pattern, an English-made muzzle-loading rifle, a 12-bore breech-loading shot-gun, some Eley's ammunition, and an English gun-case. The reports of Russian arms found in Tibet have been very much exaggerated. During the whole campaign we did not come across more than thirty Russian Government rifles, and these were weapons that must have drifted into Tibet from Mongolia, just as rifles of British pattern found their way over the Indian frontier into Lhasa. Also it must be remembered that the weapons locally made in Lhasa were of British pattern, and manufactured by experts decoyed from a British factory. Had these men been Russian subjects, we should have regarded their presence in Lhasa as an unquestionable proof of Muscovite assistance. Jealousy and suspicion make nations wilfully blind. Russia fully believes that we are giving underhand assistance to the Japanese, and many Englishmen, who are unbiassed in other questions, are ready to believe, without the slightest proof, that Russia has been supplying Tibet with arms and generals. We had been informed that large quantities of Russian rifles had been introduced into the country, and it was rumoured that the Tibetans were reserving these for the defence of Lhasa itself. But it is hardly credible that they should have sent levies against us armed with their obsolete matchlocks when they were well supplied with weapons of a modern pattern. Russian intrigue was active in Lhasa, but it had not gone so far as open armament.

At Nagartse we came across the great Yamdok or Palti Lake, along the shores of which winds the road to Lhasa. Nagartse Jong is a striking old keep, built on a bluff promontory of hill stretching out towards the blue waters of the lake. In the distance we saw the crag-perched monastery of Samding, where lives the mysterious Dorje Phagmo, the incarnation of the goddess Tara.

The wild mountain scenery of the Yamdok Tso, the most romantic in Tibet, has naturally inspired many legends. When Samding was threatened by the Dzungarian invaders early in the eighteenth century, Dorje Phagmo miraculously converted herself and all her attendant monks and nuns into pigs. Serung Dandub, the Dzungarian chief, finding the monastery deserted, said that he would not loot a place guarded only by swine, whereupon Dorje Phagmo again metamorphosed herself and her satellites. The terrified invaders prostrated themselves in awe before the goddess, and presented the monastery with the most priceless gifts. Similarly, the Abbot of Pehte saved the fortress and town from another band of invaders by giving the lake the appearance of green pasturelands, into which the Dzungarians galloped and were engulfed. I quote these tales, which have been mentioned in nearly every book on Tibet, as typical of the country. Doubtless similar legends will be current in a few years about the British to account for the sparing of Samding, Nagartse, and Pehte Jong.

Special courtesy was shown the monks and nuns of Samding, in recognition of the hospitality afforded Sarat Chandra Dass by the last incarnation of Dorje Phagmo, who entertained the Bengali traveller, and saw that he was attended to and cared for through a serious illness. A letter was sent Dorje Phagmo, asking if she would receive three British officers, including the antiquary of the expedition. But the present incarnation, a girl of six or seven years, was invisible, and the convent was reported to be bare of ornament and singularly disappointing. There were no pigs.

If only one were without the incubus of an army, a month in the Noijin Kang Sang country and the Yamdok Plain would be a delightful experience. But when one is accompanying a column one loses more than half the pleasure of travel. One has to get up at a fixed hour--generally uncomfortably early--breakfast, and pack and load one's mules and see them started in their allotted place in the line, ride in a crowd all day, often at a snail's pace, and halt at a fixed place. Shooting is forbidden on the line of march. When alone one can wander about with a gun, pitch camp where one likes, make short or long marches as one likes, shoot or fish or loiter for days in the same place. The spirit which impels one to travel in wild places is an impulse, conscious or unconscious, to be free of laws and restraints, to escape conventions and social obligations, to temporarily throw one's self back into an obsolete phase of existence, amidst surroundings which bear little mark of the arbitrary meddling of man. It is not a high ideal, but men often deceive themselves when they think they make expeditions in order to add to science, and forsake the comforts of life, and endure hunger, cold, fatigue and loneliness, to discover in exactly what parallel of unknown country a river rises or bends to some particular point of the compass. How many travellers are there who would spend the same time in an office poring over maps or statistics for the sake of geography or any other science? We like to have a convenient excuse, and make a virtue out of a hobby or an instinct. But why not own up that one travels for the glamour of the thing? In previous wanderings my experience had always been to leave a base with several different objectives in view, and to take the route that proved most alluring when met by a choice of roads-- some old deserted city or ruined shrine, some lake or marshland haunted by wild-fowl that have never heard the crack of a gun, or a strip of desert where one must calculate how to get across with just sufficient supplies and no margin. I like to drift to the magnet of great watersheds, lofty mountain passes, frontiers where one emerges among people entirely different in habit and belief from folk the other side, but equally convinced that they are the only enlightened people on earth. Often in India I had dreamed of the great inland waters of Tibet and Mongolia, the haunts of myriads of duck and geese--Yamdok Tso, Tengri Nor, Issik Kul, names of romance to the wild-fowler, to be breathed with reverence and awe. I envied the great flights of mallard and pochard winging northward in March and April to the unknown; and here at last I was camping by the Yamdok Tso itself--with an army.

Yet I have digressed to grumble at the only means by which a sight of these hidden waters was possible. When we passed in July, there were no wild-fowl on the lake except the bar-headed geese and Brahminy duck. The ruddy sheldrake, or Brahminy, is found all over Tibet, and will be associated with the memory of nearly every march and camping-ground. It is distinctly a Buddhist bird. From it is derived the title of the established Church of the Lamas, the Abbots of which wear robes of ruddy sheldrake colour, Gelug-pa.[15] In Burmah the Brahminy is sacred to Buddhism as a symbol of devotion and fidelity, and it was figured on Asoka's pillars in the same emblematical character.[16] The Brahminy is generally found in pairs, and when one is shot the other will often hover round till it falls a victim to conjugal love. In India the bird is considered inedible, but we were glad of it in Tibet, and discovered no trace of fishy flavour.

[15] Waddell, 'Lamaism in Tibet,' p. 200.

[16] Ibid., p. 409.

Early in April, when we passed the Bam Tso and Kala Tso we found the lakes frequented by nearly all the common migratory Indian duck; and again, on our return large flights came in. But during the summer months nothing remained except the geese and sheldrake and the goosander, which is resident in Tibet and the Himalayas. I take it that no respectable duck spends the summer south of the Tengri Nor. At Lhasa, mallard, teal, gadwall, and white-eyed pochard were coming in from the north as we were leaving in the latter half of September, and followed us down to the plains. They make shorter flights than I imagined, and longer stays at their fashionable Central Asian watering-places.

We marched three days along the banks of the Yamdok Tso, and halted a day at Nagartse. Duck were not plentiful on the lake. Black-headed gulls and redshanks were common. The fields of blue borage by the villages were an exquisite sight. On the 22nd we reached Pehte. The jong, a medieval fortress, stands out on the lake like Chillon, only it is more crumbling and dilapidated. The courtyards are neglected and overgrown with nettles. Soldiers, villagers, both men and women, had run away to the hills with their flocks and valuables. Only an old man and two boys were left in charge of the chapel and the fort. The hide fishing-boats were sunk, or carried over to the other side. On July 24 we left the lake near the village of Tamalung, and ascended the ridge on our left to the Khamba Pass, 1,200 feet above the lake level. A sudden turn in the path brought us to the saddle, and we looked down on the great river that has been guarded from European eyes for nearly a century. In the heart of Tibet we had found Arcadia--not a detached oasis, but a continuous strip of verdure, where the Tsangpo cleaves the bleak hills and desert tablelands from west to east.

All the valley was covered with green and yellow cornfields, with scattered homesteads surrounded by clusters of trees, not dwarfish and stunted in the struggle for existence, but stately and spreading--trees that would grace the valley of the Thames or Severn.

We had come through the desert to Arcady. When we left Phari, months and months before, and crossed the Tang la, we entered the desert.

Tuna is built on bare gravel, and in winter-time does not boast a blade of grass. Within a mile there are stunted bushes, dry, withered, and sapless, which lend a sustenance to the gazelle and wild asses, beasts that from the beginning have chosen isolation, and, like the Tibetans, who people the same waste, are content with spare diet so long as they are left alone.

Every Tibetan of the tableland is a hermit by choice, or some strange hereditary instinct has impelled him to accept Nature's most niggard gifts as his birthright, so that he toils a lifetime to win by his own labour and in scanty measure the necessaries which Nature deals lavishly elsewhere, herding his yaks on the waste lands, tilling the unproductive soil for his meagre crop of barley, and searching the hillsides for yak-dung for fuel to warm his stone hut and cook his meal of flour.

Yet north and south of him, barely a week's journey, are warm, fertile valleys, luxuriant crops, unstinted woodlands, where Mongols like himself accept Nature's largess philosophically as the most natural thing in the world.

It seems as if some special and economical law of Providence, such a law as makes at least one man see beauty in every type of woman, even the most unlovely, had ordained it, so that no corner of the earth, not even the Sahara, Tadmor, Tuna, or Guru, should lack men who devote themselves blindly and without question to live there, and care for what one might think God Himself had forgotten and overlooked.

These men--Bedouin, Tibetans, and the like--enjoy one thing, for which they forego most things that men crave for, and that is freedom. They do not possess the gifts that cause strife, and divisions, and law-making, and political parties, and changes of Government. They have too little to share. Their country is invaded only at intervals of centuries. On these occasions they fight bravely, as their one inheritance is at stake. But they are bigoted and benighted; they have not kept time with evolution, and so they are defeated. The conservatism, the exclusiveness, that has kept them free so long has shut the door to 'progress,' which, if they were enlightened and introspective, they would recognise as a pestilence that has infected one half of the world at the expense of the other, making both unhappy and discontented.

The Tuna Plain is like the Palmyra Desert at the point where one comes within view of the snows of Lebanon. It is not monotonous; there is too much play of light and shade for that. Everywhere the sun shines, the mirage dances; the white calcined plain becomes a flock of frightened sheep hurrying down the wind; the stunted sedge by the lakeside leaps up like a squadron in ambush and sweeps rapidly along without ever approaching nearer. Sometimes a herd of wild asses is mingled in the dance, grotesquely magnified; stones and nettles become walls and men. All the country is elusive and unreal.

A few miles beyond Guru the road skirts the Bamtso Lake, which must once have filled the whole valley. Now the waters have receded, as the process of desiccation is going on which has entirely changed the geographical features of Central Asia, and caused the disappearance of great expanses of water like the Koko Nor, and the dwindling of lakes and river from Khotan to Gobi. The Roof of the World is becoming less and less inhabitable.

From the desert to Arcady is not a long journey, but armies travel slowly. After months of waiting and delay we reached the promised land. It was all suddenly unfolded to our view when we stood on the Khamba la. Below us was a purely pastoral landscape. Beyond lay hills even more barren and verdureless than those we had crossed. But every mile or so green fan-shaped valleys, irrigated by clear streams, interrupted the barrenness, opening out into the main valley east and west with perfect symmetry. To the north-east flowed the Kyi Chu, the valley in which Lhasa lay screened, only fifty-six miles distant.

To the south of the pass lay the great Yamdok Lake, wild and beautiful, its channels twining into the dark interstices of the hills--valleys of mystery and gloom, where no white man has ever trod. Lights and shadows fell caressingly on the lake and hills. At one moment a peak was ebony black, at another--as the heavy clouds passed from over it, and the sun's rays illumined it through a thin mist--golden as a field of buttercups. Often at sunset the grassy cones of the hills glow like gilded pagodas, and the Tibetans, I am told, call these sunlit plots the 'golden ground.'

In bright sunlight the lake is a deep turquoise blue, but at evening time transient lights and shades fleet over it with the moving clouds, light forget-me-not, deep purple, the azure of a butterfly's wing--then all is swept away, immersed in gloom, before the dark, menacing storm-clouds.

On the 25th I crossed the river with the 1st Mounted Infantry and 40th Pathans. My tent is pitched on the roof of a rambling two-storied house, under the shade of a great walnut-tree. Crops, waist-deep, grow up to the walls--barley, wheat, beans, and peas. On the roof are garden flowers in pots, hollyhocks, and marigolds. The cornfields are bright with English wild-flowers--dandelions, buttercups, astragalus, and a purple Michaelmas daisy.

There is no village, but farmhouses are dotted about the valley, and groves of trees--walnut and peach, and poplar and willow--enclosed within stone walls. Wild birds that are almost tame are nesting in the trees--black and white magpies, crested hoopoes, and turtle-doves. The groves are irrigated like the fields, and carpeted with flowers. Homelike butterflies frequent them, and honey-bees.

Everything is homelike. There is no mystery in the valley, except its access, or, rather, its inaccessibility. We have come to it through snow passes, over barren, rocky wildernesses; we have won it with toil and suffering, through frost and rain and snow and blistering sun.

And now that we had found Arcady, I would have stayed there. Lhasa was only four marches distant, but to me, in that mood of almost immoral indolence, it seemed that this strip of verdure, with its happy pastoral scenes, was the most impassable barrier that Nature had planted in our path. Like the Tibetans, she menaced and threatened us at first, then she turned to us with smiles and cajoleries, entreating us to stay, and her seduction was harder to resist.

* * * * *

To trace the course of the Tsangpo River from Tibet to its outlet into Assam has been the goal of travellers for over a century. Here is one of the few unknown tracts of the world, where no white man has ever penetrated. Until quite recently there was a hot controversy among geographers as to whether the Tsangpo was the main feeder of the Brahmaputra or reappeared in Burmah as the Irawaddy. All attempts to explore the river from India have proved fruitless, owing to the intense hostility of the Abor and Passi Minyang tribes, who oppose all intrusion with their poisoned arrows and stakes, sharp and formidable as spears, cunningly set in the ground to entrap invaders; while the vigilance of the Lamas has made it impossible for any European to get within 150 miles of the Tsangpo Valley from Tibet. It was not until 1882 that all doubt as to the identity of the Tsangpo and Brahmaputra was set aside by the survey of the native explorer A. K. And the course of the Brahmaputra, or Dihong, as it is called in Northern Assam, was never thoroughly investigated until the explorations of Mr. Needham, the Political Officer at Sadiya, and his trained Gurkhas, who penetrated northwards as far as Gina, a village half a day's journey beyond Passi Ghat, and only about seventy miles south of the point reached by A. K. from Tibet.

The return of the British expedition from Tibet was evidently the opportunity of a century for the investigation of this unexplored country. We had gained the hitherto inaccessible base, and were provided with supplies and transport on the spot; we had no opposition to expect from the Tibetans, who were naturally eager to help us out of the country by whatever road we chose, and had promised to send officials with us to their frontier at Gyala Sendong, who would forage for us and try to impress the villagers into our service. The hostile tribes beyond the frontier were not so likely to resist an expedition moving south to their homes after a successful campaign as a force entering their country from our Indian frontier. In the latter case they would naturally be more suspicious of designs on their independence. The distance from Lhasa to Assam was variously estimated from 500 to 700 miles. I think the calculations were influenced, perhaps unconsciously, by sympathy with, or aversion from, the enterprise.

* * * * *

The Shap, it is true, though they promised to help us if we were determined on it, advised us emphatically not to go by the Tsangpo route. They said that the natives of their own outlying provinces were bandits and cut-throats, practically independent of the Lhasa Government, while the savages beyond the frontier were dangerous people who obeyed no laws. The Shap' notions as to the course of the river were most vague. When questioned, they said there was a legend that it disappeared into a hole in the earth. The country near its mouth was inhabited by savages, who went about unclothed, and fed on monkeys and reptiles. It was rumoured that they were horned like animals, and that mothers did not know their own children. But this they could not vouch for.

It was believed that tracks of a kind existed from village to village all along the route, but these, of course, after a time would become impracticable for pack transport. The mules would have to be abandoned, and sent back to Gyantse by our guides, or presented to the Tibetan officials who accompanied us. Then we were to proceed by forced marches through the jungle, with coolie transport if obtainable; if not, each man was to carry rice for a few days. The distance from the Tibet frontier to Sadiya is not great, and the unexplored country is reckoned not to be more than seven stages. The force would bivouac, and, if their advance were resisted, would confine themselves solely to defensive tactics. In case of opposition, the greatest difficulty would be the care of the wounded, as each invalid would need four carriers. Thus, a few casualties would reduce enormously the fighting strength of the escort.

But opposition was unlikely. Mr. Needham, who has made the tribes of the Dihong Valley the study of a lifetime, and succeeded to some extent in gaining their confidence, considered the chances of resistance small. He would, he said, send messages to the tribes that the force coming through their country from the north were his friends, that they had been engaged in a punitive expedition against the Lamas (whom the Abors detested), that they were returning home by the shortest route to Assam, and had no designs on the territory they traversed. It was proposed that Mr. Needham should go up the river as far as possible and furnish the party with supplies.

All arrangements had been made for the exploring-party, which was to leave the main force at Chaksam Ferry, and was expected to arrive in Sadiya almost simultaneously with the winding up of the expedition at Siliguri. Captain Ryder, R.E., was to command the party, and his escort was to be made up of the 8th Gurkhas, who had long experience of the Assam frontier tribes, and were the best men who could be chosen for the work. Officers were selected, supply and transport details arranged, everything was in readiness, when at the last moment, only a day or two before the party was to start, a message was received from Simla refusing to sanction the expedition. Colonel Younghusband was entirely in favour of it, but the military authorities had a clean slate; they had come through so far without a single disaster, and it seemed that no scientific or geographical considerations could have any weight with them in their determination to take no risks. Of course there were risks, and always must be in enterprises of the kind; but I think the circumstances of the moment reduced them to a minimum, and that the results to be obtained from the projected expedition should have entirely outweighed them.

In European scientific circles much was expected of the Tibetan expedition. But it has added very little to science. The surveys that were made have done little more than modify the previous investigations of native surveyors.[17]

[17] The only expedition sanctioned is that which is now exploring the little-known trade route between Gyantse and Gartok, where a mart has been opened to us by the recent Tibetan treaty. The party consists of Captain Ryder, R.E., in command, Captain Wood, R.E., Lieutenant Bailey, of the 32nd Pioneers, and six picked men of the 8th Gurkhas. They follow the main feeder of the Tsangpo nearly 500 miles, then strike into the high lacustrine tableland of Western Tibet, passing the great Mansarowar Lake to Gartok; thence over the Indus watershed, and down the Sutlej Valley to Simla, where they are expected about the end of January. The party will be able to collect useful information about the trade resources of the country; but the route has already been mapped by Nain Singh, the Indian surveyor, and the geographical results of the expedition will be small compared with what would have been derived from the projected Tengri Nor and Brahmaputra trips.

An expedition to the mountains bordering the Tengri Nor, only nine days north of Lhasa, would have linked all the unknown country north of the Tsang po with the tracts explored by Sven Hedin, and left the map without a hiatus in four degrees of longitude from Cape Comorin to the Arctic Ocean. But military considerations were paramount.

For myself, the abandonment of the expedition was a great disappointment. I had counted on it as early as February, and had made all preparations to join it.

CHAPTER XIII

LHASA AND ITS VANISHED DEITY

The passage of the river was difficult and dangerous. If we had had to depend on the four Berthon boats we took with us, the crossing might have taken weeks. But the good fortune that attended the expedition throughout did not fail us. At Chaksam we found the Tibetans had left behind their two great ferry-boats, quaint old barges with horses' heads at the prow, capacious enough to hold a hundred men. The Tibetan ferrymen worked for us cheerfully. A number of hide boats were also discovered. The transport mules were swum over, and the whole force was across in less than a week.

But the river took its toll most tragically. The current is swift and boisterous; the eddies and whirlpools are dangerously uncertain. Two Berthon boats, bound together into a raft, capsized, and Major Bretherton, chief supply and transport officer, and two Gurkhas were drowned. It seemed as if the genius of the river, offended at our intrusion, had claimed its price and carried off the most valuable life in the force. It was Major Bretherton's foresight more than anything that enabled us to reach Lhasa. His loss was calamitous.

We left our camp at the ferry on July 31, and started for Lhasa, which was only forty-three miles distant. It was difficult to believe that in three days we would be looking on the Potala.

The Kyi Chu, the holy river of Lhasa, flows into the Tsangpo at Chushul, three miles below Chaksam ferry, where our troops crossed. The river is almost as broad as the Thames at Greenwich, and the stream is swift and clear. The valley is cultivated in places, but long stretches are bare and rocky. Sand-dunes, overgrown with artemisia scrub, extend to the margin of cultivation, leaving a well-defined line between the green cornfields and the barren sand. The crops were ripening at the time of our advance, and promised a plentiful harvest.

For many miles the road is cut out of a precipitous cliff above the river. A few hundred men could have destroyed it in an afternoon, and delayed our advance for another week. Newly-built sangars at the entrance of the gorge showed that the Tibetans had intended to hold it. But they left the valley in a disorganized state the day we reached the Tsangpo. Had they fortified the position, they might have made it stronger than the Karo la.

The heat of the valley was almost tropical. Summer by the Kyi Chu River is very different from one's first conceptions of Tibet. To escape the heat, I used to write my diary in the shade of gardens and willow groves. Hoopoes, magpies, and huge black ravens became inquisitive and confidential. I have a pile of little black notebooks I scribbled over in their society, dirty and torn and soiled with pressed flowers. For a picture of the valley I will go to these. One's freshest impressions are the best, and truer than reminiscences.

NETHANG.

In the most fertile part of the Kyi Chu Valley, where the fields are intersected in all directions by clear-running streams bordered with flowers, in a grove of poplars where doves were singing all day long, I found Atisa's tomb.

It was built in a large, plain, barn-like building, clean and sweet-smelling as a granary, and innocent of ornament outside and in. It was the only clean and simple place devoted to religion I had seen in Tibet.

In every house and monastery we entered on the road there were gilded images, tawdry paintings, demons and she-devils, garish frescoes on the wall, hideous grinning devil-masks, all the Lama's spurious apparatus of terrorism.

These were the outward symbols of demonolatry and superstition invented by scheming priests as the fabric of their sacerdotalism. But this was the resting-place of the Reformer, the true son of Buddha, who came over the Himalayas to preach a religion of love and mercy.

I entered the building out of the glare of the sun, expecting nothing but the usual monsters and abortions--just as one is dragged into a church in some tourist-ridden land, where, if only for the sake of peace, one must cast an apathetic eye at the lions of the country. But as the tomb gradually assumed shape in the dim light, I knew that there was someone here, a priest or a community, who understood Atisa, who knew what he would have wished his last resting-place to be; or perhaps the good old monk had left a will or spoken a plain word that had been handed down and remembered these thousand years, and was now, no doubt, regarded as an eccentric's whim, that there must be no gods or demons by his tomb, nothing abnormal, no pretentiousness of any kind. If his teaching had lived, how simple and honest and different Tibet would be to-day!

The tomb was not beautiful--a large square plinth, supporting layers of gradually decreasing circumference and forming steps two feet in height, the last a platform on which was based a substantial vat-like structure with no ornament or inscription except a thin line of black pencilled saints. By climbing up the layers of masonry I found a pair of slant eyes gazing at nothing and hidden by a curve in the stone from gazers below. This was the only painting on the tomb.

Never in the thousand years since the good monk was laid to rest at Nethang had a white man entered this shrine. To-day the courtyard was crowded with mules and drivers; Hindus and Pathans in British uniform: they were ransacking the place for corn. A transport officer was shouting:

'How many bags have you, babu?'

'A hundred and seven, sir.'

'Remember, if anyone loots, he will get fifty beynt' (stripes with the cat-o'-nine-tails).

Then he turned to me.

'What the devil is that old thief doing over there?' he said, and nodded at a man with archeological interests, who was peering about in a dark corner by the tomb. 'There is nothing more here.'

'He is examining Atisa's tomb.'

'And who the devil is Atisa?'

And who is he? Merely a name to a few dry-as-dust pedants. Everything human he did is forgotten. The faintest ripple remains to-day from that stone cast into the stagnant waters so many years ago. A few monks drone away their days in a monastery close by. In the courtyard there is a border of hollyhocks and snapdragon and asters. Here the unsavoury guardians of

Atisa's tomb watch me as I write, and wonder what on earth I am doing among them, and what spell or mantra I am inscribing in the little black book that shuts so tightly with a clasp.

TOILUNG.

To-morrow we reach Lhasa.

A few hours ago we caught the first glimpse of the Potala Palace, a golden dome standing out on a bluff rock in the centre of the valley. The city is not seen from afar perched on a hill like the great monasteries and jongs of the country. It is literally 'hidden.' A rocky promontory projects from the bleak hills to the south like a screen, hiding Lhasa, as if Nature conspired in its seclusion. Here at a distance of seven miles we can see the Potala and the Lamas' Medical College.

Trees and undulating ground shut out the view of the actual city until one is within a mile of it.

To-morrow we camp outside. It is nearly a hundred years since Thomas Manning, the only Englishman (until to-day) who ever saw Lhasa, preceded us. Our journey has not been easy, but we have come in spite of everything.

The Lamas have opposed us with all their material and spiritual resources. They have fought us with medieval weapons and a medley of modern firearms. They have held Commination Services, recited mantras, and cursed us solemnly for days. Yet we have come on.

They have sent delegates and messengers of every rank to threaten and entreat and plead with us--emissaries of increasing importance as we have drawn nearer their capital, until the Dalai Lama despatched his own Grand Chamberlain and Grand Secretary, and, greater than these, the Ta Lama and Yutok Shap? members of the ruling Council of Five, whose sacred persons had never before been seen by European eyes. To-morrow the Amban himself comes to meet Colonel Younghusband. The Dalai Lama has sent him a letter sealed with his own seal.

Every stretch of road from the frontier to Lhasa has had its symbol of remonstrance. Cairns and chortens, and mani walls and praying-flags, demons painted on the rock, writings on the wall, white stones piled upon black, have emitted their ray of protest and malevolence in vain.

The Lamas knew we must come. Hundreds of years ago a Buddhist saint wrote it in his book of prophecies, Ma-ong Lung-Ten, which may be bought to-day in the Lhasa book-shops. He predicted that Tibet would be invaded and conquered by the Philings (Europeans), when all of the true religion would go to Chang Shambula, the Northern Paradise, and Buddhism would become extinct in the country.

And now the Lamas believe that the prophecy will be fulfilled by our entry into Lhasa, and that their religion will decay before foreign influence. The Dalai Lama, they say, will die, not by violence or sickness, but by some spiritual visitation. His spirit will seek some other incarnation, when he can no longer benefit his people or secure his country, so long sacred to Buddhists, from the contamination of foreign intrusion.

The Tibetans are not the savages they are depicted. They are civilized, if medieval. The country is governed on the feudal system. The monks are the overlords, the peasantry their serfs. The poor are not oppressed. They and the small tenant farmers work ungrudgingly for their spiritual masters, to whom they owe a blind devotion. They are not discontented, though they give more than a tithe of their small income to the Church. It must be remembered that every family contributes at least one member to the priesthood, so that, when we are inclined to abuse the monks for consuming the greater part of the country's produce, we should remember that the laymen are not the victims of class prejudice, the plebeians groaning under the burden of the patricians, so much as the servants of a community chosen from among themselves, and with whom they are connected by family ties.

No doubt the Lamas employ spiritual terrorism to maintain their influence and preserve the temporal government in their hands; and when they speak of their religion being injured by our intrusion, they are thinking, no doubt, of another unveiling of mysteries, the dreaded age of materialism and reason, when little by little their ignorant serfs will be brought into contact with the facts of life, and begin to question the justness of the relations that have existed between themselves and their rulers for centuries. But at present the people are medieval, not only in their system of government and their religion, their inquisition, their witchcraft, their incantations, their ordeals by fire and boiling oil, but in every aspect of their daily life.

I question if ever in the history of the world there has been another occasion when bigotry and darkness have been exposed with such abruptness to the inroad of science, when a barrier of ignorance created by jealousy and fear as a screen between two peoples living side by side has been demolished so suddenly to admit the light of an advanced civilization.

The Tibetans, no doubt, will benefit, and many abuses will be swept away. Yet there will always be people who will hanker after the medieval and romantic, who will say: 'We men are children. Why could we not have been content that there was one mystery not unveiled, one country of an ancient arrested civilization, and an established Church where men are still guided by sorcery and incantations, and direct their mundane affairs with one eye on a grotesque spirit world, which is the most real thing in their lives--a land of topsy-turvy and inverted proportions, where men spend half their lives mumbling unintelligible mantras and turning mechanical prayers, and when dead are cut up into mincemeat and thrown to the dogs and vultures?'

To-morrow, when we enter Lhasa, we will have unveiled the last mystery the of the East. There are no more forbidden cities which men have not mapped and photographed. Our children will laugh at modern travellers' tales. They will have to turn again to Gulliver and Haroun al Raschid. And they will soon tire of these. For now that there are no real mysteries, no unknown land of dreams, where there may still be genii and mahatmas and bottle-imps, that kind of literature will be tolerated no longer. Children will be sceptical and matter-of-fact and disillusioned, and there will be no sale for fairy-stories any more.

But we ourselves are children. Why could we not have left at least one city out of bounds?

LHASA, August 3.

We reached Lhasa to-day, after a march of seven miles, and camped outside the city. As we approached, the road became an embankment across a marsh.

Butterflies and dragon-flies were hovering among the rushes, clematis grew in the stonework by the roadside, cows were grazing in the rich pastureland, redshanks were calling, a flight of teal passed overhead; the whole scene was most homelike, save for the bare scarred cliffs that jealously preclude a distant view of the city.

Some of us climbed the Chagpo Ri and looked down on the city. Lhasa lay a mile in front of us, a mass of huddled roofs and trees, dominated by the golden dome of the Jokhang Cathedral.

It must be the most hidden city on earth. The Chagpo Ri rises bluffly from the river-bank like a huge rock. Between it and the Potala hill there is a narrow gap not more than thirty yards wide. Over this is built the Pargo Kaling, a typical Tibetan chorten, through which is the main gateway into Lhasa. The city has no walls, but beyond the Potala, to complete the screen, stretches a great embankment of sand right across the valley to the hills on the north.

LHASA, August 4.

An epoch in the world's history was marked to-day when Colonel Younghusband entered the city to return the visit of the Chinese Amban. He was accompanied by all the members of the mission, the war correspondents, and an escort of two companies of the Royal Fusiliers and the 2nd Mounted Infantry. Half a company of mounted infantry, two guns, a detachment of sappers, and four companies of infantry were held ready to support the escort if necessary.

In front of us marched and rode the Amban's escort--his bodyguard, dressed in short loose coats of French gray, embroidered in black, with various emblems; pikemen clad in bright red with black embroidery and black pugarees; soldiers with pikes and scythes and three-pronged spears, on all of which hung red banners with devices embroidered in black.

We found the city squalid and filthy beyond description, undrained and unpaved. Not a single house looked clean or cared for. The streets after rain are nothing but pools of stagnant water frequented by pigs and dogs searching for refuse. Even the Jokhang appeared mean and squalid at close quarters, whence its golden roofs were invisible. There was nothing picturesque except the marigolds and hollyhocks in pots and the doves and singing-birds in wicker cages.

The few Tibetans we met in the street were strangely incurious. A baker kneading dough glanced at us casually, and went on kneading. A woman weaving barely looked up from her work.

The streets were almost deserted, perhaps by order of the authorities to prevent an outbreak. But as we returned small crowds had gathered in the doorways, women were peering through windows, but no one followed or took more than a listless interest in us. The monks looked on sullenly. But in most faces one read only indifference and apathy. One might think the entry of a foreign army into Lhasa and the presence of English Political Officers in gold-laced uniform and beaver hats were everyday events.

The only building in Lhasa that is at all imposing is the Potala.

It would be misleading to say that the palace dominated the city, as a comparison would be implied--a picture conveyed of one building standing out signally among others. This is not the case.

The Potala is superbly detached. It is not a palace on a hill, but a hill that is also a palace. Its massive walls, its terraces and bastions stretch upwards from the plain to the crest, as if the great bluff rock were merely a foundation-stone planted there at the divinity's nod. The divinity dwells in the palace, and underneath, at the distance of a furlong or two, humanity is huddled abjectly in squalid smut-begrimed houses. The proportion is that which exists between God and man.

If one approached within a league of Lhasa, saw the glittering domes of the Potala, and turned back without entering the precincts, one might still imagine it an enchanted city, shining with turquoise and gold. But having entered, the illusion is lost. One might think devout Buddhists had excluded strangers in order to preserve the myth of the city's beauty and mystery and wealth, or that the place was consciously neglected and defaced so as to offer no allurements to heretics, just as the repulsive women one meets in the streets smear themselves over with grease and cutch to make themselves even more hideous than Nature ordained.

The place has not changed since Manning visited it ninety years ago, and wrote:--'There is nothing striking, nothing pleasing, in its appearance. The habitations are begrimed with smut and dirt. The avenues are full of dogs, some growling and gnawing bits of hide that lie about in profusion, and emit a charnel-house smell; others limping and looking livid; others ulcerated; others starved and dying, and pecked at by ravens; some dead and preyed upon. In short, everything seems mean and gloomy, and excites the idea of something unreal.' That is the Lhasa of to-day. Probably it was the same centuries ago.

Above all this squalor the Potala towers superbly. Its golden roofs, shining in the sun like tongues of fire, are a landmark for miles, and must inspire awe and veneration in the hearts of pilgrims coming from the desert parts of Tibet, Kashmir, and Mongolia to visit the sacred city that Buddha has blessed.

The secret of romance is remoteness, whether in time or space. If we could be thrown back to the days of Agincourt we should be enchanted at first, but after a week should vote everything commonplace and dull. Falstaff, the beery lout, would be an impossible companion, and Prince Hal a tiresome young cub who wanted a good dressing-down. In travel, too, as one approaches the goal, and the country becomes gradually familiar, the husk of romance falls off. Childe Roland must have been sadly disappointed in the Dark Tower; filth and familiarity very soon destroyed the romance of Lhasa.

But romance still clings to the Potala. It is still remote. Like Imray, its sacred inmate has achieved the impossible. Divinity or no, he has at least the divine power of vanishing. In the material West, as we like to call it, we know how hard it is for the humblest subject to disappear, in spite of the confused hub of traffic and intricate network of communications. Yet here in Lhasa, a city of dreamy repose, a King has escaped, been spirited into the air, and nobody is any the wiser.

When we paraded the city yesterday, we made a complete circuit of the Potala. There was no one, not even the humblest follower, so unimaginative that he did not look up from time to time at the frowning cliff and thousand sightless windows that concealed the unknown. Those hidden corridors and passages have been for centuries, and are, perhaps, at this very moment, the scenes of unnatural piety and crime.

Within the precincts of Lhasa the taking of life in any form is sacrilege. Buddha's first law was, 'Thou shalt not kill'; and life is held so sacred by his devout followers that they are careful not to kill the smallest insect. Yet this palace, where dwells the divine incarnation of the Bodhisat, the head of the Buddhist Church, must have witnessed more murders and instigations to crime than the most blood-stained castle of medieval Europe.

Since the assumption of temporal power by the fifth Grand Lama in the middle of the seventeenth century, the whole history of the Tibetan hierarchy has been a record of bloodshed and intrigue. The fifth Grand Lama, the first to receive the title of Dalai, was a most unscrupulous ruler, who secured the temporal power by inciting the Mongols to invade Tibet, and received as his reward the kingship. He then established his claim to the godhead by tampering with Buddhist history and writ. The sixth incarnation was executed by the Chinese on account of his profligacy. The seventh was deposed by the Chinese as privy to the murder of the regent. After the death of the eighth, of whom I can learn nothing, it would seem that the tables were turned: the regents systematically murdered their charge, and the crime of the seventh Dalai Lama was visited upon four successive incarnations. The ninth, tenth, eleventh, and twelfth all died prematurely, assassinated, it is believed, by their regents.

There are no legends of malmsey-butts, secret smotherings, and hired assassins. The children disappeared; they were absorbed into the Universal Essence; they were literally too good to live. Their regents and protectors, monks only less sacred than themselves, provided that the spirit in its yearning for the next state should not be long detained in its mortal husk. No questions were asked. How could the devout trace the comings and goings of the divine Avalokita, the Lord of Mercy and Judgment, who ordains into what heaven or hell, demon, god, hero, mollusc, or ape, their spirits must enter, according to their sins?

So, when we reached Lhasa the other day, and heard that the thirteenth incarnation had fled, no one was surprised. Yet the wonder remains. A great Prince, a god to thousands of men, has been removed from his palace and capital, no one knows whither or when. A ruler has disappeared who travels with every appanage of state, inspiring awe in his prostrate servants, whose movements, one would think, were watched and talked about more than any Sovereign's on earth. Yet fear, or loyalty, or ignorance keeps every subject tongue-tied.

We have spies and informers everywhere, and there are men in Lhasa who would do much to please the new conquerors of Tibet. There are also witless men, who have eyes and ears, but, it seems, no tongues.

But so far neither avarice nor witlessness has betrayed anything. For all we know, the Dalai Lama may be still in his palace in some hidden chamber in the rock, or maybe he has never left his customary apartments, and still performs his daily offices in the Potala, confident that there at least his sanctity is inviolable by unbelievers.

The British Tommy in the meanwhile parades the streets as indifferently as if they were the New Cut or Lambeth Palace Road. He looks up at the Potala, and says: 'The old bloke's done a bunk. Wish we'd got 'im; we might get 'ome then.'

LHASA, August --.

We had been in Lhasa nearly three weeks before we could discover where the Dalai Lama had fled. We know now that he left his palace secretly in the night, and took the northern road to Mongolia. The Buriat, Dorjieff met him at Nagchuka, on the verge of the great desert that separates inhabited Tibet from Mongolia, 100 miles from Lhasa. On the 20th the Amban told us that he had already left Nagchuka twelve days, and was pushing on across the desert to the frontier.

I have been trying to find out something about the private life and character of the Grand Lama. But asking questions here is fruitless; one can learn nothing intimate. And this is just what one might expect. The man continues a bogie, a riddle, undivinable, impersonal, remote. The people know nothing. They have bowed before the throne as men come out of the dark into a blinding light. Scrutiny in their view would be vain and blasphemous. The Abbots, too, will reveal nothing; they will not and dare not. When Colonel

Younghusband put the question direct to a head Lama in open durbar, 'Have you news of the Dalai Lama? Do you know where he is?' the monk looked slowly to left and right, and answered, 'I know nothing.' 'The ruler of your country leaves his palace and capital, and you know nothing?' the Commissioner asked. 'Nothing,' answered the monk, shuffling his feet, but without changing colour.

From various sources, which differ surprisingly little, I have a fairly clear picture of the man's face and figure. He is thick-set, about five feet nine inches in height, with a heavy square jaw, nose remarkably long and straight for a Tibetan, eyebrows pronounced and turning upwards in a phenomenal manner--probably trained so, to make his appearance more forbidding--face pockmarked, general expression resolute and sinister. He goes out very little, and is rarely seen by the people, except on his annual visit to Depung, and during his migrations between the Summer Palace and the Potala. He was at the Summer Palace when the messenger brought the news that our advance was inevitable, but he went to the Potala to put his house in order before projecting himself into the unknown.

His face is the index of his character. He is a man of strong personality, impetuous, despotic, and intolerant of advice in State affairs. He is constantly deposing his Ministers, and has estranged from himself a large section of the upper classes, both ecclesiastical and official, owing to his wayward and headstrong disposition. As a child he was so precociously acute and resolute that he survived his regent, and so upset the traditional policy of murder, being the only one out of the last five incarnations to reach his majority. Since he took the government of the country into his own hands he has reduced the Chinese suzerainty to a mere shadow, and, with fatal results to himself, consistently insulted and defied the British. His inclination to a rapprochement with Russia is not shared by his Ministers.

The only glimpse I have had into the man himself was reflected in a conversation with the Nepalese Resident, a podgy little man, very ugly and good-natured, with the manners of a French comedian and a face generally expanded in a broad grin. He shook with laughter when I asked him if he knew the Dalai Lama, and the idea was really intensely funny, this mercurial, irreverent little man hobnobbing with the divine. 'I have seen him,' he said, and exploded again. 'But what does he do all day?' I asked. The Resident puckered up his brow, aping abstraction, and began to wave his hand in the air solemnly with a slow circular movement, mumbling 'Om man Padme om' to the revolutions of an imaginary praying-wheel. He was immensely pleased with the effort and the effect it produced on a sepoy orderly. 'But has he no interests or amusements?' I asked. The Resident could think of none. But he told me a story to illustrate the dulness of the man, for whom he evidently had no reverence. On his return from his last visit to India, the Maharaja of Nepal had given him a phonograph to present to the Priest-King. The impious toy was introduced to the Holy of Holies, and the Dalai Lama walked round it uneasily as it emitted the strains of English band music, and raucously repeated an indelicate Bhutanese song. After sitting a long while in deep thought, he rose and said he could not live with this voice without a soul; it must leave his palace at once. The rejected phonograph found a home with the Chinese Amban, to whom it was presented with due ceremonial the same day. 'The Lama is gumar,' the Resident said, using a Hindustani word which may be translated, according to our charity, by anything between 'boorish' and 'unenlightened.' I was glad to meet a man in this city of evasiveness whose views were positive, and who was eager to communicate them. Through him I tracked the shadow, as it were, of this impersonality, and found that to many strangers in Lhasa, and perhaps to a few Lhasans themselves, the divinity was all clay, a palpable fraud, a pompous and puritanical dullard masquerading as a god.

For my own part, I think the oracle that counselled his flight wiser than the statesmen who object that it was a political mistake. He has lost his prestige, they say. But imagine him dragged into durbar as a signatory, gazed at by profane eyes, the subject of a few days' gossip and comment, then sunk into commonplace, stripped of his mystery like this city of Lhasa, through which we now saunter familiarly, wondering when we shall start again for the wilds.

To escape this ordeal he has fled, and to us, at least, his flight has deepened the mystery that envelops him, and added to his dignity and remoteness; to thousands of mystical dreamers it has preserved the effulgence of his godhead unsoiled by contact with the profane world.

From our camp here the Potala draws the eye like a magnet. There is nothing but sky and marsh and bleak hill and palace. When we look out of our tents in the morning, the sun is striking the golden roof like a beacon light to the faithful. Nearly every day in August this year has opened fine and closed with storm-clouds gathering from the west, through which the sun shines, bathing the eastern valley in a soft, pearly light. The western horizon is dark and lowering, the eastern peaceful and serene. In this division of darkness and light the Potala stands out like a haven, not flaming now, but faintly luminous with a restful mystic light, soothing enough to rob Buddhist metaphysics of its pessimism and induce a mood, even in unbelievers, in which one is content to merge the individual and become absorbed in the universal spirit of Nature.

No wonder that, when one looks for mystery in Lhasa, one's thoughts dwell solely on the Dalai Lama and the Potala. I cannot help dwelling on the flight of the thirteenth incarnation. It plunges us into medievalism. To my mind, there is no picture so romantic and engrossing in modern history as that exodus, when the spiritual head of the Buddhist Church, the temporal ruler of six millions, stole out of his palace by night and was borne away in his palanquin, no one knows on what errand or with what impotent rage in his heart. The flight was really secret. No one but his immediate confidants and retainers, not even the Amban himself, knew that he had gone. I can imagine the awed attendants, the burying of treasure, the locking and sealing of chests, faint lights flickering in the passages, hurried footsteps in the corridors, dogs barking intermittently at this unwonted bustle--I feel sure the Priest-King kicked one as he stepped on the terrace for the last time. Then the procession by moonlight up the narrow valley to the north, where the roar of the stream would drown the footsteps of the palanquin-bearers.

A month afterwards I followed on his track, and stood on the Phembu Pass twelve miles north of Lhasa, whence one looks down on the huge belt of mountains that lie between the Brahmaputra and the desert, so packed and huddled that their crests look like one continuous undulating plain stretching to the horizon. Looking across the valley, I could see the northern road to Mongolia winding up a feeder of the Phembu Chu. They passed along here and over the next range, and across range after range, until they reached the two conical snow-peaks that stand out of the plain beside Tengri Nor, a hundred miles to the north. For days they skirted the great lake, and then, as if they feared the Nemesis of our offended Raj could pursue them to the end of the earth, broke into the desert, across which they must be hurrying now toward the great mountain chain of Burkhan Buddha, on the southern limits of Mongolia.

LHASA, August 19.

The Tibetans are the strangest people on earth. To-day I discovered how they dispose of their dead.

To hold life sacred and benefit the creatures are the laws of Buddha, which they are supposed to obey most scrupulously. And as they think they may be reborn in any shape of mammal, bird, or fish, they are kind to living things.

During the morning service the Lamas repeat a prayer for the minute insects which they have swallowed inadvertently in their meat and drink, and the formula insures the rebirth of these microbes in heaven. Sometimes, when a Lama's life is despaired of, the monks will ransom a yak or a bullock from the shambles, and keep him a pensioner in their monastery, praying the good Buddha to spare the sick man's life for the life ransomed. Yet they eat meat freely, all save the Gelug-pa, or Reformed Church, and square their conscience with their appetite by the pretext that the sin rests with the outcast assassin, the public butcher, who will be born in the next incarnation as some tantalized spirit or agonized demon. That, however, is his own affair.

But it is when a Tibetan dies that his charity to the creatures becomes really practical. Then, by his own tacit consent when living, his body is given as a feast to the dogs and vultures. This is no casual or careless gift to avoid the trouble of burial or cremation. All creatures who have a taste for these things are invited to the ceremony, and the corpse is carved to their liking by an expert, who devotes his life to the practice.

When a Tibetan dies he is left three days in his chamber, and a slit is made in his skull to let his soul pass out. Then he is rolled into a ball, wrapped in a sack, or silk if he is rich, packed into a jar or basket, and carried along to the music of conch shells to the ceremonial stone. Here a Lama takes the corpse out of its vessel and wrappings, and lays it face downwards on a large flat slab, and the pensioners prowl or hop round, waiting for their dole. They are quite tame. The Lamas stand a little way apart, and see that strict etiquette is observed during the entertainment. The carver begins at the ankle, and cuts upwards, throwing little strips of flesh to the guests; the bones he throws to a second attendant, who pounds them up with a heavy stone.

I passed the place to-day as I rode in from a reconnaissance. The slab lies a stone's-throw to the left of the great northern road to Tengri Nor and Mongolia, about two miles from the city.

A group of stolid vultures, too demoralized to range in search of carrion, stood motionless on a rock above, waiting the next dispenser of charity.

A few ravens hopped about sadly; they, too, were evidently pauperized. One magpie was prying round in suspicious proximity, and dogs conscious of shame slunk about without a bark in them, and nosed the ground diligently. They are always there, waiting.

There was hardly a stain on the slab, so quick and eager are the applicants for charity. Only a few rags lay around, too poor to be carried away.

I have not seen the ceremony, and I have no mind to. My companion this morning, a hardened young subaltern who was fighting nearly every day in April, May, and June, and has seen more bloodshed than most veterans, saw just as much as I have described. He then felt very ill, dug his spurs into his horse, and rode away.

CHAPTER XIV

THE CITY AND ITS TEMPLES

By the first week in September I had visited all the most important temples and monasteries in Lhasa. We generally went in parties of four and five, and a company of Sikhs or Pathans was left in the courtyard in case of accidents. We were well armed, as the monks were sullen, though I do not think they were capable of any desperate fanaticism. If they had had the abandon of dervishes, they might have rushed our camp long before. They missed their chance at Gyantse, when a night attack pushed home by overwhelming numbers could have wiped out our little garrison. In Lhasa there was the one case of the Lama who ran amuck outside the camp with the coat of mail and huge paladin's sword concealed beneath his cloak, a medieval figure who thrashed the air with his brand like a flail in sheer lust of blood. He was hanged medievally the next day within sight of Lhasa. Since then the exploit has not been repeated, but no one leaves the perimeter unarmed.

I have written of the squalor of the Lhasa streets. The environs of the city are beautiful enough--willow groves intersected by clear-running streams, walled-in parks with palaces and fish-ponds, marshes where the wild-duck flaunt their security, and ripe barley-fields stretching away to the hills. In September the trees were wearing their autumn tints, the willows were mostly a sulphury yellow, and in the pools beneath the red-stalked polygonum and burnished dock-leaf glowed in brilliant contrast. Just before dusk there was generally a storm in the valley, which only occasionally reached the city; but the breeze stirred the poplars, and the silver under the leaves glistened brightly against the background of clouds. Often a rainbow hung over the Potala like a nimbus.

On the Lingkhor, or circular road, which winds round Lhasa, we saw pilgrims and devotees moving slowly along in prayer, always keeping the Potala on their right hand. The road is only used for devotion. One meets decrepit old women and men, halting and limping and slowly revolving their prayer-wheels and mumbling charms. I never saw a healthy yokel or robust Lama performing this rite. Nor did I see the pilgrims whom one reads of as circumambulating the city on their knees by a series of prostrations, bowing their heads in the dust and mud. All the devotees are poor and ragged, and many blind. It seems that the people of Lhasa do not begin to think of the next incarnation until they have nothing left in this.

When one leaves the broad avenues between the walls of the groves and pleasure-gardens, and enters the city, one's senses are offended by everything that is unsightly and unclean. Pigs and pariah dogs are nosing about in black oozy mud. The houses are solid but dirty. It is hard to believe that they are whitewashed every year.

Close to the western entrance are the huts of the Ragyabas, beggars, outcasts, and scavengers, who cut up the dead. The outer walls of their houses are built of yak-horns.

Some of the houses had banks of turf built up outside the doors, with borders of English flowers. The dwellings are mostly two or three storied.

Bird-cages hang from the windows.

The outside of the cathedral is not at all imposing. From the streets one cannot see the golden roof, but only high blank walls, and at the entrance a forest of dingy pillars beside a massive door. The door is thrown open by a sullen monk, and a huge courtyard is revealed with more dingy pillars that were once red. The entire wall is covered with paintings of Buddhist myth and symbolism. The colours are subdued and pleasing. In the centre of the yard are masses of hollyhocks, marigolds, nasturtiums, and stocks. Beside the flower-borders is a pyramidical structure in which are burnt the leaves of juniper and pine for sacrifice.

The cloisters are two-storied; on the upper floor the monks have their cells. Looking up, one can see hundreds of them gazing at us with interest over the banisters. The upper story, as in every temple in Tibet, is coated with a dark red substance which looks like rough paint, but is really sacred earth, pasted on to evenly-clipped brushwood so as to seem like a continuation of the masonry. On the face of the wall are emblems in gilt, Buddhist symbols, like our Prince of Wales's feathers, sun and crescent moon, and various other devices. A heavy curtain of yak-hair hangs above the entrance-gate. On the roof are large cylinders draped in yak-hair cloth topped by a crescent or a spear. Every monastery and jong, and most houses in Tibet, are ornamented with these. When one first sees them in the distance they look like men walking on the roof.

Generally one ascends steps from the outer courtyard to the temple, but in the Jokhang the floors are level. We enter the main temple by a dark passage. The great doorway that opens into the street has been closed behind us, but we leave a company of Pathans in the outer yard, as the monks are sullen. Our party of four is armed with revolvers.

Service is being held before the great Buddhas as we enter, and a thunderous harmony like an organ-peal breaks the interval for meditation. The Abbot, who is in the centre, leans forward from his chair and takes a bundle of peacock-feathers from a vase by his side. As he points it to the earth there is a clashing of cymbals, a beating of drums, and a blowing of trumpets and conch shells.

Then the music dies away like the reverberation of cannon in the hills. The Abbot begins the chant, and the monks, facing each other like singing-men in a choir, repeat the litany. They have extraordinary deep, devotional voices, at once unnatural and impressive. The deepest bass of the West does not approach it, and their sense of time is perfect.

The voice of the thousand monks is like the drone of some subterranean monster, musically plaintive--the wail of the Earth God praying for release to the God of the Skies.

The chant sounds like the endless repetition of the same formula; the monks sway to it rhythmically. The temple would be dark if it were not for the flickering of many thousands of votive candles and butter lamps. Rows upon rows of them are placed before every shrine.

In an inner temple we found the three great images of the Buddhist trinity--the Buddhas of the past, present, and future. The images were greater than life-size, and set with jewels from foot to crown. As in the cloisters of an English cathedral, there were little side-chapels, which held sacred relics and shrines.

There were lamps of gold, and solid golden bowls set on altars, and embossed salvers of copper and bronze.

A hanging grille of chainwork protected the precincts from sacrilege, and an extended hand, bloody and menacing, was stretched from the wall, terrible enough when suddenly revealed in that dim light to paralyze and strike to earth with fright any profane thief who would dare to enter.

In the upper story we found a place which we called 'Hell,' where some Lamas were worshipping the demon protectress of the Grand Lama. The music here was harsh and barbaric. There were displayed on the pillars and walls every freak of diabolical invention in the shape of scrolls and devil-masks. The obscene object of this worship was huddled in a corner--a dwarfish abortion, hideous and malignant enough for such rites.

All about the Lamas' feet ran little white mice searching for grain. They are fed daily, and are scrupulously reverenced, as in their frail white bodies the souls of the previous guardians of the shrine are believed to be reincarnated.

In another temple we found the Lamas holding service in worship of the many-handed Buddha, Avalokitesvara. The picture of the god hung from pillars by the altar. The chief Lamas were wearing peaked caps picturesquely coloured with subdued blue and gold, and vestments of the same hue. The lesser Lamas were bare-headed, and their hair was cropped.

When we first entered, an acolyte was pouring tea out of a massive copper pot with a turquoise on the spout. Each monk received his tea in a wooden bowl, and poured in barley-flour to make a paste.

During this interval no one spoke or whispered. The footsteps of the acolytes were noiseless. Only the younger ones looked up at us self-consciously as we watched them from a latticed window in the corridor above.

Centuries ago this service was ordained, and the intervals appointed to further the pursuit of truth through silence and abstraction. The monks sat there quiet as stone. They had seen us, but they were seemingly oblivious.

One wondered, were they pursuing truth or were they petrified by ritual and routine? Did they regard us as immaterial reflexes, unsubstantial and illusory, passing shadows of the world cast upon them by an instant's illusion, to pass away again into the unreal, while they were absorbed in the contemplation of changeless and universal truths? Or were we noted as food for gossip and criticism when their self-imposed ordeal was done?

The reek of the candles was almost suffocating. 'Thank God I am not a Lama!' said a subaltern by my side. An Afridi Subadar let the butt of his rifle clank from his boot to the pavement.

At these calls to sanity we clattered out of this unholy atmosphere of dreams as if by an unquestioned impulse into the bright sunshine outside.

In the bazaar there is a gay crowd. The streets are thronged by as good-natured a mob as I have met anywhere. Sullenness and distrust have vanished. Officers and men, Tommies, Gurkhas, Sikhs, and Pathans, are stared at and criticised good-humouredly, and their accoutrements fingered and examined. It is a bright and interesting crowd, full of colour. In a corner of the square a street singer with a guitar and dancing children attracts a small crowd. His voice is a rich baritone, and he yodels like the Tyrolese. The crowd is parted by a Shap?riding past in gorgeous yellow silks and brocades, followed by a mounted retinue whose head-gear would be the despair of an operatic hatter. They wear red lamp-shades, yellow motor-caps, exaggerated Gainsboroughs, inverted cooking-pots, coal-scuttles, and medieval helmets. And among this topsy-turvy, which does not seem out of place in Lhasa, the most eccentrically-hatted man is the Bhutanese Tongsa Penlop, who parades the streets in an English gray felt hat.

The Mongolian caravan has arrived in Lhasa, after crossing a thousand miles of desert and mountain tracks. The merchants and drivers saunter about the streets, trying not to look too rustic. But they are easily recognisable--tall, sinewy men, very independent in gait, with faces burnt a dark brick red by exposure to the wind and sun. I saw one of their splendidly robust women, clad in a sheepskin cloak girdled at the waist, bending over a cloth stall, and fingering samples as if shopping were the natural business of her life.

On fine days the wares are spread on the cobbles of the street, and the coloured cloth and china make a pretty show against the background of garden flowers. At the doors of the shops stand pale Nuwaris, whose ancestors from Nepal settled in Lhasa generations ago. They wear a flat brown cap, and a dull russet robe darker than that of the Lamas. The Cashmiri shopkeepers are turbaned, and wear a cloak of butcher's blue. They and the Nuwaris and the Chinese seem to monopolize the trade of the city.

British officers haunt the bazaars searching for curios, but with very little success. Lhasa has no artistic industries; nearly all the knick-knacks come from India and China. Cloisonn?ware is rare and expensive, as one has to pay for the 1,800 miles of transport from Peking. Religious objects are not sold. Turquoises are plentiful, but coarse and inferior. Hundreds of paste imitations have been bought. There is a certain sale for amulets, rings, bells, and ornaments for the hair, but these and the brass and copper work can be bought for half the price in the Darjeeling bazaar. The few relics we have found of the West must have histories. In the cathedral there was a bell with the inscription 'Te Deum laudamus,' probably a relic of the Capuchins. In the purlieus of the city we found a bicycle without tyres, and a sausage-machine made in Birmingham.

With the exception of the cathedral, most of the temples and monasteries are on the outskirts of the city. There is a sameness about these places of worship that would make description tedious. Only the Ramo-ch?and Moru temples, which are solely devoted to sorcery, are different. Here one sees the other soul-side of the people.

The Ramo-ch?is as dark and dingy as a vault. On each side of the doorway are three gigantic tutelary demons. In the vestibule is a collection of bows, arrows, chain-armour, stag-horns, stuffed animals, scrolls, masks, skulls, and all the paraphernalia of devil-worship. On the left is a dark recess where drums are being beaten by an unseen choir.

A Lama stands, chalice in hand, before a deep aperture cut in the wall like a buttery hatch, and illumined by dim, flickering candles, which reveal a malignant female fiend. As a second priest pours holy water into a chalice, the Lama raises it solemnly again and again, muttering spells to propitiate the fury.

In the hall there are neither ornaments, gods, hanging canopies, nor scrolls, as in the other temples. There is neither congregation nor priests. The walls are apparently black and unpainted, but here and there a lamp reveals a Gorgon's head, a fiend's eye, a square inch or two of pigment that time has not obscured.

The place is immemorially old. There are huge vessels of carved metal and stone, embossed, like the roof, with griffins and skulls, which probably date back to before the introduction of Buddhism into Tibet, and are survivals of the old Bon religion. There is nothing bright here in colour or sound, nothing vivid or animated.

Stricken men and women come to remove a curse, vindictive ones to inflict one, bereaved ones to pay the initiated to watch the adventures of the soul in purgatory and guide it on its passage to the new birth, while demons and furies are lurking to snatch it with fiery claws and drag it to hell.

All these beings must be appeased by magic rites. So in the Ramo-ch?there is no rapture of music, no communion with Buddha, no beatitudes, only solitary priests standing before the shrines and mumbling incantations, dismal groups of two or three seated Buddha-fashion on the floor, and casting spells to exercise a deciding influence, as they hope, in the continual warfare which is being waged between the tutelary and malignant deities for the prize of a soul.

In the chancel of the temple, behind the altar, is a massive pile of masonry stretching from floor to roof, under which, as folk believe, an abysmal chasm leads down to hell. Round this there is a dark and narrow passage which pilgrims circumambulate. The floor and walls are as slippery as ice, worn by centuries of pious feet and groping hands. One old woman in some urgent need is drifting round and round abstractedly.

Elsewhere one might linger in the place fascinated, but here in Lhasa one moves among mysteries casually; for one cannot wonder, in this isolated land where the elements are so aggressive, among these deserts and wildernesses, heaped mountain chains, and impenetrable barriers of snow, that the children of the soil believe that earth, air, and water are peopled by demons who are struggling passionately over the destinies of man.

I will not describe any more of the Lhasa temples. One shrine is very like another, and details would be tedious. Personally, I do not care for systematic sightseeing, even in Lhasa, but prefer to loiter about the streets and bazaars, and the gardens outside the city, watch the people, and enjoy the atmosphere of the place. The religion of Tibet is picturesque enough in an unwholesome way, but to inquire how the layers of superstition became added to the true faith, and trace the growth of these spurious accretions, I leave to archeologists. Perhaps one reader in a hundred will be interested to know that a temple was built by the illustrious Konjo, daughter of the Emperor Tai-Tsung and wife of King Srong-btsan-gombo, but I think the other ninety and nine will be devoutly thankful if I omit to mention it.

Yet one cannot leave the subject of the Lhasa monasteries without remarking on the striking resemblance between Tibetan Lamaism and the Romish Church. The resemblance cannot be accidental. The burning of candles before altars, the sprinkling of holy water, the chanting of hymns in alternation, the giving alms and saying Masses for the dead, must have their origin in the West. We know that for many centuries large Christian communities have existed in Western China near the Tibetan frontier, and several Roman Catholic missionaries have penetrated to Lhasa and other parts of Tibet during the last three centuries. As early as 1641 the Jesuit Father Grueber visited Lhasa, and recorded that the Lamas wore caps and mitres, that they used rosaries, bells, and censers, and observed the practice of confession, penance, and absolution. Besides these points common to Roman Catholicism, he noticed the monastic and conventual system, the tonsure, the vows of poverty, chastity, and obedience, the doctrine of incarnation and the Trinity, and the belief in purgatory and paradise.[18]

[18] It is interesting to compare Grueber's account with the journal of Father Rubruquis, who travelled in Mongolia in the thirteenth century. In 1253 he wrote of the Lamas:

'All their priests had their heads shaven quite over, and they are clad in saffron-coloured garments. Being once shaven, they lead an unmarried life from that time forward, and they live a hundred or two of them in one cloister.... They have with them also, whithersoever they go, a certain string, with a hundred or two hundred nutshells thereupon, much like our beads which we carry about with us; and they do always mutter these words, "Om mani pectavi (om mani padme hom)"--"God, Thou knowest," as one of them expounded it to me; and so often do they expect a reward at God's hands as they pronounce these words in remembrance of God.... I made a visit to their idol temple, and found certain priests sitting in the outward portico, and those which I saw seemed, by their shaven beards, as if they had been our countrymen; they wore certain ornaments upon their heads like mitres made of paper.'

We occasionally saw a monk with the refined ascetic face of a Roman Cardinal. Te Rinpoche, the acting regent, was an example. One or two looked as if they might be humane and benevolent--men who might make one accept the gentle old Lama in 'Kim' as a not impossible fiction; but most of them appeared to me to be gross and sottish. I must confess that during the protracted negociations at Lhasa I had little sympathy with the Lamas. It is a mistake to think that they keep their country closed out of any religious scruple. Buddhism in its purest form is not exclusive or fanatical. Sakya Muni preached a missionary religion. He was Christlike in his universal love and his desire to benefit all living creatures. But Buddhism in Tibet has become more and more degenerate, and the Lamaist Church is now little better than a political mechanism whose chief function is the uncompromising exclusion of foreigners. The Lamas know that intercourse with other nations must destroy their influence with the people.

And Tibet is really ruled by the Lamas. Outside Lhasa are the three great monasteries of Depung, Sera, and Gaden, whose Abbots, backed by a following of nearly 30,000 armed and bigoted monks, maintain a preponderating influence in the national assembly.[19] These men wield a greater influence than the four Shap 閣 or the Dalai Lama himself, and practically dictate the policy of the country.

[19] 'It may be asked how the monastic influence is brought to bear on a Government in which three out of the four principal Ministers (Shap? are laymen. The fact seems to be that lying behind the Tak Lama, the Shap 閣, and all the machinery of the Tibetan Government, as we have hitherto been acquainted with it, there is an institution called the "Tsong-du-chembo," or "Tsong-dugze-tsom," which may reasonably be compared with what we call a "National Assembly," or, as the word implies, "Great Assembly." It is constituted of the Kenpas or Abbots of the three great monasteries, representatives from the four lings or small monasteries actually in Lhasa city, and from all the other monasteries in the province of U; and besides this, all the officials of the Government are present--laymen and ecclesiastics alike--to the number of several hundreds.'--Captain O'Connor's Diary at Khamba Jong (Tibetan Blue-Book, 1904).

The three great monasteries are of ancient foundation, and intimately associated with the history of the country. They are, in fact, ecclesiastical Universities,[20] and resemble in many ways our Universities of Oxford and Cambridge. The Universities are divided into colleges. Each has its own Abbot, or Master, and disciplinary staff. The undergraduates, or candidates for ordination, must attend lectures and chapels, and pass examinations in set books, which they must learn from cover to cover before they can take their degree. Failure in examination, as well as breaches in discipline and manners, are punished by flogging. Corporal punishment is also dealt out to the unfortunate tutors, who are held responsible for their pupils' omissions. If a candidate repeatedly fails to pass his examination, he is expelled from the University, and can only enter again on payment of increased fees. The three leading Universities are empowered to confer degrees which correspond to our Bachelor and Doctor of Divinity. The monks live in rooms in quadrangles, and have separate messing clubs, but meet for general worship in the cathedral. If their code is strictly observed, which I very much doubt, prayers and tedious religious observances must take up nearly their whole day. But the Lamas are adept casuists, and generally manage to evade the most irksome laws of their scriptures.

[20] I have derived most of my information regarding the discipline and constitution of Depung from 'Lamaism in Tibet,' by Colonel Augustine Waddell, who accompanied the expedition as Archeologist and Principal Medical Officer.

Soon after our arrival in Lhasa we had occasion to visit Depung, which is probably the largest monastery in the world. It stands in a natural amphitheatre in the hillside two miles from the city, a huge collection of temples and monastic buildings, larger, and certainly more imposing, than most towns in Tibet.

The University was founded in 1414, during the reign of the first Grand Lama of the Reformed Church. It is divided into four colleges, and contains nearly 8,000 monks, amongst whom there is a large Mongolian community. The fourth Grand Lama, a Mongolian, is buried within the precincts. The fifth and greatest Dalai Lama, who built the Potala and was the first to combine the temporal and spiritual power, was an Abbot of Depung. The reigning Dalai Lama visits Depung annually, and a palace in the university is reserved for his use. The Abbot, of course, is a man of very great political influence.

All these facts I have collected to show that the monks have some reason to be proud of their monastery as the first in Tibet. One may forgive them a little pride in its historic distinctions. Even in our own alma mater we meet the best of men who seem to gather importance from old traditions and association with a long roll of distinguished names. What, then, can we expect of this Tibetan community, the most conservative in a country that has prided itself for centuries on its bigotry and isolation--men who are ignorant of science, literature, history, politics, everything, in fact, except their own narrow priestcraft and confused metaphysics? We call the Tibetan 'impossible.' His whole education teaches him to be so, and the more educated he is the more 'impossible' he becomes.

Imagine, then, the consternation at Depung when a body of armed men rode up to the monastery and demanded supplies. We had refrained from entering the monasteries of Lhasa and its neighbourhood at the request of the Abbots and Shap 閣, but only on condition that the monks should bring in supplies, which were to be paid for at a liberal rate. The Abbots failed to keep their promise, supplies were not forthcoming, and it became necessary to resort to strong measures. An officer was sent to the gate with an escort of three men and a letter saying that if the provisions were not handed over within an hour we would break into the monastery and take them, if necessary, by force. The messengers were met by a crowd of excited Lamas, who refused to accept the letter, waved them away, and rolled stones towards them menacingly, as an intimation that they were prepared to fight. As the messengers rode away the tocsin was heard, warning the villagers, women and children, who were gathered outside with market produce, to depart.

General Macdonald with a strong force of British and native troops drew up within 1,300 yards of the monastery, guns were trained on Depung, the infantry were deployed, and we waited the expiration of the period of grace intimated in the letter. An hour passed by, and it seemed as if military operations were inevitable, when groups of monks came out with a white flag, carrying baskets of eggs and a complimentary scarf.

Even in the face of this military display they began to temporize. They bowed and chattered and protested in their usual futile manner, and condescended so far as to say they would talk the matter over if we retired at once, and send the supplies to our camp the next day, if they came to a satisfactory decision. The Lamas are trained to wrangle and dispute and defer and vacillate.[21] They seem to think that speech was made only to evade conclusions. The curt ultimatum was repeated, and the deputation was removed gently by two impassive sepoys, still chattering like a flock of magpies.

[21] The highest degree which is conferred on the Lamas by their

Universities is the Rabs-jam-pa (verbally overflowing endlessly).--Waddell, 'Lamaism in Tibet.'

In the meanwhile we sat and waited and smoked our pipes, and wondered if there were going to be another Guru. It seemed the most difficult thing in the world to save these poor fools from the effects of their obstinate folly. The time-limit had nearly expired, the two batteries were advanced 300 yards, the gunners took their sights again, and trained the 10-pounders on the very centre of the monastery.

There were only five minutes more, and we were stirred, according to our natures, by pity or exasperation or the swift primitive instinct for the dramatic, which sweeps away the humanities, and leaves one to the conflict of elemental passions.

At last a thin line of red-robed monks was seen to issue from the gate and descend the hill, each carrying a bag of supplies. The crisis was over, and we were spared the necessity of inflicting a cruel punishment. I waited to see the procession, a group of sullen ecclesiastics, who had never bowed or submitted to external influence in their lives, carrying on their backs their unwilling contribution to the support of the first foreign army that had ever intruded on their seclusion. It must have been the most humiliating day in the history of Depung.

It must be admitted that it was not a moment when the monks looked their best. Yet I could not help comparing their appearance with that of the simple honest-looking peasantry. Many of them looked sottish and degraded; other faces showed cruelty and cunning; their brows were contracted as if by perpetual scheming; some were almost simian in appearance, and looked as if they could not harbour a thought that was not animal or sensual. They waddled in their walk, and their right arms, exposed from the shoulder, looked soft and flabby, as if they had never done an honest day's work in their life.

One man had the face of an inquisitor--round, beady eyes, puffed cheeks, and thin, tightly-shut mouth.

How they hated us! If one of us fell into their hands secretly, I have no doubt they would rack him limb from limb, or cut him into small pieces with a knife.

The Depung incident shows how difficult it was to make any headway with the Tibetans without recourse to arms. We were present in the city to insist on compliance with our demands. But an amicable settlement seemed hopeless, and we could not stay in Lhasa indefinitely. What if these monks were to say, 'You may stay here if you like. We will not molest you, but we refuse to accept your terms'? We could only retire or train our guns on the Potala. Retreat was, of course, impossible.

CHAPTER XV

THE SETTLEMENT

The political deadlock continued until within a week of the signing of the treaty.

For a long time no responsible delegates were forthcoming. The Shap 閣, who were weak men and tools of the fugitive Dalai Lama, protested that any treaty they might make with us would result in their disgrace. If, on the other hand, they made no treaty, and we were compelled to occupy the Potala, or take some other step offensive to the hierarchy, their ruin would be equally certain. Ruin, in fact, faced them in any case.

The highest officials in Tibet visited Colonel Younghusband, expressed their eagerness to see differences amicably settled, and, when asked to arrange the simplest matter, said they were afraid to take on themselves the responsibility. And this was not merely astute evasiveness. It was really a fact that there was no one in Lhasa who dared commit himself by an action or assurance of any kind.

Yet there existed some kind of irresponsible disorganized machine of administration which sometimes arrived at a decision about matters of the moment. The National Assembly was sufficiently of one mind to depose and imprison the Ta Lama, the ecclesiastical member of Council. His disgrace was due to his failure to persuade us to return to Gyantse.

The National Assembly held long sessions daily, and after more than a week of discussion they began to realize that there was at least one aim that was common to them all--that the English should be induced to leave Lhasa. They then appointed accredited delegates, whose decisions, they said, would be entirely binding on the Dalai Lama, should he come back. The Dalai Lama had left his seal with Te Rinpoche, the acting regent, but with no authority to use it.

The terms of the treaty were disclosed to the Amban, who communicated them to the Tsong-du. The Tsong-du submitted the draft of their reply to the Amban before it was presented to Colonel Younghusband. The first reply of the Assembly to our demands ought to be preserved as a historic epitome of national character. The indemnity, they said, ought to be paid by us, and not by them. We had invaded their territory, and spoiled their monasteries and lands, and should bear the cost. The question of trade marts they were obstinately opposed to; but, provided we carried out the other terms of the treaty to their satisfaction, they would consider the advisability of conceding us a market at Rinchengong, a mile and a half beyond the present one at Yatung. They would not be prepared, however, to make this concession unless we undertook to pay for what we purchased on the spot, to respect their women, and to refrain from looting. Road-making they could not allow, as the blasting and upheaval of soil offended their gods and brought trouble on the neighbourhood. The telegraph-wire was against their customs, and objectionable on religious grounds. With regard to foreign relations, they had never had any dealings with an outside race, and they intended to preserve this policy so long as they were not compelled to seek protection from another Power.

The tone of the reply indicates the attitude of the Tibetans. Obstinacy could go no further. The document, however, was not forwarded officially to the Commissioner, but returned to the Assembly by the Amban as too impertinent for transmission. The Amban explained to Colonel Younghusband that the Tibetans regarded the negotiations in the light of a huckster's bargain. They did not realize that we were in a position to enforce terms, and that our demands were unconditional, but thought that by opening negotiations in an unconciliatory manner, and asking for more than they expected, they might be able to effect a compromise and escape the full exaction of the penalty.

The first concession on the part of the Tibetans was the release of the two Lachung men, natives of Sikkim and British subjects, who had been captured and beaten at Tashilunpo in July, 1903, while the Commission was waiting at Khamba Jong. Their liberation was one of the terms of the treaty. Colonel Younghusband made the release the occasion of an impressive durbar, in which he addressed a solemn warning to the Tibetans on the sanctity of the British subject. The imprisonment of the two men from Sikkim, he said, was the most serious offence of which the Tibetans had been guilty. It was largely on that account that the Indian Government had decided to advance to Gyantse. The prisoners were brought straight from the dungeon to the audience-hall. They had been incarcerated in a dark underground cell for more than a year, and they knew nothing of the arrival of the English in Lhasa until the morning when Colonel Younghusband told them they were free by the command of the King-Emperor. I shall never forget the scene--the bewilderment and delight of the prisoners, their drawn, blanched features, and the sullen acquiescence of the Tibetans, who learnt for the first time the meaning of the old Roman boast, 'Civis Romanus sum.'

On August 20 Colonel Younghusband received through the Amban the second reply to our demands. The tone of the delegates was still impossible, though slightly modified and more reasonable. Several durbars followed, but they did not advance the negociations. Instead of discussing matters vital to the settlement, the Tibetan representatives would arrive with all the formalities and ceremonial of durbar to beg us not to cut grass in a particular field, or to request the return of the empty grain-bags to the monasteries. The Amban said that he had met with nothing but shuffling from the 'barbarians' during his term of office. They were 'dark and cunning adepts at prevarication, children in the conduct of affairs.'

The counsellors, however, began to show signs of wavering. They were evidently eager to come to terms, though they still hoped to reduce our demands, and tried to persuade the Commissioner to agree to conditions proposed by themselves.

Throughout this rather trying time our social relations with the Tibetans were of a thoroughly friendly character. The Shap 閣 and one or two of the leading monks attended race-meetings and gymkanas, put their money on the totalizator, and seemed to enjoy their day out. When their ponies ran in the visitors' race, the members of Council temporarily forgot their stiffness, waddled to the rails to see the finish, and were genuinely excited. They were entertained at lunch and tea by Colonel Younghusband, and were invited to a Tibetan theatrical performance given in the courtyard of the Lhalu house, which became the headquarters of the mission. On these occasions they were genial and friendly, and appreciated our hospitality.

The humbler folk apparently bore us no vindictiveness, and showed no signs of resenting our presence in the city. Merchants and storekeepers profited by the exaggerated prices we paid for everything we bought. Trade in Lhasa was never brisker. The poor were never so liberally treated. One day a merry crowd of them were collected on the plain outside the city, and largess was distributed to more than 11,000. Every babe in arms within a day's march of Lhasa was brought to the spot, and received its dole of a tanka (5d.).

I think the Tibetans were genuinely impressed with our humanity during this time, and when, on the eve of our departure, the benign and venerable Te Rinpoche held his hands over General Macdonald in benediction, and solemnly blessed him for his clemency and moderation in sparing the monasteries and people, no one doubted his thankfulness was sincere. The golden Buddha he presented to the General was the highest pledge of esteem a Buddhist priest could bestow.

When, on September 1, the Tibetans, after nearly a month's palaver, had accepted only two of the terms of the treaty,[22] Colonel Younghusband decided that the time had come for a guarded ultimatum. He told the delegates that, if the terms were not accepted in full within a week, he would consult General Macdonald as to what measures it would be necessary to take to enforce compliance. Their submission was complete, and immediate.

[22] The liberation of the Lachung men and the destruction of the Yatung and Gob-sorg barriers.

Colonel Younghusband had achieved a diplomatic triumph of the highest order. If the ultimatum had been given three weeks, or even a fortnight, earlier, I believe the Tibetans would have resisted. When we reached Lhasa on August 3, the Nepalese Resident said that 10,000 armed monks had been ready to oppose us if we had decided to quarter ourselves inside the city, and they had only dispersed when the Shap who rode out to meet us at Toilung returned with assurances that we were going to camp outside. At one time it seemed impossible to make any progress with negociations without further recourse to arms. But patience and diplomacy conquered. We had shown the Tibetans we could reach Lhasa and yet respect their religion, and left an impression that our strength was tempered with humanity.

The treaty was signed in the Potala on August 7, in the Dalai Lama's throne-room. The Tibetan signatories were the acting regent, who affixed the seal of the Dalai Lama; the four Shap 閣; the Abbots of the three great monasteries, Depung, Sera, and Gaden; and a representative of the National Assembly. The Amban was not empowered to sign, as he awaited 'formal sanction' from Peking. Lest the treaty should be afterwards disavowed through a revolution in Government, the signatories included representatives of every organ of administration in Lhasa.

On the afternoon of the 7th our troops lined the causeway on the west front of the Potala. Towards the summit the rough and broken road became an ascent of slippery steps, where one had to walk crabwise to prevent falling, and plant one's feet on the crevices of the age-worn flagstones, where grass and dock-leaves gave one a securer foothold. Then through the gateway and along a maze of slippery passages, dark as Tartarus, but illumined dimly by flickering butter lamps held by aged monks, impassive and inscrutable. In the audience-chamber Colonel Younghusband, General Macdonald, and the Chinese Amban sat beneath the throne of the Dalai Lama. On either side of them were the British Political Officer and Tibetan signatories. In another corner were the Tongsa Penlop of Bhutan and his lusty big-boned men, and the dapper little Nepalese Resident, wreathed in smiles. British officers sat round forming a circle. Behind them stood groups of Tommies, Sikhs, Gurkhas, and Pathans. In the centre the treaty, a voluminous scroll, was laid on a table, the cloth of which was a Union Jack.

When the terms had been read in Tibetan, the signatories stepped forward and attached their seals to the three parallel columns written in English, Tibetan, and Chinese. They showed no trace of sullenness and displeasure. The regent smiled as he added his name.

After the signing Colonel Younghusband addressed the Tibetans:

'The convention has been signed. We are now at peace, and the misunderstandings of the past are over. The bases have been laid for mutual good relations in the future.

'In the convention the British Government have been careful to avoid interfering in the smallest degree with your religion. They have annexed no part of your territory, have made no attempt to interfere in your internal affairs, and have fully recognised the continued suzerainty of the Chinese Government. They have merely sought to insure--

'1. That you shall abide by the treaty made by the Amban in 1890.

'2. That trade relations between India and Tibet, which are no less advantageous to you than to us, should be established as they have been with every other part of the Chinese Empire, and with every other country in the world except Tibet.

'3. That British representatives should be treated with respect in future.

'4. That you should not depart from your traditional policy in regard to political relations with other countries.

'The treaty which has now been made I promise you on behalf of the British Government we will rigidly observe, but I also warn you that we will as rigidly enforce it. Any infringement of it will be severely punished in the end, and any obstruction of trade, any disrespect or injury to British subjects, will be noticed and reparation exacted.

'We treat you well when you come to India. We do not take a single rupee in Customs duties from your merchants. We allow any of you to travel and reside wherever you will in India. We preserve the ancient buildings of the Buddhist faith, and we expect that when we come to Tibet we shall be treated with no less consideration and respect than we show you in India.

'You have found us bad enemies when you have not observed your treaty obligations and shown disrespect to the British Raj. You will find us equally good friends if you keep the treaty and show us civility.

'I hope that the peace which has at this moment been established between us will last for ever, and that we may never again be forced to treat you as enemies.

'As the first token of peace I will ask General Macdonald to release all prisoners of war. I expect that you on your part will set at liberty all those who have been imprisoned on account of dealings with us.'

At the conclusion of the speech, which was interpreted to the Tibetans sentence by sentence, and again in Chinese, the Shap expressed their intention to observe the treaty faithfully.[23]

[23] The following is a draft of the terms as communicated by The Times Correspondent at Peking. The terms have not yet been disclosed in their final form, but I understand that Dr. Morrison's summary contains the gist of them:

'1. Tibetans to re-erect boundary-stones at the Tibet frontier.

'2. Tibetans to establish marts at Gyangtse, Yatung, Gartok, and facilitate trade with India.

'3. Tibet to appoint a responsible official to confer with the British officials regarding the alteration of any objectionable features of the treaty of 1893.

'4. No further Customs duties to be levied upon merchandise after the tariff shall have been agreed upon by Great Britain and the Tibetans.

'5. No Customs stations to be established on the route between the Indian frontier and the three marts mentioned above, where officials shall be appointed to facilitate diplomatic and commercial intercourse.

'6. Tibet to pay an indemnity of ?00,000 in three annual instalments, the first to be paid on January 1, 1906.

'7. British troops to occupy the Chumbi Valley for three years, or until such time as the trading posts are satisfactorily established and the indemnity liquidated in full.

'8. All forts between the Indian frontier on routes traversed by merchants from the interior of Tibet to be demolished.

'9. Without the consent of Great Britain no Tibetan territory shall be sold, leased, or mortgaged to any foreign Power whatsoever; no foreign Power whatsoever shall be permitted to concern itself with the administration of the government of Tibet, or any other affairs therewith connected; no foreign Power shall be permitted to send either official or non-official persons to Tibet--no matter in what pursuit they may be engaged--to assist in the conduct of Tibetan affairs; no foreign Power shall be permitted to construct roads or railways or erect telegraphs or open mines anywhere in Tibet.

'In the event of Great Britain's consenting to another Power constructing roads or railways, opening mines, or erecting telegraphs, Great Britain will make a full examination on her own account for carrying out the arrangements proposed. No real property or land containing minerals or precious metals in Tibet shall be mortgaged, exchanged, leased, or sold to any foreign Power.

'10. Of the two versions of the treaty, the English text to be regarded as operative.'

The ninth clause, which precludes Russian interference and consequent absorption, is of course the most vital article of the treaty.

The next day in durbar a scene was enacted which reminded one of a play before the curtain falls, when the characters are called on the stage and apprised of their changed fortunes, and everything ends happily. Among the mutual pledges and concessions and evidences of goodwill that followed we secured the release of the political captives who had been imprisoned on account of assistance rendered British subjects. An old man and his son were brought into the hall looking utterly bowed and broken. The old man's chains had been removed from his limbs that morning for the first time in twenty years, and he came in blinking at the unaccustomed light like a blind man miraculously restored to sight. He had been the steward of the Phalla estate near Dongste; his offence was hospitality shown to Sarat Chandra Das in 1884. An old monk of Sera was released next. He was so weak that he had to be supported into the room. His offence was that he had been the teacher of Kawa Guchi, the Japanese traveller who visited Lhasa in the disguise of a Chinese pilgrim. We who looked on these sad relics of humanity felt that their restitution to liberty was in itself sufficient to justify our advance to Lhasa.

On August 14 the Amban posted in the streets of Lhasa a proclamation that the Dalai Lama was deposed by the authority of the Chinese Emperor, owing to the desertion of his trust at a national crisis. Temporal power was vested in the hands of the National Assembly and the regent, while the spiritual power was transferred to Panchen Rinpoche, the Grand Lama of Tashilunpo, who is venerated by Buddhists as the incarnation of Amitabha, and held as sacred as the Dalai Lama himself. The Tashe Lama, as he is called in Europe, has always been more accessible than the Dalai Lama. It was to the Tashe Lama that Warren Hastings despatched the missions of Bogle and Turner, and the intimate friendship that grew up between George Bogle and the reigning incarnation is perhaps the only instance of such a tie existing between an Englishman and a Tibetan. The officials of the Tsang province, where the Tashe Lama resides, are not so bigoted as the Lhasa oligarchy. It was a minister of the Tashe Lama who invited Sarat Chandra Das to Shigatze, learnt the Roman characters from him, and sat for hours listening to his talk about languages and scientific developments. The exile of this man, and the execution of the Abbot of Dongste, who was drowned in the Tsangpo, for hospitality shown to the Bengali explorer, are the most recent marks of the difference in attitude between the Lhasans and the people of Tsang.

The present incarnation has not shown himself bitterly anti-foreign. During the operations in Tibet he remained as neutral and inactive as safety permitted, and it is not impossible that the hope of Mr. Ular may be realized, and an Anglophile Buddhist Pope established at Shigatze. Herein lies a possible simplification of the Tibetan problem, which has already lost some of its complexity by the flight of the Dalai Lama to Urga.

In estimating the practical results of the Tibet Expedition, we should not attach too much importance to the exact observance of the terms of the treaty. Trade marts and roads, and telegraph-wires, and open communications are important issues, but they were never our main objective. What was really necessary was to make the Tibetans understand that they could not afford to trifle with us. The existence of a truculent race on our borders who imagined that they were beyond the reach of our displeasure was a source of great political danger. We went to Tibet to revolutionize the whole policy of the Lhasa oligarchy towards the Indian Government.

The practical results of the mission are these: The removal of a ruler who threatened our security and prestige on the North-East frontier by overtures to a foreign Power; the demonstration to the Tibetans that this Power is unable to support them in their policy of defiance to Great Britain, and that their capital is not inaccessible to British troops.

We have been to Lhasa once, and if necessary we can go there again. The knowledge of this is the most effectual leverage we could have in removing future obstruction. In dealing with people like the Tibetans, the only sure basis of respect is fear. They have flouted us for nearly twenty years because they have not believed in our power to punish their defiance. Out of this contempt grew the Russian menace, to remove which was the real object of the Tibet Expedition. Have we removed it? Our verdict on the success or failure of Lord Curzon's Tibetan policy should, I think, depend on the answer to this question.

There can be no doubt that the despatch of British troops to Lhasa has shown the Tibetans that Russia is a broken reed, her agents utterly unreliable, and her friendship nothing but a hollow pretence. The British expedition has not only frustrated her designs in Tibet: it has made clear to the whole of Central Asia the insincerity of her pose as the Protector of the Buddhist Church.

But the Tibetans are not an impressionable people. Their conduct after the campaign of 1888 shows us that they forget easily. To make the results of the recent expedition permanent, Lord Curzon's original policy should be carried out in full, and a Resident with troops left in Lhasa. It will be objected that this forward policy is too fraught with possibilities of political trouble, and too costly to be worth the end in view. But half-measures are generally more expensive and more dangerous in the long-run than a bold policy consistently carried out.

We have left a trade agent at Gyantse with an escort of fifty men, as well as four or five companies at Chumbi and Phari Jong, at distances of 100 and 130 miles. But no vigilance at Gyantse can keep the Indian Government informed of Russian or Chinese intrigue in Lhasa. Lhasa is Tibet, and there alone can we watch the ever-shifting pantomime of Tibetan politics and the manoeuvres of foreign Powers. If we are not to lose the ground we have gained, the foreign relations of Tibet must stand under British surveillance.

But putting aside the question of vigilance, our prestige requires that there should be a British Resident in Lhasa. That we have left an officer at Gyantse, and none at Lhasa, will be interpreted by the Tibetans as a sign of weakness.

Then, again, diplomatic relations with Tibet can only continue a farce while we are ignorant of the political situation in Lhasa. Influences in the capital grow and decay with remarkable rapidity. The Lamas are adepts in intrigue. When we left Lhasa, the best-informed of our political officers could not hazard a guess as to what party would be in power in a month's time, whether the Dalai Lama would come back, or in what manner his deposition would affect our future relations with the country. We only knew that our departure from Lhasa was likely to be the signal for a conflict of political factions that would involve a state of confusion. The Dalai Lama still commanded the loyalty of a large body of monks. Sera Monastery was known to support him, while Gaden, though it contained a party who favoured the deposed Shata Shap? numbered many adherents to his cause. The only political figure who had no following or influence of any kind was the unfortunate Amban.[24] Whatever party gains the upper hand, the position of the Chinese Amban is not enviable.

[24] The Amban or Chinese Resident in Lhasa is in the same position as a British Resident in the Court of a protected chief in India. Of late years, however, the Amban's authority has been little more than nominal.

At the moment of writing China has not signed the treaty; she may do so yet, but her signature is not of vital importance. The Tibetans will decide for themselves whether it is safe to provoke our hostility. If they decide to defy us, then of course trouble may arise from their refusing to recognise the treaty of 1904 on the pretext that it was not signed by the Amban.

It will be remembered that after the campaign of 1888 the convention we drew up in Calcutta was signed by China, and afterwards repudiated by Tibet. For many years the Tibetans have ignored China's suzerainty, and refused to be bound by a convention drawn up by her in their behalf; but now the plea of suzerainty is convenient, they may use it as a pretext to escape their new obligations.

It is even possible that the Amban advised the Tibetan delegates in Lhasa to agree to any terms we asked, if they wanted to be rid of us, as any treaty we might make with them would be invalid without the acquiescence of China. Thus the 'vicious circle' revolves, and a more admirable political device from the Chino-Tibetan point of view cannot be conceived.

But the permanence of the new conditions in Tibet does not depend on China. If the Tibetans think they are still able to flout us, they will do so, and one pretext will serve as well as another. But if they have learnt that our displeasure is dangerous they will take care not to provoke it again.

The success or failure of the recent expedition depends on the impression we have left on the Tibetans. If that impression is to be lasting, we must see that our interests are well guarded in Lhasa, or in a few months we may lose the ground we gained, with what cost and danger to ourselves only those who took part in the expedition can understand.

THE END

Printed in Great Britain
by Amazon